B O

FALL
OF THE
SIX

MATT RYAN

THE **PRESTON SIX** SERIES

For information on new releases
or if you want to chat with me, you can find me at:
www.facebook.com/authormattryan
or www.authormattryan.com

Cover: Regina Wamba
www.maeidesign.com
Editor: Victoria Schmitz | Crimson Tide Editorial
Formatting: Inkstain Interior Book Designing
www.inkstainformatting.com

FALL OF THE SIX

CHAPTER 1

"HOW COULD YOU LET THIS happen?" Lucas yelled, pointing to the sky as he approached Harris and Julie.

Poly had been taken and now three of his friends were gone to Marcus. The surrounding crowd, who had once been ruckus and violent, had fallen silent. They stared at a mere vapor trail—a cruel reminder of Emmett's departure with his friend.

Harris regarded him with a distant look, shaking his head absentmindedly. "I wasn't expecting Emmett."

"And what's this about, you being a rank nine? You were *part* of them?" Lucas asked.

Julie let go of Harris and the fog lifted from her eyes as she looked around. She made eye contact with Lucas and ran for him. He embraced her sobbing face into his chest, feeling the strange fabric wrapping around her like a shawl. Leaning close, he whispered in her ear, "You look ridiculous."

She chuckled and raised her head. Lucas pulled a few strands of hair back from her teary eyes. "We made these clothes to blend in. Poly glued a lot of the seams." She looked up at the sky.

Lucas glanced at Travis. He stood behind Harris, a sword trembling in his hand. Harris either didn't notice him, or more than likely chose to ignore him, as Lucas didn't think Harris could miss Travis's rushed breaths as he stared at the back of his head.

The crowd began to rumble with conversation. Travis turned his attention to the mob and lowered his sword. He jumped on a pile of broken lumber, the remnants of the broken stage. A camera flew close to his face and he spoke loud. "MM wants us to put our weapons down, they want us to give in." The people booed. "But not *this* time, my friends. We will be oppressed no longer. Let's take our city back!" He raised his sword.

The crowd became a tornado of cheers and movement.

"What's going on?" Hank asked, walking up next to the group.

Lucas spun to face him. "Naptime over, sleeping beauty?" He wanted to hug the guy, but that meant letting go of Julie.

Hank rubbed his eyes and shook his head. "What the hell happened back there? The last thing I remember was taking off on that plane, surrounded by the mutants."

"Oh, you didn't miss much. I just single-handedly took down the MM pilot and co-pilot of our aircraft, flew us over to Sanct, to where Poly killed Max, *live* in front of the entire world, just before she was kidnapped by some MM guy named Emmett. Oh, and Harris used to work for MM," Lucas said.

Hank surveyed the surrounding chaos. "Where is she?" he said in a slight panic.

"They took her, Hank. They took Poly. Freaking dude just jet-packed right out of here with her."

Hank looked to the sky. The vapor had faded to just a whisper of a cloud, soon there would be nothing. He punched the air and screamed.

Harris broke into the middle of their reunion. "We'll get her back. We'll get them all back." He struggled with the words, as if they were the third or fourth thing going on in his mind. Or maybe he was at a loss.

Lucas frowned, he'd never seen Harris stumbling and running his hands through his hair in frustration. If Harris was losing it, Lucas didn't think they had a chance of getting his friends back. "What are we supposed to do now?"

Harris turned and looked past Lucas. "Travis," he called.

Travis seethed. "What?"

"Can you take care of them for a while?"

"I think they're safer in my hands anyway. Death follows you," Travis said.

"That it does." Harris let out a long breath. "Julie, we'll have to set up a new way to communicate, I think Almadon has a few other servers out there. I have a plan and I don't want to risk any more of your lives. It's a long shot but know that I'm truly sorry and I'll do whatever I can to get them back, I promise."

Harris stood and took each of them in. It felt like a goodbye, but Lucas didn't know what to say to the man and the rest must have felt the same. Harris nodded and walked to the aircraft he came in on and closed the door. Dust stirred up under the craft and a few boards rattled as it lifted into the air.

"Where is he going?" Lucas asked the closed door and turned to his friends. "Did he *promise* to get them back?" He wrapped his bow over his chest and adjusted the quiver on his back. He'd spent a lot of time with Harris over the last couple weeks and the man didn't promise anything. But he didn't need Harris's promises, he would find them.

Gunfire sounded at a distance.

"We should go as well. The MM guards will regroup," Travis said.

The crowd cheered as they entered the aircraft. Out of the open door, Lucas watched the crowd tearing down MM banners. The guards in black were all gone. In the sky, a few black aircrafts could be seen leaving the city. Lucas looked over the crowd and shook his head. Take away a city's internet and this is what happens. He closed the door and the din of the crowd silenced.

"I think I can get the motors back on—" Julie stopped in her tracks. "Holy crap, what happened in here?"

Lucas sighed as he looked at the man strapped to a pipe in the corner of the cargo bay, just as he'd left him. A muffled moan sounded as the man moved his head. There was another man in the ship, but Lucas avoided looking at him, shivering at the thought of their last encounter.

"We should let that one go," Travis said and walked to the MM guard. "Try anything and I'll make you join your friend there."

The man nodded and grunted through his gag. Travis cut his ties and the man rubbed his wrist and pulled his gag out of his mouth. "Marcus will kill you all for this," he sputtered with rage.

Travis laughed and grabbed the man by the back of his shirt. "You think he cares about some rank six?" He led him to the door, opened it and pushed him out onto the ground. The crowd cheered at the offering and pulled the man away.

Lucas sighed and closed the door. He didn't like being cruel, even to the enemy, and a crowd charged up as much as they were, was only looking for a reason to lose control.

"Got it," Julie exclaimed and tapped on the screen of her Panavice.

The motors of the craft hummed to life. Lucas adjusted his footing as they lifted off the ground and leveled.

"So we got set up with the mutants?" Hank said, rubbing his head.

"It was a total setup," Lucas said. "It wasn't Harris's people picking us up, it was MM. They must have found out about the plan. This whole room filled with gas, knocking everyone out. I don't know what they did with the mutants, but when I woke up, it was just me and you."

"Yep, they tricked us as well," Julie said. "They hacked into our server and placed fake messages like they came from Harris. That's how they got us to come out of hiding." She folded her arms and tears formed. "And now Poly's gone."

"I bet they wanted to put on a show," Lucas said. "Arrest you in front of a worldwide audience."

"Yeah, well, Poly gave them something to talk about alright," Travis added.

"I doubt there's a person on Vanar who doesn't know of her now." He walked to the cockpit and pushed numbers into the craft's screen. Once they were airborne, Lucas looked out the front windows as buildings moved by, and then just sky.

"Where we going?" Julie asked.

"My office," Travis replied.

They landed on top of Travis's building and took the elevator to his floor. The doors slid open. Gladius sat behind her desk and upon seeing her dad, she bolted out of the chair and ran for him, jumping into his arms. Her doll scurried across the room and joined in by hugging his leg. He kicked it off with a gentle nudge. Lucas would have booted the creepy doll to the sun.

"Dad, I thought you were going to be killed," Gladius said with her small red hat sitting on the side of her head.

"I'm fine." Travis petted her head.

It was heartwarming to see a father-daughter reunion, but Lucas wanted to get going and everything else seemed to be a waste of time. He tapped his foot impatiently.

"We need to tell Opal," Hank said.

Lucas nodded his head in agreement. Poly's mom needed to know what had happened. All the parents had a right to know. "Can we use your stone?" He looked to Travis.

"Of course," he said.

"What stone?" Gladius asked.

"Nothing, dear."

She scowled at her dad. "You shouldn't keep secrets from me."

Travis took in a deep breath. "Let's go into my office. Gladius, can you make sure the shorefront house is ready? I don't want to stay here any longer than necessary. Gather your things."

Her face crunched up in anger, but she walked to her desk and started typing into her screen.

Lucas remembered Travis's office, the weapon-filled chamber where he conducted business. He adjusted Prudence on his shoulder as he crossed the door.

"How do you like the bow?" Travis asked.

"It's fine, thank you." He held back his glee over such a superior weapon, with the idea Travis might want it back.

Travis nodded once. "I'm happy it has a good home."

"Speaking of *home*," Julie said. She seemed rather annoyed by him.

"Oh, yes." Travis pulled the key from around his neck and opened the secret elevator. "I'm sorry you lost Poly, she's an amazing woman."

"We'll get her back," Julie said as they loaded onto the elevator. She held her arm out to stop the door from closing. "We are going home briefly and then we are coming back to find her. I will expect you to help find viable options upon our return." She scowled at him.

Travis lowered his head. "I can and will. And Julie, I apologize it took me so long to come around. When you have a city on your shoulders, you just can't jump."

Julie rolled her eyes and crossed her arms. "Just do it."

Lucas wanted to hear what happened to them over the last couple weeks, but they needed to get moving. Plus, the way Travis looked at Julie, like he knew her better than she did, annoyed him as well.

"You really should get going. Send me a message when you get back and I'll get you to safety." Travis grabbed a few things from his desk and stuffed them in his pocket. "Make the trip quick. When you do something like I just did, there can be swift consequences." He pulled the picture of Maya off the wall and walked toward the door. "Good luck to you." He left.

"What's his deal?" Lucas asked.

"Let's just get out of here," Julie huffed.

Making it to the stone room, Lucas bent over the stone in preparation. "You guys ready?"

The ground shook and a rumble blasted its way through the room. The shock wave sent Lucas to his backside. Julie and Hank spread their arms out to keep balance. Lucas stared at the ceiling, hoping it didn't cave in on them. Then it stopped. The stirred up dust lingered in the air.

"What'd you do?" Julie asked.

"Nothing, I didn't even touch the stone yet."

Hank walked to the door. "Sounded like a bomb to me."

"Oh my God, something's gone terribly wrong," Julie said looking at her Panavice.

CHAPTER 2

JOEY SAT AT THE HEAD of the kitchen table, with Samantha and Poly to either side of him. Poly grabbed a piece of bread made by Samantha and tore into it. Samantha looked at her lap and messed with her hands. In the silence, Poly's chewing seemed exceedingly loud.

He'd barely recovered from the heart attack she'd caused upon her arrival in the yard. Flinging Samantha off his body, he'd ran to her, touching her, making sure she wasn't a mirage or some projection of a person. He'd hugged her limp body and felt her, verifying she was real.

Now, he couldn't stop staring at her from across the kitchen table, questioning his eyesight. She had died. In his mind, he'd buried her and said his goodbye. But there she was, eating bread in front of him.

Samantha had tried to explain to Poly how they were being watched, and as long as they acted like a couple, Joey was left alone.

Poly scowled at her words and hadn't said much for the last two hours, except to confirm the rest of the Six were indeed still alive. This news felt heavier than Joey could handle and he only let a few pounds soak in at a time. He glanced at Poly, wanting to jump across the table and embrace her. He needed a physical connection with her, but her stiff body language told him no.

"So this is where you two have been this whole time?" she asked.

Joey jerked in his chair from the break of silence.

"No," Samantha said. "They kept us in an amusement park at first."

Poly dropped the bread on the table and wiped crumbs from her hands. She took a deep breath and looked at Joey. "An amusement park? Were there other people there?"

"No, it was just us. How did you get here?" Joey dared a question.

"I don't know, some guy from the crowd grabbed me."

"What crowd?" Joey asked.

Poly huffed, crossed her arms and leaned back in her chair. "I've spent every waking second trying to get back to you. Remember Max, the man who took you?"

"Yes," Joey said.

"I killed him in a duel on a stage, in front of a huge crowd and on live TV."

His mouth hung open. "You killed him?"

"That is just part of the path I've taken to get back to you. And then I get here to find you in the arms of Samantha. I knew you liked her but . . . I am so stupid." She looked away and shook her head.

"We thought you were dead," Samantha said.

"Sorry to interrupt your perfect fantasy world, but I am alive."

"It's not like that at all, Poly," Joey said.

"Isn't it?"

"We thought you were dead, all of you—that it was just us left."

Poly leaned forward. "Was it nice here? Did you two enjoy your time?"

"Some of it, yes," Joey glanced at Samantha as she glanced at him. There were nice moments, but with Poly sitting in front of him, it muddied the memories.

She stood from the table. "I'll tell you one thing, I am not staying in this place."

"This house is empty, there is a guest room—"

"I am not staying in your guest room like some third wheel," she burst out. "I am leaving this," she flung her hands in the air, "simulation—this fabrication of reality. I can't stand to be in it for another minute." She stormed out of the kitchen, flinging the front door open.

Joey and Samantha chased after her. Poly, for not knowing where she was going, kept a brisk pace. They passed the fountain and she veered off the path and stomped over bushes, creating a new path into the forest.

The fog seemed thinner. Joey could see more of the trees and he realized he had never gone beyond the paths, never had a reason to. The forest leaves crunched under his feet and he felt the pull of Preston. Knowing the Six were still alive made everything different.

Poly stopped and Joey nearly bumped into her.

"Look." She pointed ahead. "Is that normal?"

Joey stood next to her, staring at the peculiar black rectangle standing in the middle of the forest. It was a door. He squinted and thought he saw artificial light flicker in the crack at the bottom. "No."

"What is it?" Samantha asked.

"Let's find out." Poly continued her hurried pace through the fog, straight toward the door. She turned the knob and the door opened.

Joey walked passed her and into the dark room beyond. As his eyes adjusted to the darkness, he made out shapes—a locker room with benches in the middle. Black streaks ran down the face of some lockers, paint peeled on others. The musty smell of dirty laundry filled the room.

At the end of the lockers, another door stood open. One fluorescent light bulb on the ceiling lit their way into the next room. Joey turned back to the women and held a finger over his mouth. They both nodded. Poly scanned the room and had her throwing knives in each hand, while Samantha stayed close to him.

Joey pushed open the swinging door and studied the long hallway. A few lights flickered and he pushed onward. Further down the hall, a brighter light shone on a clean, hinged door.

When he got close enough, a shiny label that read *Office* hung on the door.

"What do you think?" Samantha whispered, grabbing onto his arm.

He shrugged and grasped the handle, opening the door. Joey put his hands against Poly and Julie, holding them back as he locked eyes with a man sitting behind the desk. He wore a MM black uniform with an R9 on his chest. His face gave no expression of interest or concern to the new arrivals in his office. Joey thought the man might have been dead until he blinked.

Poly pointed at the man behind the desk, her aggressive stance putting the hairs up on Joey's arm. "That's him," she said. "That's the man who took me."

CHAPTER 3

"WHAT?" LUCAS ASKED.

"I don't know, but my Panavice isn't detecting a single device. Usually there are hundreds, if not thousands of names detected. But, there's nothing." Julie looked at the ceiling.

"Nothing?"

"Why is it so hot?" Hank asked, wiping the sweat from his head.

The dome rumbled again. Lucas walked to the door and put his hand on the handle when Julie yelled, "Don't open that door." But he was already turning the handle.

Yanking his hand back, he rubbed it against his shirt. "It's hot."

"You hear that?" Julie asked.

"Water," Lucas said and got closer to the door. Water splashed around on the other side and hissed as it struck the door. The room cooled in a matter of seconds and Lucas dared another go at the door handle. Tapping the metal, it felt cool and he turned the handle.

"Wait!" Julie said.

But he already turned the handle too far to go back. The door flung open, knocking him to the ground with water rushing in, soaking them. It kept pouring in and Lucas jumped back to his feet. "We need to get out of here." He took big steps, making his way through the knee deep water. Looking down the hall of the next room, he saw the water pouring from the elevator.

"This place is going to fill," Julie said.

Half swimming, half walking, they got to the open elevator and pushed up on the top hatch. Water cascaded down on them. Through the steady stream, Lucas spotted daylight, but that couldn't be right. An entire building sat above. "We've got to get back to the stone."

"No, it's filled up," Julie said. "Help!"

The water pushed them to the top of the elevator and Lucas pulled his way through the opening. Hank and Julie filed through behind him, until they were all standing on top of the elevator.

Water rained down from above, but the daylight shined through the opening a hundred feet above. The sound of rushing water filled the space and it wasn't slowing down. Water bubbled up from the open hatch of the elevator and reached their ankles.

"How can we get up there?" Lucas asked. "You got a freaking grappling hook attachment on that thing?" He pointed at her Panavice.

Julie wiped the water from her face and studied the walls around them. "We wait. This water is filling up several inches a minute. We can ride it straight to the top."

Lucas saw the strain on her face. "What is it?"

"The water is going to be aerated, making it difficult to stay on top."

Water reached Lucas's waist and he pushed around the rising liquid with his hands. Bubbles swirled around as the steady streams from above crashed into the surface. "You talking about these bubbles?"

"Yes, we're going to have to swim hard." The water reached her chest.

"Hank, can we use you as a floatation device?" Lucas asked.

Hank responded with a grunt, looking as nervous as Lucas felt.

The water crested his chest and rushed to his neck. Julie paddled hard and Lucas let go of the foot hold and started swimming. It took a few seconds to find out what Julie was talking about. He fought to keep on top and already saw Julie struggling. He looked to the sunlight and it felt a mile away.

The water rose and took on a different smell as they ascended. If he hadn't been swimming for his life, he might have dwelled on the thoughts of possible sewer water getting mixed in.

Halfway up, Julie went under.

"Julie!" Lucas stopped swimming and dove down. She'd only dropped a foot and he grabbed her around the waist with one arm and kicked hard. They breached the surface.

"I can't, my arms are dead." She swam as hard as she could, but was losing the battle.

"No." He looked at the opening not twenty feet up. "Just a little longer. You have to." She dipped again, but Lucas had a hand on her and pushed her up. The strain of carrying two people with one less arm dragged on Lucas and he felt himself fading. "We can do this," he screamed.

Both of their faces dipped under and Lucas took in a mouthful of water. Coughing it out, he lost his rhythm and they both plunged. He kicked hard and swam but couldn't get back to the top.

Something grabbed his shirt and Lucas tried to free it, but it pulled him, propelling them to the surface. He held Julie tight and emerged, taking deep breaths. Looking up at the hole about the size of the elevator, he could see the edges were broken chunks of concrete and rebar. He reached for the top, and with Hanks help, pulled himself up halfway before turning back and grabbing Julie. He pulled, while Hank pushed, and she grabbed at the broken concrete, pulling herself from the hole.

Lucas rushed out, layingon the rubble next to Julie, panting hard. "Hank," he said between breaths, looking toward the opening.

"Don't worry about me. I'm just fine." Hank appeared, climbing from the hole.

"You're Julie," a man said. "Guys, I have Julie over here! Are you okay?"

Lucas jumped up at the appearance of the man.

"Yes, we're fine." Her face turned a light shade of red as the man gushed over her presence. She sat up and smiled.

Lucas, dumbfounded, stared at the man. What had Julie left out of her story?

"There may have been some banners of us around the city," Julie whispered.

"So, you're some kind of celebrity?"

"No, I'm a side kick. Poly's the star."

He leaves the girls alone for a couple weeks and they go and become famous. "Excuse me, sir," Lucas said. "What happened here?"

"A bomb exploded. It isn't safe here. You need to leave the area. More of the building could collapse at any second. A medical staff is forming on the street. You sure you're okay?"

"Yes, thank you."

The man nodded and walked away, holding out what looked like a metal detector in front of him.

Above them stood a tangled mess of metal and concrete, Lucas dreaded the thought of any people in the building. They followed a path through the rubble and onto the street where several rescue personnel waited.

"Julie, we're so glad you're alive." A woman in a white shirt with an oak tree logo wrapped a blanket around her. Julie looked confused, but took the blanket and used it to dry her hair.

Lucas took a blanket from a man and thanked him. The man gave long looks at his quiver and bow. He tried to dry his clothes as best he could but they were soaked. He wiped his face and hair and handed it back to the man.

"Is there anything we can do to help?" Julie asked.

"I don't think so, the building was empty from all the commotion today. The trick with Poly flying off with that guy was pretty cool."

"She was kidnapped," Julie said flatly.

The woman's mouth stood open as she stammered for words. "Who would do such a thing?"

"MM, that's who."

"I am just about fed up with the way MM is treating us here. I mean they kept orange from us! Look, you can see a *wrinkle* near my eye."

"What about them blowing up your buildings?" Lucas asked.

"I bet it was the mutants," the man in the yellow vest said.

"Oh please, they don't have anything capable of this." Lucas shook his head. These people had no clue who the mutants were.

"Who knows what they have out there?" the woman said.

Lucas wanted to argue the point further, explain how they had just come from the island. How they would never blow up a building. Even if they wanted to, they didn't have the resources. He took a deep breath and held back.

"Has Travis been located?" Julie asked.

"I haven't heard," the woman said. "Before you go, can I get a picture with you?"

Julie looked at her Panavice and ignored the woman. "Okay, well thanks for your help," she said, nodding her head to the right, indicating we should follow her.

"Wait," the man in yellow raised his hands and ran after them, "can you follow me?"

"Dude," Lucas said. "Thanks for the help, but we'll be on our way now. We don't need to follow you anywhere."

The man looked confused and switched his attention from Lucas to Julie. "No . . . what? Not like follow me, follow me, I mean . . ." he held his Panavice up and held it close to Julie. "If you follow me, I'll get like a thousand social points, at least."

Julie closed her eyes for a second. Lucas chuckled, he knew Julie was rolling her eyes under those closed lids. "I am not connected in that way, sorry, I can't follow you." Julie turned and motioned with her eyes for Lucas to follow her.

"Again, thanks for your help," Lucas said with finality and rushed after Julie.

The man stood with a blank expression, holding his Panavice. The poor guy's social score was going to have to stay where it was. Julie walked down the street, away from the building and damage. They crossed over a few barriers and into the city.

The dust hung in the air and people filled the streets, pointing at the destroyed building. Cameras zoomed by, rushing to the disaster. Lucas looked for any signs of MM, but none appeared. Julie walked fast through the crowd, keeping the blanket over her head like a hood. She took a left down an alleyway and stopped when no one was around. The narrow path was enough room for the three of them to face each other in a circle.

"What is it?" Lucas asked.

"Travis sent me a text back. They barely made it out in time, but he's at his shore house with Gladius."

"Well, that's good, I guess."

"He helped us stay alive here." Julie looked as if she was trying to figure out a difficult problem. He loved that look, it crunched up her nose and squinted her eyes in a cute way. She must have been contemplating this Travis guy.

Lucas didn't have such confusion with the tool. "He also stood next to Max for over a week. Or what about when he tricked us into that hell, Ryjack. Or when he dueled Poly. He's tried to kill us all at some point."

"He's different now. I think his hate is truly reserved for Harris."

"What is it with them?" Hank asked. "I thought Travis was going to stab Harris on the stage."

"I don't know, but he's sending Gladius to pick us up."

Lucas didn't like depending on someone else, but it wasn't safe to be running the streets of Sanct. He adjusted his bow. "Where are we going?"

"It's not far."

They were at the edge of a dock. The boards had rotted away long ago, leaving only concrete pillars and a few cross support beams. The waves crashed around the pillars, sending a salty mist into the air. After his lengthy excursion in the small rubber raft, he didn't have quite the same fascination with the ocean as he once did.

"She'll be here any a minute," Julie said, looking out on the horizon.

Lucas pointed to a small craft heading their way. It bounced on the waves and churned up a mist. Gladius stood behind the wheel, her red hat flapping in the wind, hair damp and matted against her head. She didn't look happy and drove the boat to the shores' edge. The boat sprayed water on them. He closed his eyes and spit the water from his mouth. It wasn't like he could get any wetter.

"Get on," Gladius said.

Her doll sat on the seat next to her. It creeped Lucas out when the doll's eyes followed him as he boarded.

"Thanks," Julie said.

"Yeah, thanks for the lift," Lucas said.

"Hey, Hank." Gladius flashed her brilliant smile. "Can you sit next to me and hold Gem? She almost fell out getting here."

"Uh, sure," Hank said and picked up Gem and sat in the passenger seat.

Lucas was happy to take a seat next to Julie on the back bench. Gladius turned the boat around and headed into the ocean. The circular boat glided over the waves and made for a smooth ride if you didn't mind the constant mist blowing in your face.

Lucas scooted closer to Julie, put his arm around her and pulled her closer. "I missed you," he whispered in her ear.

She looked weary and tired, but she wrapped her arm around his waist and placed her head on his chest. It was the closest moment they had to being alone in way too long. He held her tight and didn't say anything. Before they knew it, they pulled up to a massive house built into the cliffs of the shoreline.

Gladius pulled the boat into a cave below the house and parked it at a dock. The motor silenced as she placed her hand on a screen.

"Oh no, look at Gem, her outfit's a mess," Gladius pouted.

Lucas snorted, "Silver lining, she looks exactly like you."

Gladius gave him a sharp look as Hank lifted Gem to her. Gem's arms extended out, searching for her owner's embrace. The matching red hats they both wore were soggy and their hair was matted down. Gem's hands pulled at her hair and looked at it.

"I'm so sorry, Gem, I should have left you behind, but I just couldn't leave you alone, not right now." She hugged the doll and got off the boat. "Come on, people, I didn't get all soaked just so you could cuddle." Gladius glared at Lucas and Julie, then walked up the wood staircase and through the door at the top.

Hank hopped out and started up the stairs as Lucas helped Julie out of the boat.

Travis greeted them at the door. "I'm so glad you guys made it, when I saw the building go down . . . well, I thought the worst."

Lucas shook the man's hand and gawked at his house. Floor to ceiling glass covered one wall, giving a stunning view of the ocean. Works of art hung on the wall, sculptures of men and women and shiny metal decorated the corners. Not to be outdone by the weapons lining much of the free space on the walls. Even with everything competing for attention, Lucas couldn't look at anything but the motorcycle displayed in the center of the room, gleaming with high polish.

Travis must have noticed his eyes lingering on the bike. "You like this motorcycle?"

Lucas glanced at Travis. "Yeah, cool bike."

"The gas engine was last built in Vanar five hundred years ago." He moved his hand close to the handle bars but stopped. He stared at the bike, shaking his head. "This bike still runs. Sometimes I think of taking it to the city." His eyes brightened with the thought. "But it would be a little flashy."

"Yeah, sorry about your building, I hope no one was in it," Lucas said.

Travis stared at the white marble floors. "I'd had it cleared hours before. I suppose I knew MM might try to kill me when I helped Poly."

"So you were going to help us the whole time?" Julie asked.

"Yes," he said loudly. In a quieter voice, he continued, "It destroyed me to have to stand behind the man who killed my daughter."

Julie looked away from Travis, she gritted her teeth. Lucas knew she was holding back something, maybe something about Compry? Lucas pictured Compry pushing the lunch cart into their table during training, making the plates crash around. She must have hated being a servant in any capacity. Lucas wished he could have learned more about her.

"I'm sorry about Compry, she was a great woman. I'm glad to have known her for the time I did," Julie said.

"Thank you," Travis said. "You're all soaked. Gladius, why don't you take them to the guest rooms and get them some clothes."

"Fine," she said. "Come on, Gem."

The bedrooms were as elegant as the rest of the house. Ocean views from the solid glass walls and works of art on the others. How rich was Travis? Lucas didn't understand the collection of artifacts. He liked the weapons and such, but did you need to have so much of everything? He didn't want to be flashy with his bike, yet he displayed it front and center.

Lucas didn't like men who said one thing and did another. But Julie seemed to trust the guy and that was enough for him in the end.

Gladius took Julie to another room and closed the door.

"You want to take a shower first?" he asked Hank.

"Sure." He headed into the bathroom.

Lucas sat on the soft bed and disrobed down to his underwear. He searched the room for a spot to place the clothes. A bronze statue in the corner of the room of a man flexing his large muscles looked like a coat rack. He draped his clothes over his bronze arms.

"That's a statue of Articus, and it's probably worth as much as this house."

Lucas spun around to find Gladius standing in the doorway holding a stack of clothes. She eyed him up and down in his boxers and raised an approving eyebrow as she walked into the room.

"You don't knock, do you?"

"What's the purpose?"

Lucas shrugged. "Thanks for the clothes." He took the stack of clothes from her, trying to act as comfortable as she seemed.

"You and Hank aren't like the men around here."

Lucas put on the shirt, the fabric was softer than anything he ever felt. "What do you mean?"

"Most men see my advances and it's game on. But you two back away and avert your eyes. I haven't even seen you look at my fantastic body." She pushed her chest up for a second.

"I only have eyes for Julie. And Hank . . . well, he's just Hank. I don't think he would hit on a woman, even if his life depended on it."

She appeared to soak in his words, nodding at the right times. He never noticed before, but she was beautiful in a quirky way, with her over-the-top clothes and strange personality. Then it hit him, she didn't have Gem with her. With that thing around, he had never looked at her directly.

"Yes, I saw you and Julie on the boat, cozying up. I don't mind, most of the men I play with are married, she would never know." She smirked.

He didn't know if she was playing with him or serious, but he didn't want to find out—his danger meter was peaking. "Where's that doll of yours?"

Her coy face changed to a scowl. "She's getting cleaned, and her name is Gem."

"Hey, Lucas, can you—" Hank halted his steps into the bedroom when he noticed their company. Eyes bulging, he brought his hands down and covered his parts, scooting back behind the door. "Sorry . . . Gladius," his sputtered, face turning a deep shade of red.

"You two are so weird," she said and left the room.

Lucas chuckled and brought the clothes to Hank, who snatched them and closed the bathroom door.

AFTER EVERYONE WAS SHOWERED, THEY met in the family room.

Travis sat in a chair, holding a glass of liquid. "Would anyone like a drink?" he asked, standing at their arrival.

"Yeah," Lucas said. Julie shot him a look and he rolled his eyes.

"I'm going to find Poly," she said and brought out her Panavice.

Travis walked to the bar and dropped a few cubes of ice in a glass and poured two fingers.

"Thanks." Lucas took the glass, raised it to Travis, and swallowed the contents. His eyes watered a bit and he almost coughed, but choked it down. He didn't want to seem like a noob. Looking to Julie, he found her glaring into her screen.

Hank picked at his too-small shirt, the fabric making him look like some bodybuilder. Lucas wasn't sure what to do next, but sitting in a fancy house and looking at each other wasn't going to get anything done. He slapped his legs and let out a long breath.

"Patience," Julie said.

She knew him so well. He slowed his mind and stared out the window. The dark ocean churned and slammed into the rocks below. He wasn't a fan of quiet moments anymore. When his mind had a chance to catch up with him, it would wander to the terrors of what he'd seen. The bite on his leg, feeling himself changing into a grinner, Nathen and Compry being shot, Almadon's body, killing the pilot on the aircraft. He took a deep breath. He felt his heart beating hard. He needed to do something to get away from the thoughts.

"You have an interesting collection of art," Lucas said.

"Thank you."

"I never got to thank you for the bow and arrows, Travis. It is the most remarkable weapon I have ever shot."

Travis grinned. "I'm glad you have it. A bow of that caliber is supposed to be used. It was a waste on my wall."

Lucas glanced at Julie who moved her fingers across her screen. He hated small talk. This Travis guy seemed okay, but how could he trust a man who sent them to Ryjack? They could've died in the bank if it wasn't for Julie. He continued his conversation to eat up the silence. "You ever use that Alius stone yourself?"

"What's an Alius stone?" Gladius asked. She walked into the family room holding Gem. They wore a matching blue dress and hat.

"Oh, just a type of weapon," Travis brushed her question off and addressed Lucas. "And no, I haven't. Most don't even know they exist."

Lucas eyed Travis, he saw the pleading in his eyes to drop the subject and while everything inside was telling him to stir it up, he moved on. "Yeah, it's pretty hardcore." He stared at Julie, trying to get her attention by sheer brain power. It wasn't working.

She started talking without looking up. "I'm following a lead. They have some strange diversions. Emmett signed off on a bunch of packages to be moved. It could be Poly, but let me keep digging."

"I'm sorry you guys lost Poly," Gladius said. She sat down on the other armchair and petted Gem's hair. "I originally thought she was some obnoxious girl after my dad, but she turned out to be a little more interesting than that."

Lucas raised an eyebrow at her words, but didn't make his thoughts into words.

Julie stood from the couch, clutching the screen with shaky hands. "Ryjack," Julie said. "They were taken to Ryjack, in their LA bunker."

Hank swore and Lucas leaned his head back, shutting his eyes.

"Gladius, can you go get the boat ready?" Travis said.

She huffed and picked up Gem, storming off to a back room.

"There's no stone anywhere near it." Julie sounded panicked.

Lucas took in a deep breath and opened his eyes. They were in the largest city in the country. Ten million people equaled ten million grinners. "Do you know where, exactly?"

"Yep."

"Then, let's go," Lucas said. "What's the closest stone?"

"Vegas."

Great, the last time he left Vegas was in a pit full of grinners. They were probably ten deep by now all piled up around the stone. "Let me guess, Ferrell's is the next closest?"

"Yep, and there's another weird thing," Julie said. "I think they left a trail for me to follow. They *want* us to go there."

"Trap," Hank said.

"Most definitely," Julie agreed and looked at Travis.

"I would go with you in a second, if present circumstances were different," Travis said.

Lucas eyed him, trying to decide how legitimate he was. Travis seemed to brighten up when they mentioned Poly's name and Julie trusted the man, but he seemed to be hiding something.

"There is also the issue of the stone being under water here," Hank said.

"The backup pumps will kick in and get rid of most of it," Travis answered.

"Well, thanks for having us," Lucas said, before standing up and walking next to Julie.

"Wait, let me get you a few toys to take with you," Travis said.

If he brought out a weird Gem doll, Lucas would leave—with or without his friends.

Travis placed his palm on a screen next to a large steel door. A green light lit above before the door hissed and clicked as it opened. Lucas entered the small steel room, smiling. Similar to his now destroyed office, the walls were lined with weapons and steel cabinets he was sure contained more weapons. He had to give the man credit for his collection of killables. They were mostly blade weapons, but a few bows and strange guns lined the walls.

"My vault is your vault."

Lucas didn't need any more of an invitation. He went to the display case with a bow on the wall and many arrows lined up below it. He could never trade out Prudence, but she would love to have new things to shoot. He touched their narrow shafts, feeling the smooth surface of the arrows.

"I thought you might like these. Let me show you something," Travis said and opened a drawer below the display.

"These might look small and weak, but I assure you they are as strong as any arrow you've ever used. And look, you can store a hundred in a quiver.

"Thank you," Lucas said. He took the box from Travis and filled his quiver with the thin arrows.

"I think I have something you might like, Julie." Travis walked to a drawer and pulled out a bag with an oak tree leaf on it. "It's a combat med pack. Poly mentioned you saved their lives. It also has water filters and enough food rations to last you guys days out there. "

Julie took the bag. "Thank you. I hope we don't need it though." She glanced at Lucas.

Lucas took in a deep breath and felt the hint of pain where he had been bitten. She saved his life those days following. He never told his friends about the night shift he had with Hank in the woods of Ryjack. Hank had fallen asleep and left him with the thoughts he was going turn and kill his friends in their sleep. He had searched for Joey's guns, but the guy slept with them on. Chills ran down his body and he closed his eyes trying to forget the past.

"Here, Hank. You should take this gun. It's a railgun designed to fire hundreds of tiny projectiles. You could mow down a herd of those dead with this gun," Travis handed Hank a gun with a square barrel.

"Thanks." Hank took the weapon and didn't know what to do with it and ended up stuffing it in his pocket.

"I bet those grinners have filled that pit back up in Vegas, you got anything for those guys?" Lucas shivered, thinking of how he got bit in that pit.

"Yeah, let me see here . . ." Travis dug into a cabinet and handed him a device. After they received instructions on how to detonate it, they were ready to go.

AFTER THE LONG, WET BOAT ride back to the dock in Sanct, they said their goodbyes to Gladius and snuck to the edge of the pit they'd ascended only hours ago. Emergency crews hovered around, and smoke tendrils swirled from the partially collapsed building.

Thankfully, they were able to sneak around the main groups and get down the elevator shaft with a rope Travis gave them. Lucas went first. He reached the bottom and looked down the elevator hole, only a small puddle of water remained. Lucas whistled and Julie descended down the rope.

"This is freaky," Julie called out. Her voice echoed throughout the chamber. She made good time and they whistled to Hank.

"Did Travis say the weight rating on this thing?" Lucas yelled up.

Hank didn't respond as he lowered himself to the landing.

They climbed down into the elevator with little more than a splash of water.

"Travis said there were pumps," Julie said.

The Alius stone room sat lower than the rest of the underground complex and two feet of water filled it as a result. Lucas shook his head. For Travis's plan to work, he had to move quickly and running through water wasn't going to make it any easier.

"How are you going to do it?" Julie asked.

"Let me practice."

Lucas stood in the knee deep water, with just the tip of the stone sticking out of the water. He held the bomb in his hand and thought of Travis's instructions. He needed to set the timer on the bomb, press in the Ryjack code and get out of the dome before it jumped, taking the ticking bomb with it.

"Time me." He walked over and placed the bomb on top of the stone and got into a running stance, facing the door. "Three, two, one." He jumped toward the door, moving his legs high as he ran to it. The water sloshed around him, soaking his pants and slowing him down. He hit the three stairs at the door way and jumped out into the room with Hank and Julie.

"Four point two five seconds."

He lay on the floor breathing hard. He would have to be less than five seconds to get out quick enough.

"Maybe we can do something else," Julie said.

"No, we're wasting time as is. Let me try again. Hank, hold my stuff." He handed Hank his quiver and bow and then slipped off his pants and tossed them on Hanks face. If it gave him fraction of a second it was worth it.

He tried much harder on the next go.

"Three point eight seconds."

Lucas slapped the wet floor. He needed to shave another second off the time. He stood up, breathing hard and stared into the dang water filled Alius stone room. Lucas considered himself athletic but did he have another second of speed in him? "I'm going to do it for real this time."

"No, you're not even close. You could get killed."

"I can do it. I've just been taking it slow the last few times. I can do it in two seconds if I really tried. Besides, how many times can I do this before I start to get slower?"

Julie raised an eyebrow. He couldn't get away from lying to her, but his logic obviously wore her down. He set the bomb Travis gave them next to the door and put a one minute timer on it as Travis showed him. The bomb showed fifty nine seconds, fifty eight . . .

He sloshed to the stone and kept a maximum distance from him and the stone. He felt the divots on the stone and placed most of the code in, the stone hummed, he put his feet in a running stance and pushed his finger into the last divot.

He rushed to the door, the heavy water slowing him down. He felt fast and placed a foot on the bottom stair and jumped toward the open door. His face hit a wall and he fell to the floor.

The door was gone and the dome had gone dark. The green digits of the bomb flashed out, sending tiny amounts of light with each passing second, counting down, forty-one, forty. He brushed the water from his face and stared at the bomb. The water sloshed behind him and he turned to face the noise. A grinner stumbled by, it hadn't seen him yet. Another grinner staggered near him but didn't react—how could they not see him?

Without Prudence, he stood still, taking advantage of the seconds the grinners were giving him. They moved around the room in no particular pattern, maybe thirty of them in total. In a matter of seconds, he knew the grinners would notice him, chew him up and kill him. This bomb could be the one thing that clears the room for his friends.

The grinners sloshed in the water toward him. They must have finally noticed the new arrival in their pit. He could make a dash for the stone . . . no, too many surrounding it now. The phantom pain in his leg returned and he reached at it with his free hand. He lifted the bomb and the flashing green light gave enough light to see their faces.

They weren't grinning.

CHAPTER 4

"WHAT DO YOU MEAN HE'S gone?" Harris asked.

Jack didn't lift his head from the computer screen in front of him. "He was scheduled to meet with two senators, but he didn't show." He swiped his fingers over the screen. "It appears they're looking for him as well."

What the hell was Marcus up to? Ever since he got Joey and Samantha's serum he'd been everywhere, showing the world he was still alive and well.

Harris leaned back in his chair. Not too long ago, Compry would've been sitting next to him. A couple decades further back and his wife would be in that seat. The longer he lived, the less he had. Everything seemed to die around him. He took in a deep breath and stared at the side of Jack's head. How long would it be until he lost another? The humming engine of the aircraft filled the silence. The young man willingly signed up for it. Who was he to stop him?

"What are the kids up to?"

"Sir, there's been an explosion."

Harris jerked upright in his seat. The screen displayed a live video of the partially collapsed building. "Isn't that Travis's building?"

"The one with his office, yes."

"Were the kids in there?"

"I don't know."

"Travis, you better have gotten them out," Harris said, clenching his fist.

"Do you want me to turn around?"

Harris stared at the screen. "No."

Jack nodded and went back to his computer.

The next hour he spent looking at the pictures of the scene at Travis's building, with emergency workers frantically searching for survivors. Travis announced he had canceled all work in the building since MM's takeover of the town and no one should have been in there. Harris shook his head, it seemed too convenient to have everyone out of the building. Travis knew he was going to betray Max and knew the consequences of his actions.

If Travis got the kids out of the building, he was further indebted to Travis. He didn't think he would live long enough to pay that debt, but if given the chance, he most certainly would. The man had every right to hate him. In Harris's hands, two of his daughters had been killed, not to mention their old history with his first wife.

"Poly's video has gone viral," Jack said.

Harris nodded. The numbers on the video had already reached a billion. The video started a debate, even within Capital, about the limits of MM's power over the world. He started the conversation a few weeks ago, and now this gave them a platform to openly criticize MM.

Where was Marcus in all this? Could Marcus be in hiding? Marcus used to enjoy this part of the game, deflecting blame and spinning the situation until he came out looking like the hero. He'd seen it first hand, many times. This time, there would be no back doors and no diversions; he wanted to knock on the front door.

The world was furious over the Sanct disaster, but they would soon forget. He had to take action with the smell of blood still fresh in the air. Even a week could be too late.

"How much longer until we arrive?" Harris asked.

"We'll be at Capital in one hour," Jack said. "Sir, I've been monitoring MM's headquarters for the last thirty minutes and something's happening. The chatter has exploded."

"What are they saying?"

"I don't know yet, they switched encryptions, but the volume is staggering."

"What do you think it is?"

Jack shook his head and crunched his eyebrows together, staring at the screen. "Their servers are going offline, I think they're crashing. Someone's attacking their systems."

Harris rubbed his chin and leaned closer to the screen. Almadon said it wasn't possible and she tried many times. Marcus himself had setup all the server's codes and it was beyond anyone to figure them out. Even if anyone got close,

Alice would interject. It was the biggest reason Marcus had a bill passed banning all A.I. development nearing the singularity.

Companies were banned from creating robots, beyond toys. Marcus figured only an A.I. computer would have a chance at beating his system. Had someone been building one, waiting until this moment of chaos to unleash it? Marcus had made so many enemies through the centuries, it wouldn't surprise him.

"I can't believe someone finally got to them," Harris said, shaking his head.

"This is too massive," Jack said, his attention bounced from screen to screen. "Everything in MM going down. The orange distribution plants around Capital are reporting massive failures as well. Wait, now the whole west coast is crashing." Jack took his fingers off the keys and squeezed his hands. Sweat beaded at his brow. He stared at Harris, looking pale.

"What is it?" Harris asked.

"The whole world's going dark. . ." Jack looked as if he might throw up.

"Calm down, this could be the very distraction we need."

"There's nothing that could do this, nothing. This is too quick, too powerful. Everything online is being wiped from the planet. Don't you see? This is going to cause global chaos." Jack shook his head. "No, there's only one man in the world that could pull this off."

Harris agreed, it just didn't make sense. Why would Marcus destroy the world he spent a lifetime building?

CHAPTER 5

JOEY STOOD BEHIND THE CHAIR and glared at Emmett. With Julie and Poly standing to either side, he felt for the guns that weren't there. How much of a chance did he have with Emmett if he moved to attack? Emmett's face didn't change as he regarded them. He could have been reading a car's maintenance schedule.

"Why did you take me?" Poly said, breaking the silence.

"He wanted me to," Emmett said. "But I didn't bring you here for his entertainment. I brought you here to be rid of you."

"What are you talking about?" Joey asked.

"Where are we?" Julie added.

"We're on Ryjack, LA, to be precise."

Joey took in a quick breath. "Why?"

"Marcus thought I was building a grand bunker here—a retreat of sorts. But in his bedridden state, I disobeyed his orders. I couldn't allow someone like him, a natural, running the company into the ground."

"And what does this have to do with us?" Joey asked.

Emmett's eyes narrowed before going back to his normal blank face. "I want you gone, but I won't kill you. It wouldn't be very sporting of me to do so. You've impressed me, going through the sevens and eights like you have." Emmett stood from his chair. "I'm going to give you a fighting chance."

Joey's heart raced and he clenched his fists in preparation. Maybe if all three of them attacked at once . . .

Emmett laughed. "I'm not fighting you, it would be like choking a baby. But don't take this as a free pass." He looked at the ceiling. "It won't be easy to leave this place alive and if you manage to get out of the bunker, I doubt you will make it out of the city."

Joey looked at the ceiling. What was above them? "We've seen worse than a rundown building."

"There are things in this place that would make the average person curl up and want to die. You kids have earned my respect." Emmett stared at Joey's wrists. "What are those bracelets for?"

Joey stared at the man behind the desk and rubbed at the metal on his wrists. "Something I made at summer camp."

The corner of Emmett's mouth cracked. "You know, once I dispose of Marcus, I could use people like you. If you can live through this, that is."

Was he offering them a chance at freedom? Joey wanted to get home, get back to his family and the awkward birthday parties. He wanted to see the Preston Six whole once again. The idea seemed whimsical, something a silly boy would dream up. The idea of going back to a normal life was so deep and tantalizing in the recesses of his mind, he didn't dare open the door, or he would get lost in the fantasy.

"We'll get out of this rat trap," Joey said.

"I'm rooting for you." Emmett stood. "I hope you make it. I, on the other hand, am leaving this place. I have to get back to Capital and pay a visit to Marcus." He turned his back to them and placed his hand on the wall, glancing back over his shoulder. "In my desk drawer, you will find a few items of use." A green light lit near his hand and a hidden door swung open next to him and he stepped inside. Once inside, the door slammed shut. A loud hum emanated before a whoosh of air, and then silence.

Poly stared at the wall, shaking her head. "Probably some escape pod. Freaking coward."

Joey ran to the door and pulled at the edges, but it wouldn't open. He kicked the steel, bruising his foot in the process. "Dammit, if I only had my guns."

"There are a couple items in here," Poly said, staring at the open drawer. She pulled out a kitchen knife and turned the blade in the light.

Joey rushed to the drawer and saw the only other item, a flashlight. He picked it up, a long flashlight with some weight to it. The steel construction might allow for it to be used as a blunt weapon of sorts.

"We should consider ourselves lucky, I think that man could've killed us instantly if he wanted to." Samantha was seemingly glad Emmett was gone. "So we are in that zombie world?"

"He said LA," Poly said.

"Yeah, don't you remember?" Joey asked. "This is where it started. I bet this was their research bunker."

"Great, grinners originated here?" Poly huffed.

"Grinners?"

"Lucas started calling them that and the name stuck."

Joey couldn't help but feel a little jealous when he heard about Lucas and Poly. They shared something while he was with Samantha.

"So now what?" Samantha asked.

"We get out of here," Poly and Joey said, smiling at each other when they realized they'd said it in unison.

After some searching, they found a staircase leading to the next floor, which turned out to be mostly living quarters. Following the staircase up many floors, the staircase ended at a single steel door.

Joey placed his hand on the cool handle and turned the knob, sighing in relief when it turned. The door opened into a hallway. A few lights flickered and he saw the distinctive oak tree symbols on the walls. He knew it was a medical wing of some kind.

"Stay behind me," he instructed and saw Poly roll her eyes. She probably had a good reason to be annoyed, as she was the one with the knives. Moving forward, he led them down the hallway, shining his flashlight in quick bursts around the dark corners of the hall.

"Where are we going?" Samantha whispered, grabbing hold of his shirt.

"We keep going up. There's got to be another staircase."

The light bounced off a glass wall on the left side of the hallway, probably an executive's office back in the day. They would stand behind their glass wall and watch over the minions below.

He stopped and put his hand out, signaling them to stop with him. The putrid smell of the half dead wafted around the space. They were close. He didn't see anything, but heard a shuffle just past the glass.

Gliding past the glass wall, Joey kept an eye on the window. He didn't want to shine a light, knowing what the room contained.

"Something moved in there," Samantha said and pointed at the glass.

Joey resigned himself. It was better for her to see one in an aquarium for the first time, versus one lunging its black mouth at her throat. He raised the light onto the glass. What used to be a woman, dressed in a black suit and tied down to a chair, wrestled against her restraints. Her skin looked dull and saggy, it drooped on her face like it was too heavy. Snarling and groaning at them with its black mouth, it shook and convulsed until the chair fell over. Its legs and hands grabbed at the floor, pulling itself closer to them.

Samantha flattened herself against the wall, sucking in a deep breath. "Is *that* a grinner?"

"Yep," Poly said. "Freaking MM tried to create some next level type human."

"To be honest, I thought you were exaggerating. I just didn't think it could be real."

43

Joey apologized to Samantha. He wished she could have kept the doubt in her mind, but now she knew it was real. Joey wanted to comfort her, but he kept his mind on scanning their surroundings. Harris hadn't spent many hours in the scene generator training him for moments like this, only to have him lose focus when it mattered.

They walked past the glass wall, ignoring the thing on the ground, clawing its way across the carpet toward them.

"Look," Samantha said. She pointed at something next to a door.

Joey shined his flashlight on what turned out to be a map. "Fire escape procedures." He leaned in closer. A star labeled *You Are Here* followed with an arrow leading through the door behind the map. He studied the drawing for a few more seconds before opening the door. Another set of stairs.

"The escape path said up," Samantha said.

He peered in between the stairs down below and shined his light. He saw motion a few floors down, a person in all black. The grinner looked up with its grayish skin and opened its mouth and yelled. The creature staggered up the stairs toward them, making a clunking sound.

"What is it?" Samantha asked. "We need to get out of here." She moved toward the door.

"Wait," Joey said. "He's wearing a guard's uniform. He could be armed."

"Let's go," Samantha pleaded.

"They can't use weapons. Poly, you think you can take this one out?"

"Please." She brandished her long kitchen knife in her hand and stood in a ready stance as the clunk sounds of footsteps grew louder. Only a few flights left.

Joey stood behind Poly, sucked in a breath and tensed his muscles in case he had to jump in. Poly awaited the thing and when it reached the last step, she lunged forward with a quick stab to the thing's head. It crumbled to its knees and fell face first on the concrete landing.

"*This* is what you've been dealing with?" Samantha asked, gasping for air. She held out her hand and pointed at the dead thing on the ground.

"Yeah," Joey said.

"And they just kill you for no reason?"

"No, they have a reason . . . they're hungry," Poly said, wiping her knife on the grinner's black jacket.

Joey pulled at the jacket and smiled when he found the gun on its side. A semi-automatic 9mm pistol. He pulled the man's belt and holster off and wrapped it around his waist. The belt had several clips as well. He breathed out a sigh of relief at the feeling of a gun at his side. He could stand next to Poly and fight these things.

"Let's move," Joey said.

A new clunk sound resonated from the steel steps below. He peered over the rail, shining the flashlight into the darkness below. Bodies moved, many of them, climbing the stairs.

"There's more?" Samantha whimpered.

"They never end," Poly said and walked past Joey up the stairs.

"Come on, move those legs." Joey gave Samantha a nudge. She tore away from the edge of the railing and climbed the stairs. A grinner screamed from below, it must have caught a glimpse of them. "Stay to the outside, they won't see us."

They ran up a few flights of stairs and the sound of the grinners diminished.

"You hear that?" Joey asked, stopping his movement to listen. It was a bell. He strained his ears, looking up to the sound, only to be greeted with the yells of grinners above. Their arms brushed the railing as they staggered down the stairs, maybe a few flights above them. "Crap, they're coming from above."

"What did that map say?" Samantha asked, her shaking hand grasping her neck.

Poly's face looked like cold steel. She held a knife in each hand. He knew she could take on whatever came down those stairs.

"It just showed this staircase led to the top."

"There must be another way?"

Joey glanced up and down the stairs. They were getting close and he wasn't going to take a chance on grinners coming in both directions. "We need to pick a floor."

"Let's get a bit higher and then we can lock the doors behind us," Poly said.

Joey liked the idea and led the way up the next two flights of stairs, stopping on the landing. He glanced up again, they were too close for another floor. The sound of dragging feet and the rotting smell of death surrounded them. They stood in front of a single steel door marked *B16*.

He took out his gun and pushed the door open. One light shown at the far end of the room, illuminating the variety of medical and office equipment stacked haphazardly around the large room. He shined his flashlight around the room, looking for movement but nothing did.

"Come on," Joey said.

Poly and Samantha entered the room and he slammed the door closed. A grinner thumped against the door. He put his back against the steel door and felt the vibrations of the bodies hitting the other side. He closed his eyes for a second and hoped the floor they were on was devoid of grinners.

"Let's stay close and figure out where we are," Joey said.

The next room was a huge, long room, filled with cubicles, desks, and papers littering the floor. A few lights blinked and shined light across the room. He shook his head. Every cubicle could harbor a grinner. He couldn't go back, but he sure didn't want to go forward.

"Stay close to my back, Samantha, we're going to move slow and low. Poly, watch our backs."

Samantha walked so close on his heels, she stumbled into him. Poly walked sideways and glanced backward as they moved. He crept up on the first cubicle. A long dead body, mostly a skeleton laid on the floor. Samantha let out a squeak. Poly put her hands on her hips and glared at Samantha.

"Sorry, I'm not used to seeing this stuff like you all," she whispered.

The next five were empty, then he heard a faint sound of scratching on the wall ahead. He moved into the next opening and a grinner walked out. He reactively shot it in the head. The thundering shot echoed throughout the area. Joey closed his eyes and cursed at what he had just done. Poly should be stealth killing these grinners.

"Sorry, it sort of jumped at me," Joey explained, breathing hard.

"I'm glad you killed that thing," Samantha said.

"Yeah, but now every Damned one of them will be coming this way," Poly said on her tiptoes, looking down the train of cubicles.

"Maybe that thing was the only . . . ." Samantha trailed off and turned toward the sounds of rustling chairs and groaning grinners.

At first it sounded as if it might only be a few, but then it grew and quickly became a horde stumbling out into the aisles, pushing their chairs over and stumbling into the open areas. Joey looked at the ceiling and thought about all the duct escapes he had seen in the movies, but there was only a regular ceiling above. The vent register was big enough for a dog.

"They're coming," Samantha said.

"We can take them, Joey," Poly said.

He looked over the tops of the cubicles and saw the heads of many grinners bobbing in and out of sight. Taking a deep breath, he spoke. "I have an idea."

CHAPTER 6

LUCAS HELD THE BOMB IN his hand and watched the ticker countdown to ten seconds. Another grinner walked by, sniffed him and continued on. He twisted the bomb and turned it off.

A rat fell in from above and the grinners lunged at it. They tore its small body apart and fought for each piece. Lucas grabbed his stomach at the sickening sight. If he had his bow, he might have a chance. He didn't see any weapons he could use, except chunks of concrete left over from the collapse. Concrete could work.

He picked up a large piece of concrete and bashed it against the head of the nearest grinner. It fell into the water and floated on top, not moving. Another grinner walked by and he did the same. Noticing his acts hadn't incited any activity in the remaining grinners, he took a deep breath of exhilaration. He wasn't going to die, the zombies for whatever reason didn't see him as food. He could mingle with them.

It wouldn't be long before Hank and Julie showed, so Lucas ran around the room killing each grinner. It took only a few minutes. He tossed the gooey concrete chunk into the water. He had done it, he had killed them all.

Julie and Hank appeared next to the stone. He made eye contact with Julie and relief washed over her face.

Hank yelled and fumbled to get his gun out of his pocket. He jostled it and ended up tossing it into the dead grinner filled water.

"What happened?" She used her foot to push a floating grinner away.

"I don't know. They didn't see me, I guess. So, I turned off the bomb and killed them all one by one with a brick."

"As in you were all fast, like Joey?"

"Nope, they just didn't care I was here, even as I killed every one of them."

"Weird," Hank said.

Julie ran her hands over his body, inspecting it. "Did any of them bite you?"

"Nah."

She spent a moment looking over the dead grinners and looked as if she might throw up. "Can we get out of this hole?"

They climbed out on a pile of concrete rubble and silently made their way through the casino, to the front entrance with its gleaming marble floors. Lucas looked up the stairs and saw Hooper's Top Hats. He thought about getting another tuxedo, but time wouldn't allow it.

Walking past their original footprints, it felt like a life time ago since they'd been here last. Daylight shone through the large windows and it heated up the lobby. When they stepped out of the front door, Lucas hoped their Hummer would still be there. It was gone.

"Dang," Lucas said.

"Who would take it?" Julie asked.

"I bet it was people from that Sanctuary place," Lucas said. Poly had spotted a building not far down the strip with *Sanctuary* written on the side.

"Oh yeah, I remember that from the balcony," Hank said, looking up.

Lucas wanted his vehicle. If they had any chance of making it to LA, they needed a car. They wouldn't last a day walking in the summer heat of the New Vegas desert.

"What are we going to do?" Hank asked.

Lucas took a deep breath. "We go to this Sanctuary place and ask for help."

Julie protested for a bit, but they had to make quick progress. Lucas felt in his core his friends were in trouble. Wasting just a few minutes might get them killed. Julie conceded to the plan, but didn't feel good about it.

They walked down the strip with cars piled on each side of the road. The desert sands covered large sections of the road and weeds grew out of control. A few palms clung to life here and there. When the large white Sanctuary sign came into view, Lucas felt his muscles tense. Something about the way Harris had talked about them. What had he said? They don't like outsiders? That couldn't be it, why would they have a huge banner advertising what they were?

They stood on the road in front of the old casino. A tall, wooden wall reached all the way to the edge of the road and made it impossible to see the entrance to the casino sitting several hundred yards behind it. Lucas scanned the front wall, searching for a way in. "You guys see anything?" he asked.

"I don't," Hank muttered, squinting with a hand over his eyes.

"Let's walk the wall, there's got to be an entrance somewhere." With Prudence in hand, he walked close to the wall. Was plywood all it took to keep the grinners out? He rubbed his free hand on the old gray wood and bits of it flaked to the ground.

They worked their way down the wall, moving closer to the casino, inspecting every inch as they did.

"Stop and place your weapon on the ground," a man's voice ordered.

Lucas froze in place and frantically looked for the person behind them. "We are here only to get our car back."

"You have five seconds to place your weapon on the ground."

Lucas's hand shook as he placed his bow on the concrete sidewalk. He unslung his quiver and laid it next to Prudence. "We don't want any trouble."

A section of plywood hinged out like a door and a rough-looking man holding a rifle stepped out. He held his gun at his hip. The man looked at them with a questioning glare, moving his eyes up and down each one of them.

"We just need a car," Lucas said.

The man smiled and shook his head as if it was a ridiculous request. "Just don't move, he'll be here in a minute."

"Who?" Julie asked.

"The mayor," the man said.

Soon, the plywood door opened again and a man in a grungy shirt and tie emerged. He wore a gun on his hip and a large hunting knife on the other side. He smiled at them and walked over with a hand extended. Lucas shook the man's hand.

"Welcome," the mayor greeted. Turning to the guard, he said, "Please, Marty, put your gun down."

"Thanks for the welcome," Lucas said. "We had a car just up the road, a Hummer, we were hoping to get it back and be on our way."

The mayor's head jerked and tilted up. "Hummer? Don't think I've seen anything like that."

Lucas sighed. The man was lying to him. A diesel hummer that ran wouldn't go unnoticed. "If you have any operating vehicles, we would appreciate it."

"There's a million cars, son."

"This one had fuel in it."

"Now that is something special. Cars with fuel aren't something we would part with, but if you need a night to stay, you are welcome to come in. You kids look so fresh—"

"Like shiny pigs," Marty finished.

The mayor turned back with a scowl. "Where you come from?"

"Ferrell's, a few hundred miles east of here."

"Must have been a nice place for you all to look the way you do."

"It was alright, if you don't mind grinners."

"Grinners?" the mayor asked.

Lucas looked around. "That's what we call the dead people walking around out here."

"Oh yes, them." The mayor took a deep breath. "We control them as much as we can. Speaking of which, we should really get behind the wall before one of them see us."

After picking up their weapons, they followed Marty and the Mayor past the plywood door. Marty slung his gun over his shoulder and closed the door. Lucas was taken aback by what he saw beyond the wall.

In the shadow of the large hotel, women and children worked on their hands and knees in small gardens. Various crops grew, from corn to tomatoes in confined planter boxes, in what looked like dried out fountains spread between the confining wall and the hotel. The strange thing was the quiet way in which they worked. Everyone moved like they were gliding on the ground and no one spoke or clattered a shovel, every motion seemed to exemplify silence. Many looked up as they passed but went back to their gardens after the mayor gave them a sweeping wave.

"Wow, you have a quiet set up here," Lucas said.

"Noises are frowned upon."

"And you grow all this stuff?"

"Veggies and stuff are great, but nothing can truly replace meat."

Lucas scanned the farm and noticed they had no livestock. Living off of fruits and vegetables . . . he cringed at the idea.

"Come with me, I think we have a room available for you."

Lucas glanced back at Hank and Julie. Julie raised her eyebrows and opened her eyes wide. It was a look he knew too well, like he was making a mistake. He felt the same way, something about the place seemed far from normal. But Ryjack was anything but a normal world. He thought of the Costco family, living in that building, raising kids, making strange requests to visitors. That was their normal. Maybe living this way was normal for them.

They walked toward the hotel and passed by a few people. A young girl in an ill-fitting garment, covered in dirt looked up from her digging and stared at Lucas as he walked by. He couldn't take his eyes from the girl, something about her was trying to tell him something. He thought of asking the girl, but her mom yanked on her hand and she went back to tilling the dirt.

Closer to the hotel, he saw the top floors of the buildings windows broken out and many trees jutting from their holes. Most of the lower windows were cracked and all of them had a thick layer of dust covering them.

Much like the Venice hotel, the entrance was the valet parking pull-up area. They left the dirt gardens and entered the greater shade of the entrance canopy. Lucas welcomed the cooler air brushing over his sweating skin.

At the large glass doors entering the hotel, several men with rifles stood guard. They watched with interest as the mayor ushered them into the main lobby. Lucas didn't like the way they were looking at Julie and he let her walk in front of him to keep a buffer.

"It isn't much, but we call it home," the mayor said. He extended his arms, presenting the huge lobby to them with a big smile. Lucas tried to look impressed, but failed. The mayor let out a breath of disappointment. He hoped he didn't offend the man.

"How many people live here?" Julie asked.

"Well, some come and go, but usually a few hundred."

"And you cleared all the grinners from this place?"

The mayor looked at the ground. "Not exactly, but who wants to talk about this kind of stuff. Let me get Laura to take you to your room." The mayor beckoned a woman standing behind a desk at the reception area.

She jumped at the attention and ran across the marble floors to them. "Hi, the usual?"

The mayor cleared his throat. "Of course, our usual room for guests."

Laura gave an uncomfortable nod. "Yes, right this way, kids."

"I have things to attend to," the mayor said with a small bow.

"Of course, thanks for the hospitality," Lucas replied.

They passed huge displays of stained glass that might have been a stunning sight if hadn't been broken with dirt covering all that remained. Then, they followed along a narrow path with more crops growing indoors. The room felt humid and had a smell of dirt and mold. The ground looked rich, dark and moist off the path. They kept following Laura and Lucas thought to ask where they were going when they reached a staircase.

"Just a few flights up," Laura said.

They followed her up a few flights, until she opened a door to floor five. A long, soft carpeted hallway appeared.

"Wonder if they have peep shows," Lucas whispered to Julie.

"Shut up," she said, whacking him in the arm.

"Laura, will there be any tricycles in today's entertainment?"

The woman glanced back but didn't answer. She walked to the second door down the hall and turned around. "Here's your room. Do you require anything?"

"No. Wait, do you know where we can get a car?"

She shook her head and looked at the floor.

"You ok?" Hank asked. "They treating you well here?"

Laura's hands brushed her pants and shook. "There's fresh water in the room. I must get going." She walked at a near run down the hall and into the staircase.

"Why are we here?" Julie asked and pushed Lucas. "This place is freaky."

Lucas turned back from the direction in which Laura had exited. "We need a car. Hello, we can't make it through the desert on our feet."

"I agree, but I get a weird vibe here," Hank said.

"Listen, we're not living here, we're getting our Hummer back and then we're gone. They must be stashing it somewhere, can your Pana help us?" Lucas asked.

"No, unless they start it, I might be able to read its electrical signal." Julie pulled her Panavice from her pocket and slid her finger around the screen. Lucas held back a laugh because he realized it had been the longest time he had seen her without it in her hands.

"Why don't we check out our room, we might see something from the windows," Hank suggested.

Lucas shrugged and opened a door marked *532*. The room looked like the hotel room he stayed in with his dad when their grandpa died, except it didn't smell of clean linen and bleach. The bed was made and several bottles of water sat on the dresser.

"Oh thank God, some water," Lucas said and grabbed a bottle. The twist cap didn't have the ring under it. The bottle had been opened before. "They refilled these."

Julie picked up a bottle and inspected it in the light of the window. "I don't know if I would trust anything coming from these people." She set the bottle of water back on the dresser.

Lucas stared at his bottle and then twisted the cap back on and set it down. He wasn't that thirsty anyway.

"Look at this," Hank said. He stood next to the window looking down. "There's a huge parking lot down there."

"I bet that's where they're keeping the Hummer," Lucas said. "Come on, let's check it out." He walked to the door and turned the metal handle, but the door wouldn't budge. "The door's locked." His heart began to beat faster.

"What do you mean?"

"It won't open."

"Back away, let me kick it open." Hank kicked the door with his feet and created a small dent in the metal door, but it held. He kicked it many times, but the door stayed in place.

"They locked us in," Lucas said.

"Hello!" Julie yelled at the door.

"Wait, I hear something." Lucas peered into the peep hole.

Marty stood in the hallway with another man holding what looked like a big metal pot with smoke coming out of it. A long hose came out of the pot and Marty moved out of view with the hose.

"Hey, the door's locked," Lucas yelled. Marty looked up and smirked. The man next to him had a large bellows he pumped near the door.

"Who's out there?" Julie asked.

"That Marty guy. They have some kind of smoke machine out there."

"Guys," Hank said, pointing to a large grate on the wall. Tendrils of smoke rose from the vent, becoming thicker with each passing second.

"Crap." Lucas's chest pounded and he readied his bow. If they were trying to smoke them out, he'd kill every person who came through that door.

"Grab that blanket, hold it over the grate. Here, soak it in water." Julie said and handed Hank the water bottles. He poured it over the blanket. Thick rancid smoke flowed from the grate. Hank stuffed the wet blanket against it and the smoke dribbled out of the sides.

Lucas breathed in. "Thanks for being the smartest person alive."

"Oh no, it's coming in from the other one." Julie pointed behind him.

The room already had a haze of smoke through it and Lucas felt it burning his lungs. It smelled of burnt tires and microwaved farts.

"I'm not feeling too good," Hank warned, wobbling around before falling to the ground. The blanket he held fell with him and the smoke poured into the room.

"Hank." Julie ran to him. "He's alive." It was the only thing she got out before she fell to the floor next to Hank.

Lucas's adrenaline and anger raged through him. These people were trying to kill him, kill Julie. He wouldn't allow it. Both of his best friends lay at his feet and he knew what he had to do. Stumbling to the back of the room, he grasped a loaded Prudence in his hands and fell to the floor.

CHAPTER 7

HARRIS STARED AT THE COMPUTER screen in disbelief. Every computer system and power grid MM controlled had been wiped out. Each bunker and factory was silent to all pings. Their security systems were blind, nothing but a black void.

"One minute until we land," Jack said.

"Can they see us entering their airspace?"

"No, I don't think they even have a radar setup, let alone GPS tracking. They're completely crippled."

"I wouldn't count them out." Harris gazed out the window to MM's headquarters just below. "I'm getting changed."

He took off his shirt and pants and pulled out something he hadn't worn in a long time. He slid his hands through the black sleeves and buttoned the shirt. They were clothes that at one time had felt like home. Now, the shirt and insignia's on the chest felt repulsive.

The aircraft leveled off and landed on a helipad on the roof. Jack and Harris left the craft, and found the roof empty. Harris holstered his gun and walked to the roof door. He pulled out his Panavice to hack into the coded door, but Jack simply pulled on the handle and the door opened. Harris's eyes went wide. Was this a trap?

They headed into the building and down the stairs. Upon exiting the first door, they walked into chaos. Men and women in various black ranked uniforms ran down the halls, several pushed by Harris and ran into the stairwell. Harris grabbed one of the women running by.

"What's going on?"

"No one knows," she said frantically. Harris eyed her rank four insignia and let her go.

He adjusted his uniform and resisted the urge to pull it off. It made him sick to have the uniform back on, but he knew it would serve a purpose. He rubbed the tips of his fingers over the R9 insignia on his chest. It hadn't faded after all the years.

A rank seven did a double take at his chest and stared into Harris's eyes. He returned with an even glare, and the seven lowered his head, running into the stairwell.

Harris had figured on fighting with people—a fight with Marcus to end it all. Not a complete collapse of MM.

"Sir, what should we do?" Jack asked. "I don't think they even care we're here."

Harris took a deep breath and watched the people run by. "We should go to the lower levels, that's where Marcus would be."

They left the chaos of the upper levels behind and descended into the bunker. The stairwell had become crowded with hordes of people running up and down the stairwell. Mostly lower ranks and service people. He tried to catch their rumors as they ran by, everything from Mutants attacking, to people getting killed in the lower levels by monsters.

The elevators had stopped working, and only the backup generators had emergency lights functioning. All of the servers had crashed, communications gone and every door hung open. Not knowing the how's and the why's, he quickened his pace. Another R7 passed by, he was sure some of the higher ranks recognized him—he probably trained them at some point. Yet they didn't slow down. Some of them looked so pale from fear they could have been grinners.

They reached floor sixteen: rank seven's floor. The people in the room didn't even look up at him as he moved through the room. One seven had the panels down on the wall next to the elevator and was trying to reactivate them manually. He would have done the same thing.

Harris hesitated at the secure steel door in front of him with a keypad he knew well. But, had the code changed? If he entered the wrong code, it would deploy a shot of knockout gas.

"Stand back," he said to Jack. He pressed in the first number and watched the door swing open. He couldn't hold back the shock in his face.

"I take it, that door isn't supposed to open?"

"No." Harris looked at the sevens around the room and pulled Jack inside, closing the door. "This isn't just some system breakdown, these doors are made for breakdowns, and they seal themselves automatically when something goes wrong."

"Why would he want everything open?"

"I don't know, but it gives me a bad feeling."

"What are we going to do now? Our plan is pretty much thrown out."

Harris looked at the small room filled with weapons of any imaginable type. If things had even been a hair the way he planned, he would be thrilled to be in that room. But this . . . this shouldn't be happening. He would have to adapt to the new situation, it's what he'd been trained to do and he wasn't one for not taking advantage of a situation. Grabbing the one item he wanted, a rail gun, they left the room.

One seven glanced his way and did a double take. Harris winced, he knew he'd been spotted. "Hey," the seven yelled, "you're Harris." The others perked up at this and dropped their tools.

Harris turned to face the man with his hand on his new gun. He quickly considered his options, fighting four sevens would take too long. "I was sent here to help. I know these systems better than anyone."

The man raised an eyebrow. "We weren't notified."

"And how would they do that? Marcus himself sent the request."

"You're the most wanted man on the planet."

"Listen, son, do you think I would just walk into this building if it wasn't okay?"

The sevens all looked at each other and shrugged. "And what do you plan to do?" The man looked at his R9 on his chest.

"I'm a nine, you don't get to question me."

The man paused, then nodded once. "How can we help you?"

"Just stay out of my way." Harris walked into the stairwell with Jack and didn't look back as he descended into the lower levels. More people ran up the stairs, they were the only ones walking down. One man limped by with a bad wound on his leg and behind the ruckus of feet on steel stairs, Harris heard a scream from deep below.

He stopped the injured man and gestured to his leg. "What happened?"

The man looked up with his pale face. "They bit me. I barely got out of there alive."

"Who bit you?" Harris asked, but the man walked up the stairs, lost to a sea of people.

Jack looked confused. "What was that about?"

"I hope it's not what I think it is."

Fewer people filled the stairs the further they descended. Streaks of blood ran on the floor and walls as they reached floor thirty-two. Harris pulled out his gun and peered through the doorway. In the dim emergency lights he saw them, with their grayish skin and blackened eyes. It was a realization of what Marcus did and everything it meant. Harris gritted his teeth and gripped his gun as he glared at the grinners.

Marcus once again was a step ahead. In the moment of his possible downfall, he didn't do the obvious and repair the damage, he did something unimaginable and fanned the fire.

Two men ran from the room, glancing back at the grinners before running up the stairs. They didn't even glance at Harris or Jack. Harris shook his head and turned his gun onto the mass of grinners approaching. They tumbled to the ground, one after another, until no more moved. He walked further into the room, Jack on his heels.

Cracks of gunfire echoing from below brought Harris back into the stairwell. He looked down several flights and saw a man stepping backward up the stairs, firing into oncoming grinners. The precision and calmness of the man's movement sent off warning alarms. Harris pointed his gun and awaited their inevitable confrontation. The man backed into view of Harris and glanced back, and in a rare instance showed shock at the presence of Harris pointing a gun in his face.

"Harris," Emmett said.

"Emmett." Rapid gunfire blared from Emmett's gun as he shot several grinners from the stairwell. "Where's Marcus?"

"I don't know."

"He's the only one who could cause this and you know it," Harris said.

Emmett looked into the darkness and fired, two grinners stumbled into the light and fell to the floor. "Can we put our stuff aside for the moment?"

Harris nodded and lowered his gun a few inches.

"We have to make a stand here," Emmett said. "Otherwise, these things will spread and the planet will die."

"It's not just here, I've already seen people with bites ascending these stairs. We'll need to seal off Capital."

Emmett flinched and shook his head. "Agreed." Emmett pulled off a radio from his waist. Harris hadn't seen that type of radio in hundreds of years, it was a relic. "Seal the city off, no one in or out." He looked back at Harris while firing a bullet into the head of a grinner. "If we can get to the lower levels, we might have a chance of stemming the tide."

"Agreed."

Jack spoke up from behind Harris. "I don't have a weapon."

Harris nodded up the stairs. "Go upstairs and get security to stop anyone who has been bitten."

"Here," Emmett tossed Jack a badge, "this will give you the authority." He moved close to Harris, keeping his gun pointed at the floor and giving Harris his back. "I think it started down on sixty-four."

"After you." Following Emmett down the stairs, Harris kept his gun pointed at his back. With the other gun, he shot five grinners. He figured Emmett didn't have a shield up with the Panavice servers down. If he was going to kill the only other rank nine, he had to time it right. "Why don't you tell me where the kids are?"

Emmett stopped. "Marcus had them moved to Ryjack."

Harris gripped the hilt. "All of them?"

"Poly, Joey, and Samantha."

"And Marcus didn't go with them?"

"No."

Harris stared down the steps. Jack mentioned they might have been moved but the information didn't make sense.

On approach, door marked sixty-four sat ajar. The dark room beyond had no emergency lights and he squinted, trying to make out the moving shapes.

Emmett used his Panavice as a flashlight and shined it into the room and exterminated the few grinners mulling about the near-empty space.

Harris stepped by, using his own Panavice to light up the area. The huge room was lined with chain-link cages on each side and a hallway in between. The first chain-link doors lay open. Black streaks ran across much of the floor. He passed another open gate and a grinner ran out. He shot it and moved on.

He'd never been on this floor, knew it existed but had no idea what Marcus had turned it into. Had this been his plan all along? What set this into motion? It didn't make sense for a man like Marcus to destroy it all unless he had an out, a better opportunity.

Harris stopped and looked at the locked keypad at the next chain link door. This was the first secured door he'd seen since arriving. He stopped and spotted the piece of paper on the gate. Lowering his gun, he grabbed the note marked *Harris*. He opened the envelope, took out the single sheet of paper, and shined his light on it.

You can have my trophies, I've grown bored of them.

Trophies? What did he mean? The kids were in Ryjack. Harris shined his light into the cage and fell to his knees. A blonde grinner came running at him with her black grin and gray skin.

Compry.

It was easier to see her die on the roof than to see her as a grinner. He'd shed tears for her in private already, but felt a wet line streak down his cheek as she slammed into the chain-link fence. She thrashed her body against it and reached her fingers out. He touched the tips of her fingers, not noticing Emmett's gun at the side of his head.

CHAPTER 8

"I TOLD YOU BURNING THE chicken feathers would work better. Did you hear how fast they fell?"

"Yeah, but they better not be dead."

"So what if they are? These are the finest looking people we've had in a long time. You see the size of that one? We will have the best BBQ ever, with him alone."

"Well, you'll have to explain to the mayor why we have a surplus of meat again."

"Yeah, what's the deal? People been flocking here like a moth to flame, lately. We've about filled up the holding pens."

"God favors us, I guess."

Lucas listened to the conversation between Marty and the other man. Holding back his cough, he inhaled the smoke-filled air through his nose. For some reason, it wasn't affecting him. He was sure Marty still had his rifle and wanted to time his jump perfectly. They hadn't walked past the bed yet, or they would've seen him on the floor.

"Let's get the big boy out first," Marty said. His voice was muffled from something, probably a gas mask. "The dang field workers were drooling when we paraded this one through the farm." He laughed.

Lucas took a deep breath and jumped to his feet, sending an arrow deep in the second man's chest. Marty dropped Hank's leg and struggled to get his rifle. Lucas shot another arrow and hit Marty. He shouted in pain and shot his rifle into the wall near Lucas, falling to the ground.

Swaying, Lucas gripped the edge of the bed to balance himself. The smoke hurt his eyes and burned his lungs. He positioned another arrow as he approached Marty. Jaw clenched, he half wanted the man to be alive so he would have reason to stuff an arrow in his face. But he lay still. Lucas pulled his bow over his back and grabbed Julie off the ground, carrying her to the hall. He laid her on the carpet and ran back to get Hank.

The two men hadn't moved and he stepped over their bodies to get to his friend. He couldn't lift him, so he grabbed his ankles and pulled. Hank's body resisted the first attempt, but when he put his entire body into it, he managed to move him a few feet. With the energy exerted, he breathed hard and the smoke filled his lungs, making the room fuzzy. He reached down and pulled Marty's mask off his face and put it on his own. The smoke dissipated and he continued the struggle of removing his friend until they were in the clean air of the hallway.

With the gunshot, he was sure there were more on their way. Lucas pulled off the mask and stared at Hank's lump of a body. He would be near impossible to move by himself. Running back into the room, he grabbed Hank's bag and Julie's Panavice. He paused, looking at the two men he killed. He wanted it to bother him more than it did.

Unzipping the bag, he found Julie's medical supplies. Grabbing the small vial he was looking for, he cracked open the tube. The odor hit his nose and stung his eyes. He wafted it under Julie's nose, and then Hank's. Both stirred awake and grabbed at their noses, coughing.

"What happened?" Julie asked between coughs.

"They were going to *eat* us."

"What?" Hank asked.

"I killed two of them when they came in and that Marty guy shot at me. I'm sure someone else must have heard it," Lucas said, watching the door. "Please tell me you can move?"

Julie sat up and looked to the room. "You killed them?"

"They were going to eat us."

Julie looked at him sideways and struggled to get to a sitting position. "Why didn't you pass out from the gas?"

"I don't know, I almost did. Head's still cloudy."

"Sniff that thing, clears it up."

Lucas took a whiff and jerked his head back. He blinked his eyes and tried to get the burning smell from his nose. His head felt clearer. With the fuzz diminished, the fear of what almost happened hit him. "I'm sorry I got you into this, we should have found a different way."

"I'm fine," she coughed. "But if I go to a doctor, I'm going to have a hard time convincing him I'm a non-smoker. My insurance rates are going to go up now."

He laughed and extended his hand, helping Julie to her feet and giving her a big hug. "You okay?"

"I'm fine. Didn't you say more were coming?"

"Please, I have Prudence." He watched Hank struggle to get to his feet. "How you feeling, buddy?"

"What, I don't get a hug?" He stood with his arms out.

Lucas ran over and jumped into his arms. Hank picked him off the ground and squeezed. "Careful, Hank, you could scuff Prudence." Hank set him down on the ground and Lucas inspected his bow for damage.

"Is Prudence so fragile?" Hank said, teasing him.

"Good lord, I almost forgot about you naming that thing," Julie said.

"*Hey*, Prudence just saved our lives." Lucas felt the string on the bow. "And if you two are all done chatting, we need to get going. That parking lot out back is a good place to start. One floor down and we can break out a room window."

"We're still getting a car from this place?" she asked.

"Is there a better option?"

She felt her pocket and her eyes went wide. "My Pana's gone."

"I got it." Lucas handed it over.

She slid her fingers across the screen. "If we had some servers out here, I could tell you where the nearest car is."

"And if I had a helicopter, I could search for one." Lucas smiled, he liked seeing Julie frustrated and without her technology, it leveled the playing field.

They collected their bags and walked down to the staircase. Sneaking to the second floor, they entered another hallway with hotel rooms. Lucas stepped from the door and put a hand to his nose. The strong smell of decay and human waste filled the hall. He looked to Hank's bag and considered getting out the smelling vial again to fight the odor.

"I think I'm going to be sick," Julie said.

"Hello, is someone out there?" A woman's voice from behind a door called out.

Julie raised her eyebrows and stared at Lucas. He looked around, should he respond to someone who could turn them in? Could he breathe in the air long enough to respond?

"Yeah," Lucas said.

"Oh God, can you get me something to drink? I'm dying in here."

"Me too!" a man in another room cried out in a raspy voice.

"I can see you," another woman said from behind a nearby door. "Just a drink." She sounded clear.

Lucas looked to Julie and shrugged. He didn't know what to do, even if he had water, how could he get through the door. Hank failed at kicking the last one down.

Julie swore quietly. "I can't believe I didn't think of this before, I bet I can use my Pana to activate the electric locks on these hotel doors." She walked next to the door with the woman asking for water. She held her Panavice next to the handle with a card swipe and a series of lights on top. How long had it been since they had a guest with a card? All the locks had a key override which is what they must have been using.

Lucas shook his head. "And to think, I said you were the smartest woman alive."

"You know that can't be true."

"Why?"

"Because, I'm with *you*."

The door lights lit green and he heard the lock click. Lucas held his bow high and waited for the door to open. "Hank." He nodded his head to the door.

Hank pushed the door open and the smell of decay wafting from the room was so bad, Lucas could barely keep his eyes open. A frail woman in what looked like a severely soiled white sheet draped over her tiny body, emerged from behind the bed.

"I'm sorry," the woman said, staring at Prudence. "I'm not thirsty, please don't take me. I'm sorry." She cried and covered her face with a skeleton of a hand.

Lucas lowered his bow and gave Julie a confused look. "Miss, were not here to hurt you, or give you water, we don't have any. How long have you been locked in here?"

"I came here with my husband, he's a few rooms down, they drugged us with water and when I woke up, I was in this room. It's been weeks since then, I think." The frail woman, maybe thirty, put her hands to her mouth and sobbed.

"Let's get you people the heck out of here," Lucas said.

"Thank you, thank you," she repeated.

"This must be their holding floor," Hank said. "I bet we would have been filling some of these rooms."

They spent the next few minutes opening the doors to each of the rooms. They didn't look into the rooms too long as the horrible conditions inside were something they wanted to forget. With the doors open, the hall filled with a dozen people. Some were so weak, they struggled to stand. Some hugged each other, reuniting. Lucas thought there were many stories to hear from the survivors, but he didn't have the time. They needed to get out of there before the Mayor came looking.

He turned to Julie who had tears in her eyes and couldn't look at the raw humanity filling the hall. "I saw a broken window in room two-thirty-two"

Julie nodded her head.

Some of the people were on their hands and knees, touching his shoes. "Please, stand up. You don't need to do that."

Entering the room with the broken window, Lucas took in the fresh hot air from outside. The ground was only a few feet below, and the parking lot was an easy hundred feet away. What a terrible view.

When he turned around to talk to Julie and Hank, he realized everyone had followed. The weary faces of the survivors begged him to save them. He lowered his head and rubbed his eyes with his fingers. The smoke still burned. "We can't take you with us, but out this window is freedom, if you can find it."

"They were going to eat us," a man in blue jeans said.

"I'm so sorry." Julie still had tears on her face. "We just narrowly escaped that same fate as well."

Out the window a bird flew by, maybe a crow. Lucas hated the lives these poor people led. They came here looking to get away from the dead who wanted to eat them, only to find brethren who wanted to eat them as well.

Lucas jumped from the window and landed on the concrete. He turned and helped Julie down and then waited for Hank. The survivors climbed down, each looked to the sky and thanked them as they went their separate ways. Julie grabbed his hand and pulled him close. He felt her wet tears against his shirt.

"Come on," Lucas said. He pulled Julie to the parking garage, a three story structure with rows and rows of cars and trucks, all of which were filthy, with layers of dirt. All but one. A beige Hummer stood out from the dull pack with its shining paint.

"No way, there it is," Hank said.

They ran to it and opened the doors. The keys were still in it. Lucas pumped his fist on top of the steering wheel in excitement. He turned the key and the engine started.

"Please, get us out of here," Julie begged, strapping her seatbelt on in the front seat.

Lucas backed the hummer out of its parking spot. He shifted into drive and looked forward. A man stood with a rifle pointed at them fifty feet ahead.

"Get down," Lucas yelled. He pushed on the gas pedal and drove at the armed man. The man fired into their windshield. Glass flew around the inside of the hummer, but Lucas pushed on the gas pedal, the only way out of the garage was through the man. Three more shots were fired before he jumped out of the way, falling to the ground.

"Julie, you okay?" Lucas asked as he sat upright. His heart pounded as he kept glancing at Julie, inspecting her for injuries.

She brushed a few bits of glass from her shirt and nodded.

"I'm okay," Hank replied.

The Hummer skidded on the concrete as they exited the garage. Lucas drove past a couple survivors and they yelled as he drove by. The road led to the plywood wall surrounding the hotel. He hoped it was as flimsy as the one out front. He braced himself as the hummer plowed into the wall. The windshield cracked more and the mirrors ripped off. Julie crouched low in the front seat and held her arms over her head but they made it through with ease.

The mammoth vehicle bounced over the crumbled wall and he heard gun fire as they left. *Goodbye Sanctuary.* He took the path they came in on with Poly driving. It was one of the few cleared roads available.

Julie turned around, looking out the back window. "You think those people are going to be okay?"

Lucas didn't think in a million years any of them would be okay, but he glanced at her and she still looked back with optimism in her eyes. "They survived this long in this world, they should be fine."

"How much gas do we have?" Hank asked.

"Crap, it's low," he said. "There should be plenty of big rigs we can siphon from on the road." Lucas stared ahead and at the piles of cars pushed to the side of Tulip Street. He cringed when he hit a parked car and adjusted his hands on the steering wheel.

"Poly was a better driver," Hank observed.

"*Ha!* Remember her jumping this thing over the mini-dunes in that field? I've never seen someone so excited." Lucas laughed and took a deep breath, feeling some of the tension leaving his body. Everything happened so fast back there, it almost didn't feel real. Some of the faces flashed through his mind, but the little girl in the garden stuck out the most. He knew now it'd been hunger he saw in her eyes. God he hated Ryjack.

Julie smiled at him and he managed to avoid the rest of the cars as he made his way through the dead city of New Vegas. The cluttered freeway out of the city made for slow time. He off-roaded when he had to, but took his time to navigate the ditches, boulders, and cars. With the city far behind them, the road started to clear out. He kept a light foot on the gas pedal and when the tires hit the asphalt again, he took a while to get up to thirty miles per hour.

A gas light lit on the dashboard. "There goes the gas alarm."

"We need to find a rig with fuel in it," Julie said, as Hank pulled himself up to look out the front window.

Soon, Hank pointed to the right. "Some of those regular trucks are diesel."

Lucas pulled up next to the freeway car pile and drove slow. "Let me know when you see one."

After a few minutes of driving Hank pointed at a large red truck. "That one's got a diesel emblem on it."

Stopping, Lucas got out of the car. "Stay in here," he said to Julie.

Hank followed, pulling the gas can off the back of the Hummer as they walked to the red truck in the middle of the car pile. The heat blazed down on them and Lucas wanted to get back in the AC as quickly as possible. Hank shoved a clear tube into the trucks gas tank and sucked on the end. Lucas watched the dark liquid run through the tube. Hank pushed it into the gas can and the liquid splashed inside the can.

"That was one jacked up place back there," Hank said.

"You're telling me."

"I don't know if I can ever stay in a hotel again."

"Dude, I hear ya," Lucas said. He turned, thinking he heard a sound of metal scraping. "You hear that?"

"Hear what?"

A banging sound, followed by a scrape of metal, alerted Lucas. He pulled out his bow. Scanning the windows and the spaces between the cars, he looked for movement.

"That thing full?" Lucas asked.

"Almost—"

The horn on the Hummer blared. Lucas grabbed the hose, Hank picked up the gas can, and they sprinted toward Julie. The horn blasted again. Lucas ran past the last car and saw several grinners around the hummer with Julie in the driver's seat. He steadied his feet and pulled out an arrow, firing into the closest grinner, then four more to kill the rest around the car. Running to the car, Hank followed closely behind.

Lucas's hand fumbled at the locked door handle. He yanked at the handle until Julie pulled up the lock. He flung the door open and Julie fell out into his arms. "You okay?"

"Yeah, just freaked me out a bit." She glanced down at the dead grinners on the ground and then buried her face into his chest.

"Guys," Hank said as he fueled the tank. "They're coming." He pointed his hand to the freeway.

Lucas turned and saw the group of grinners moving toward them. "Julie, get in." He climbed into the car and sat in the driver's seat. "Come on, Hank."

"Just a second." Hank lifted the gas can high, trying to drain out the last of the gas.

"We got to go, man."

"Almost there."

The first grinner hit the side of the car and Julie pulled at Lucas's arm. "Get in, Hank!" she screamed.

The grinner walked around the car. Hank kicked it in the chest and pulled the gas can from the tank and jumped into the car. He shook the car when he slammed the door closed. "Let's go."

Lucas started the hummer and ran over three grinners on his way out. He steered to the dirt road parallel to the freeway and kept a decent speed. The gas gage moved a bit past empty.

"We're going to have to do that all the way to LA." Lucas looked in his rearview, he couldn't see the grinners anymore. The Hummer slowed down as the motor sputtered. He pumped the gas pedal. "No, *no*." He hit the steering wheel.

"What's wrong?" Julie asked.

"I don't know, it's breaking down."

"I think gas can go bad. It's probably too old."

Lucas pushed on the gas pedal and the car jerked forward, then clunked and slowed down. He pumped the pedal, but the engine died. At least they were far enough from the grinners.

The heat crept into the cab. Lucas took in a deep breath and closed his eyes. They were probably thirty miles outside Vegas and hundreds of miles until LA. He looked far into the shimmering horizon. A large building shook in the haze, maybe ten miles out, too far to walk in the heat.

"What are we going to do?" Julie asked.

"How many miles until LA?"

Julie looked at her Panavice. "Over two hundred." She plopped the Panavice on her lap and looked at the ceiling.

"We can't walk, we have to get a ride of some sort. Maybe we can find a running car out there?" Lucas pointed to the freeway.

"Those cars have been sitting there for twenty years, none of them are going to work," Julie said.

She was right, the only thing that kept the Hummer going was Ferrell and his personal fuel supply. Frustrated, Lucas stared at all the inoperable cars. "Water, water everywhere, not a drop to drink," he said.

Julie raised an eyebrow at his comment, but he focused on the cars.

Then, he saw it. "A Prius. Too bad we couldn't have gotten one of those things going."

"You're a genius!" Julie bolted upright in her seat. "My Panavice can power up things electrical. If we can find an all-electric car . . . it might work."

They walked the path of cars and looked for the elusive all-electric vehicle. Many hybrids sprung up, but those needed gas as well.

"Look," Hank said. "A Tesla."

Lucas thought it looked like a luxury sports car. "This is all-electric?"

"Yep," Hank said.

Julie stood next to it with her Panavice in hand. "It is."

Lucas slid his hand over the dusty door, only to be met with a face of a kid grinner slapping against the window. He stumbled back and fell against the truck behind them. "I hate kid grinners." He stood upright. "Hank, get the door."

Hank stood behind the door and pulled it open. The kid funneled out of the car and fell to the ground courtesy of an arrow through the head. Lucas gritted his teeth.

"You're free now, buddy." He pulled the arrow out of the gray flesh.

The insides of the car reeked of death. Lucas went to roll down the windows, but they didn't work, so he walked around and opened both doors to air it out. "You think you can get this thing going?" he asked Julie.

"I think so, but it might be slow going," she replied. "Whoa, the battery on this thing is huge. It might take a bit for the initial charge."

"Fine, I'm going to stay outside and keep a look out." Any excuse to exit the car and its smell.

"Move some of those cars so we can get out of here," Julie said and pointed to the cars blocking its way out.

Lucas plotted a path for the car to take and thought he could move one truck and make room for their escape from the rows of cars. "Hank, can you give me a hand?" The big guy stepped out from the car. "Let's move this truck." Lucas shifted the truck into neutral and they pushed it into the dirt shoulder, giving enough space for the Tesla.

After a half hour of waiting and watching, Julie called his name. Lucas ran to the car and looked inside to see her smiling face. Hank shuffled into the back seat, jostling the small car.

"Let's see if this thing works," she said.

Lucas grinned and jumped behind the steering wheel. He turned the key and the dash lit up. He had never driven an electric car and he wondered if it was even running. Pushing the gas pedal, he got his answer as they lurched forward. He turned the wheel sharp to get in between the space he and Hank created.

Lucas beamed at Julie as he pulled the car off the shoulder and onto the adjacent dirt road. "You're a genius."

Julie laughed. "I know, right?"

He could have kissed her right then, if it didn't make it so awkward with Hank looking on. Instead, he reached over and clasped her hand and with the look she gave him, it was clear she understood how he felt.

The car crept along the dirt road. Lucas looked ahead to the large buildings in the distance. The last-chance casinos sat ahead. He hoped they were friendlier than the Sanctuary.

With the Tesla being powered by a Panavice, the car sputtered along at about fifteen miles an hour. They passed the casinos and saw the faded *Welcome to California* sign.

"I've always wanted to go to LA," Julie said.

"Yeah, maybe we can go to Hollywood. I bet there's a Robert Pattinson grinner cruising around, maybe a Jennifer Lawrence," Lucas said.

Julie looked at her feet. "There's something I've been thinking about."

"Shocking," Lucas said and gave her a friendly smile.

"What if we are on Ryjack?"

"We are."

"No, I mean another version of us."

"Not likely," Hank said. "Isaac kind of guided our parents into creating us."

Lucas glanced back at Hank and then to Julie. "If I run into myself, you'll have to kill it for me. There can only be one and I can't do it."

"Can I be the one to do it?" Hank asked enthusiastically. "You know, to help you out."

Julie didn't respond to his playful banter, and the stoic expression remained on her face. He knew that look for deep thinking and worrying.

"There could be a billion of me," Julie said. "Each one living out a slightly different life. Somewhere Isaac won and brought us all back to Marcus. Somewhere Simon killed us."

Lucas reached across the car and grasped his hand on hers. "There's only one you and one me. Hank, however is a dime a dozen."

"I would like to get in a fight with myself," Hank said, making Lucas and Julie laugh. "I would want to see what I would do and if I could beat myself up."

"I would want to talk to myself," Julie added. "I'd bet I'd be super fascinating."

"Dang, you guys are weird," Lucas said. "I wish I had another of me to put in here to listen to this."

"Couldn't be much worse than what we've got now," Julie chimed in with light heartedness. Lucas squeezed her arm and Hank barked out a laugh.

The light feeling lasted a long ways as they crossed the desert for the next few hours. The freeway had been mostly clear except when they passed a tiny town, Baker he thought, but the sign had been torn apart.

That town was tiny, but the one coming up, looked huge. He gripped the wheel and leaned forward, weaving between the ever growing clog of cars. They passed under a bridge and Lucas jerked around, thinking he saw something. Might have been a mirage or a trick in the sunlight. Then he saw it again. Slamming on the brakes, he shot the shifter into reverse.

"What is it?" Julie asked.

Lucas drove in reverse and looked behind him as he navigated. A man appeared behind them with a gun. Several trucks and cars pulled across the freeway, blocking any possible escape. Lucas slammed on the brakes. "We just drove into a trap."

CHAPTER 9

JOEY STOOD ON TOP OF a chair, yelling and waving his gun around like a crazy person. The grinner took onto his theatrics and shifted to his side of the building. "Go!" he screamed to Samantha and Poly, and then went back to giving the grinners a show. "Over here. I'm right here."

He glanced back and spotted Poly's brown hair streaking past an empty cubicle. They were going to make it. "Come get me," he called out.

The first grinner approached and he fired a shot into its head. The gunshot echoed down the floor and stirred the grinners into a fury. They clambered over fallen chairs and shoved their way toward him.

Another grinner approached, but he let this one live as it pushed against the fallen walls of the cubicle blocking Joey from the grinners.

"I'm right here!"

The cubicle wall broke.

"Oh, crap." Joey thought he had another minute, at least. He jumped off the chair and ran to his right, then down the same path the girls took. He kept low and ran, using the cubicles as cover. A dead grinner lay on the floor with a stab wound to the head. Joey jumped over it and kept running.

At the end of the row, he saw the door. He didn't see the girls and assumed they'd made it. He spotted another grinner, dead on the floor, halfway between. He stopped at the last cubicle and looked across. A mass of grinners were pushing against each other, probably stirred up from his show. If he hustled, he could make it to the door before they could get to him.

He took a deep breath and ran for it. The second step past the cubicle, he heard the grinners groaning and stumbling for him, but it didn't matter. He outran them to the exit door and flung it open. The door slammed shut behind him and he stared up at Poly and Samantha. He didn't know who to hug first, so he settled for leaning over to catch his breath. "Thought I lost you guys for a moment there," he said between pants.

"If it wasn't for Poly, I'd be freaking dead." Samantha's hands shook as she looked at the door. Grinners pounded against it and with each hit, she winced. "We should have stayed in that simulator, anything is better than this."

"I'm sorry," he said.

"I hate grinners," Poly huffed. Her hands were covered in black goo and each knife was tucked into her waistline.

Joey looked around the room. They were at the bottom of the staircase they'd been hoping to find.

Samantha looked up. "Is this safe?"

"Nothing here is safe," Poly said.

A bell sounded from above. Joey looked at them for confirmation. "You heard that, right?"

"Yeah," Samantha agreed.

The dong sound resonated down the stairs much louder. They all looked up again.

"What could it be?" he thought aloud.

"I don't know, but I bet it's not good," Poly answered.

Something made the sound. Maybe a grinner stuck in a bell tower? The thought of it seemed ridiculous but hilarious to Joey. Quasimodo turned grinner, still pulling on the rope.

"I can't wait to get out of this place," Samantha said.

Joey walked next to her up the stairs, with his gun in hand. He looked up the space between stairs for anyone coming their way. The stairway was silent though, only the sound of their own steps bounced around the concrete walls and floor.

Poly walked behind Samantha and Joey kept glancing back at her. He wanted to stare at her, take in what was different about her since the roof. But he barely got a glimpse of her colder face before they met eyes. The pain she'd exhibited when she'd found them was something he couldn't get out of his mind. He hated hurting her and even when they explained the charade, she didn't seem to buy it all the way. But he couldn't help looking at her; he wanted to look at her more, if she would let him.

The bell sounded again, louder as they climbed the stairs. The air took on a strange smell, like tar or a newly paved asphalt road.

"What is that smell?" Samantha asked.

"Smells like the stuff they used to patch our roof," Poly said.

Once at the top, they stood on a small landing with a door at the end. Natural light came through the small window on the door, giving them a glimpse of the outside world. Joey closed his eyes and lowered his head after seeing what lay beyond.

Poly swore and slunk down against the wall, holding her head with her hands.

"What are we going to do now?" Samantha asked, fear building in her voice.

"I don't know," Joey said.

The bell must be right over them. He willed himself to stare out the window one more time. Now they knew what the bell was for and why it was there. It attracted grinners, by the tens of thousands. The door sat above the crowd, giving them the gruesome site of a sea of grinners. Many were covered in black liquid and off in the distance, Joey saw a fake woolly mammoth, half way into a watery pond.

"Oh my god, I know this place," Samantha said. "It's the tar pits in LA."

CHAPTER 10

HARRIS LET HIS FINGERS TOUCH the tips of Compry's dead gray hands. The sounds in his right ear shifted. He didn't look but knew Emmett's gun was at his head. In a split second, he slid his leg into Emmett's foot and pushed the gun upward as it fired. His right ear burst in pain from the loud bang, but he kept with his plan and pulled at Emmett's wrist, forcing him to drop the gun.

Emmett backed up and glanced down at his gun sitting on the floor right in front of Harris's toes. "Go ahead, draw."

Harris slowly put his shoe on top of the fallen gun and slid it behind him with a kick. The gun clanked off into the darkness. When he pulled out his own gun, Emmett's face didn't change, even when faced with death. Harris took a step back and laid his gun on the concrete floor. He slid the gun into the darkness behind him.

Emmett's eyes narrowed before returning to his cool demeanor.

"You're more valuable to me alive," Harris said.

A hint of emotion crept into Emmett's face. "You have a second gun." Emmett eyed his side.

"The truth is, we need each other. Do you think Marcus is coming back after this? He is looking to end this planet. We could fight and maybe kill each other—"

"You would die."

Harris took a deep breath. "You once were under my command—a young ambitious man—now we have a chance to make the rights Marcus made wrong. He wrote in this note, saying I could have his trophies, he was bored of them."

Emmett crossed his arms. Harris knew from the look on his face he wasn't going to win the man over with diplomacy.

"I challenge you then."

Emmett lowered his arms and smiled. "Please, I don't even have a gun."

"No guns, we can fight with our blades and fists. If I win and you are still alive, I become the rank ten and you are my nine."

"I earned my nine, you were given it." Emmett slapped the R9 on his chest.

"Is it a deal?"

"Yeah, if you win, I'll yield. If I win, you'll be dead."

Harris took another step back and took out his second gun, set it on the floor, and slid it behind him. He reached to his side and pulled out a dagger. Emmett followed and pulled out his blade.

Compry pressed her dead face against the chain-link as a morbid spectator. Harris kept his eyes on Emmett and stepped to his right in an attempt to push his back to the fence. Emmett stepped with him, matching his move and not giving up any advantage.

Harris took two steps forward and thrust his dagger at Emmett's chest. Emmett lunged to the side and caught Harris's shoulder in a slice.

"You're out of practice, aren't you?" Emmett asked.

Harris touched his shoulder and looked at the blood. Emmett was faster than he remembered. Did Marcus share one of his modifications with him? If so, this wasn't going to be a long fight. "Don't forget who trained you."

The smell of death surrounded them and the sight of blood and commotion sent Compry into a frenzy. Harris attacked again and watched as Emmett countered each of his attacks without taking a step back.

"The only reason I didn't strike you down then," Emmett said as he blocked. "Was out of respect for your rank."

Harris laid out his attacks favoring the right side of Emmett, pushing him to the backs of his feet. Emmett seemed to refuse to take a step back. Harris found the moment he was looking for and struck at his lower stomach. Emmett took a step back and blocked Harris's plunge. Harris stared at Emmett's blank face; neither of them would wear out or give in. He sighed at the time wasting away as Capital fell to the grinners. If not contained, they could lose the whole planet and become another Ryjack.

"This is a waste of time," he said, looking at the ceiling.

"I can end this quick if you like."

"Better to die by a sword, than a bite."

The corner of Emmett's mouth moved back, in a smirk, or a smile maybe. "Marcus had such hate for you after you left."

"And who has left now?"

Emmett's eye twitched and his hand gripped his sword. "Don't try and get out of this." He lunged forward and swung at Harris's neck.

Harris had waited for a strike filled with emotion. He calmed his mind and watched Emmett's blade glide near his neck. Harris countered and stuck his blade into Emmett's shoulder. Emmett dropped his dagger and grabbed the wound. Blood streamed down his arm.

He grit his teeth and sneered at Harris, making a dash toward the guns on the floor. Harris matched his movement, sweeping feet out from under him. Once down, Harris jumped on his back, placing a blade across his neck. Emmett's saliva fell to the ground as he grunted in anger.

"Yield," Harris commanded. "Let's save this damned planet."

"And if Marcus returns?"

"We kill him together. He can't take us both on."

Harris kept his knee on his back, not giving the man an inch to wiggle. Emmett spit on the ground. "Agreed."

Harris pulled his blade away and got off his back. Emmett sprang to his feet and faced Harris. "You know *I* would have killed you?"

"Yes."

"I should tell you the kids are supposed to die in Ryjack. They're walking into a trap."

Harris resisted the urge to plunge his dagger into Emmett's throat. "When?"

"I was there earlier today."

"Take me there."

"I can't, there's no stone in LA and I destroyed the last transport pod."

Harris gritted his teeth. "You left them there?"

"Yeah, do you really need them? Without them, Marcus never gets out of bed and dies like a natural should."

Harris back-stepped and picked up the three guns on the floor, stuffing two into holsters and one into his waistband.

"Those kids are the only pure things left in these worlds, don't you see what and who they are? To have them die would be like burning the finest work of art."

Emmett looked confused and Harris bit his lips, maybe he said too much. "What am I missing?"

"They're my friends. I won't leave them behind."

Emmett's blank face returned and with his bloody arm, he lifted his ancient radio. "Status?"

The radio gargled back in a static voice. "Sir, they're attacking the gates. I think a few of those things got by. We need back up!"

"Listen," Emmett stuffed the radio close to his mouth. "You seal the gates to the city. No one in, no one out."

Harris cleared his throat.

"And Harris Boone is reinstated with full rank ten. Marcus is gone."

"Sir?"

"Seal those gates!"

"Yes, sir."

"Let's get up there," Emmett said and waited for Harris to walk by first.

Harris didn't like having him at his back, but he knew it was protocol. You filed in as rank. "Wait," he said, turning around at the bottom of the stairs to face Emmett. He was rank ten now. There could be only one. He stared into Emmett's face and tried to imagine his plan going this way when he left Sanct for Capital. There were few moments he was truly shocked and this could be added to the short list.

Harris walked up to Compry, still shaking her cage. Raising his gun, he held a breath and fired. Nodding to Emmett, he ran up the stairs. They encountered a few grinners, but Harris shot them down without missing a step. In ten minutes they were at the top of the stairs, breathing hard and looking upon the chaos of the lobby.

The MM soldiers had set up barriers, blocking the exits, Harris spotted Jack behind one of the barricades. The men fired into the grinners running at them. There was already a large pile and with each bullet the pile grew.

Behind the barrier, people in plain clothes ran down the street, chased by grinners. Harris felt his useless Panavice in his pocket. In a world dependent on instant access to everything, there was no way to warn them, to tell them to stay in their houses, to tell them not to talk to strangers. Harris paused in the lobby, the gunshots seemed dim, Emmett spoke, but the words were dull, distant.

He should have felt like he won, Marcus would no longer be the thumb on the world. But what had he left behind?

CHAPTER 11

LUCAS SLAMMED THE SHIFTER INTO park and hit the top of the steering wheel with his palm.

"Great. What do they want?" Hank said as he looked out the window.

"I don't know, but I'm guessing it's not good for us." Lucas looked at the barricade ahead and the few cars pushed together behind him. They fell into a damned trap. Two men carrying guns walked toward the car. Lucas watched them from the rearview mirror as they approached the car. He rolled down the window. "Is there a problem?"

The clean shaven man with decent clothes smiled. He looked nothing like the sickly people of the Sanctuary. "You were driving fifteen in a seventy five."

"These darned electric cars," Lucas said.

"We don't see many driving, where you coming from?"

"Vegas."

The man looked back at another man and then turned back to Lucas. "We can't let you through without seeing Bob."

"Tell him to come on out so I can shake his hand and we can be on our way."

The friendly smile faded from the man's face. "I'm going to need you all to get out of the car." He took a step back and raised his gun.

Lucas looked around and counted seven men outside the car.

"Don't try anything," Julie said.

It did cross Lucas's mind, maybe if he was by himself . . . "I'm going to be nice until they give me reason not to be."

Without much choice, Lucas kept his hands raised and got out of the car. Julie got out from her side and Hank followed behind her, making his way between her and the men.

"Thing's battery was dead anyhow," Lucas said so everyone nearby could hear. He held Prudence in his hand and slung his quiver across his back. The man raised an eyebrow at the bow, but Lucas wasn't going anywhere without it.

"Don't try anything stupid and you can be on your way after Bob sees ya," the armed man said. "Follow me."

Lucas caught up to Julie as they climbed the stairs next to the freeway. Most of the men hung back in the rear. No one spoke, but he heard voices above and what sounded like children's laughter. He stared at the top of the stairs and wondered who would have children in such a terrible world.

The cool air swept into the area as the sun lowered. Hank crested the top first and halted his steps. Turning around, he looked at Lucas with wide eyes. Making it to the top, Lucas stumbled back at the sight. It was a carnival. A real carnival, with moving rides.

"It's festival day," the man said and shrugged.

Lucas frowned at the man's strange smile and kept the other men from getting too close to Julie as they walked toward the carnival entrance.

A large gate opened for the men as they entered. Lucas stood there and took in the Ferris wheel spinning. The wheel slowly moved around in a jerky motion as if the gears were grinding away, but it was definitely moving. A few lights flickered here and there around the many tents and booths.

"You guys are really lucky to be here during festival day," the man said with all smiles.

"We would really like to get back to our car and be on our way," Julie said.

"Sorry, rules are rules. Anyone who passes through has to see Bob."

The sound of drums and laughter spilled out of the open door as they entered the festival. Lucas expected popcorn and funnel cakes, but instead it was cooked meat and a burnt smell he couldn't place. It wasn't packed with people, but it had a feeling of being busy. The people looked different, cleaner than the people in Vegas. Their faces didn't have the haunted look either. Some of the people laughed and slapped each other's back as good friends might. A few kids ran around in joyful enthusiasm he'd previously thought impossible on Ryjack.

Lucas frowned at the first game he saw on his left. Julie gasped and grabbed at his arm. He looked back at Hank who had the same disgusted look he thought he had.

"Come take a shot at the game, son," the carny yelled from behind his booth. "Knock three heads down and win the lady a bar of chocolate."

Lucas glanced at the living grinner heads on the platform at the back of the booth. A stack of whiffle balls were on the table in front.

"How 'bout you, sir," the carny yelled at another passerby.

The next booth displayed fish bowls with ping pong balls. Lucas looked at the balls to make sure nothing was grotesquely wrong with the game, but it appeared to be just like the one he would play at the fair when it came to Preston. Was this a traveling fair? Did it just end up being here when the grinner invasion started?

They approached the Ferris wheel and the man with his gun stopped and turned back to them.

"I bet this is the only functioning Ferris wheel in the world." His admiration spread over his face.

"You have a generator?" Julie asked.

"That's the genius of Bob. Take a look at this."

They followed the man to the other side of the ride. A group of girls laughed and made faces at a glass cage. Inside, several grinners were chained together and placed on a conveyer belt. They ran at the girls making faces, spinning the belt under their feet and moving the Ferris wheel.

"Wow," Julie said. She got closer to the glass. "Aren't you scared of them getting loose?"

"Nah, ever since Bob showed us how to treat the dead as a tool, not a monster, we've turned this small community into a home. You guys are probably too young to have ever even seen anything like this, but back when I was your age, there were fairs and carnivals all the time. So many lights, you might go blind."

"I bet it was something to see," Lucas said.

The Ferris wheel inched along under its grinner power. Lucas didn't like the idea of having grinners around, but he had to admit, they were finding a use for them.

The man walked toward a huge tattered circus tent. Lucas hesitated at the flapping door, but the man's smiling face didn't seem to warrant any danger. He could kill the man quicker than he could ever raise that gun, if need be.

They entered the tent. Beams of light shot through the large holes in the tent and the smell of decay, death, and body odor filled it. Partially filled stands surrounded most of the enclosure. As they walked by the people staring at the center ring, Lucas turned to see what they were watching.

"Now, behold the dead. I will try to tame one, can they be our friend?" A man in a red jumpsuit asked the crowd.

"No," the audience roared back.

"Send it out!"

A door opened on the other side of the ring and a grinner stepped out. It rushed at the nearby people and slammed against the glass wall. The people in the stands screamed and moved back. When the glass held the grinner back, they moved, laughed, and mocked the grinner.

The man at the center of the ring cracked his whip. "Over here, you beast."

The grinner ignored the people behind the glass and ran at the man in red. At the last second, the man slid his foot out and tripped the grinner. It fell on its face and the crowd roared with applause and laughter.

"Please, I only want to be friends." The man picked up a long stick from the ground and pinned it against the grinner's chest after it stood. The grinner flailed at him, but the stick held steady.

The man they followed stopped and leaned down to a man's ear. "Bob, we have some new people. They drove up in a Tesla," the man leading them said.

Bob's smile changed to a questioning look. The man wore a black shirt and pants, and kept his hair slicked back like an old time greaser. He motioned with his finger for them to get closer. "Let's talk out back, where we can hear each other," he said and rose from his seat.

They followed the men downstairs to the back of the tent. Bob pushed the flaps of the tent open, letting the sun pour into the opening. Lucas squinted and kept Julie between him and Hank as they walked out. The crowd roared again at some unseen event behind them.

"Please, let's go to my trailer, right over here," Bob said. He had a hint of an accent Lucas had heard before. He looked to Julie, but she only gave him a questioning look back. Maybe he imagined it?

"If you don't mind, Bob, we would like to get going soon," Lucas spoke up.

"Oh, this will only take a second." Bob said in a sigh and climbed up the three steps that led to his trailer door. "Please wait here." He entered his trailer and closed the door.

"What's your name again?" Lucas asked.

The man holding his rifle perked up at the question. "Jeff."

"Hey, Jeff. Is this something normal here?" Lucas nodded toward the closed door.

Jeff chuckled. "Yeah, he has us bring anyone we cross here, I think he's checking you guys for something." He shrugged.

Lucas slid his fingers along Prudence's string, when the trailer door flung open and hit the stair railing with a loud thud. Bob stepped from the open door and looked to each of them. He looked like a different man, his face pale and his hair disheveled.

"Get in here, quick," Bob said.

"You need me?" Jeff asked.

"Get the hell out of here, Jeff."

Lucas took in the situation, trying to remember his training with Nathen. Something was going on way beyond the surface. Then Lucas saw it, with wide eyes he looked at the Panavice in Bob's hand. "Come on," he said, trying to get Julie and Hank into the trailer.

"I'm not going into that freak's trailer," Julie said.

"We'll be fine," Lucas said, walking into the trailer and leaving the door open. Lucas took in the maps nailed to the walls. Pins and Post-it notes covered many sections of the map, each one with notes. Lucas thought of the many times he saw this in movies when detectives were trying to figure out a crime. He thought he knew what Bob was searching for.

Hank closed the door and Bob stood with his Panavice in hand.

Julie shot her hand to her pocket with a shocked look and pulled her Panavice out. "Where did you get that?"

"It's mine. Do you know how long I've waited for someone to show up? I've nearly given up so many times." Bob plopped into an office chair.

"You're from Vanar?" Julie clarified.

"Yeah, Marcus sent me here as a punishment. I was in charge of . . . well, he blamed me for a lot of stuff."

"Whoa, you've been stuck here for that long? Why didn't you use a stone?"

"What's a stone?" Bob's face ignited with hope.

"There are portals," Lucas answered vaguely.

"I knew it. I woke up at the bottom of some kind of casino, everything was so crazy at first and . . . well, I eventually made it here."

"So what do you want from us?" Hank asked.

Bob sprang from the chair and stepped to the trailer window. He pulled down the metal shades with a finger and peeked through the opening. He turned to each of them with a determined expression. "I want out of this hell."

"We're going to LA to find a friend," Lucas said.

"LA?" Bob shook his head. "No, no, you can't go there. I have many contacts from neighboring tribes and they all say the same thing. LA's gone, there was something like ten million people there."

"That's where we're going."

Bob stepped from the window and paced for a bit. Lucas adjusted his bow. In these tight quarters, he wouldn't have enough time to use it, but with Hank he knew he didn't need to.

"Before you go to your death, can you show me how this stone works and where it is?" Bob asked.

Lucas raised a questioning eyebrow to Julie who shrugged. "If you get us transportation to LA, we'll show you how to get back to Vanar."

Bob's eyes widened and he opened his mouth, but instead of words he stepped to Lucas and hugged him. Lucas sent Julie a panicked look and waited for the man to let him go.

"Thank you so much, you can have whatever you need." Bob stepped back and looked at the back of his hands. "Look at my hands, I was promised to be a young man for my whole life, now I look like an old man. I need to get back before this becomes irreversible."

"Give us our car back and show us the safest route to LA, and, like I said, we'll tell you what you need to know," Lucas said.

"Of course, of course, anything you want."

"Now."

Bob jerked back at the order, but recovered quickly. "As long as you keep your end of the bargain, I expect full details about how to get back."

"You'll have them."

BOB ESCORTED THEM BACK TO the freeway. Their car sat in the center lane with a group of people surrounding it. He brought a couple of men with him to carry two bags of supplies. Lucas loosened his bow over his shoulder and tightened the quiver on his back. Bob looked giddy, but the two other men seemed emotionless.

Lucas eyed Hank and nodded his head; Hank nodded in return. He didn't need words with the big guy. Lucas leaned close to Julie and whispered, "Charge the car as soon as you're in range."

The men around the car cleared a path. Lucas kept his chin high as he walked past them and opened the front door. He motioned for Julie to get in with a wave of his hand and she obliged, climbing into the driver seat and over to the passenger side. She locked her door.

The two men carrying bags walked to the back of the car and opened the trunk.

"You know, Bob, on second thought, we've taken enough from your people. Please keep the bags," Lucas said. The two men held the bags and looked to Bob.

"Oh no, I couldn't in good conscience send you off without something."

"It's fine, really."

"I insist." Bob pointed to the two men and they placed the bags in the trunk and closed the door.

"Hank, get in the car." Hank opened the back door and got into the car. "We will tell you what you want to know in the car, as we are driving away. Once we are out of view from your men, we'll let you out."

Bob laughed and Lucas narrowed his eyes. He stopped laughing and took in a deep breath, looking at his two men and pointing to the trunk. They opened it and took out the bags. "On second thought, I think it's very generous of you to give your supplies back to the people." Bob slid into the car next to Hank.

Lucas glanced around, got into the front seat, and closed the door. He turned to look into the back of the car, Bob showed him a warm smile. "I said I'd do anything to get out of this hell."

"Even kill us?"

"Hey, it was just insurance. No hard feelings. Oh, and if anything should happen to me, there are men surrounding this car who will not hesitate to kill each one of you and feed your dying bodies to the dead."

Julie let out a long breath and slid lower in her seat.

"You really think there will be another chance for you to meet someone who knows how to get off this planet?"

Bob fidgeted in his seat and he grimaced. "No."

"All we want is to be on our way."

"Tell me about this stone and you have my blessing."

"Let's get to a private place."

Bob nodded his head.

Lucas pressed down on the pedal and the silent electrical motor moved them forward. He spotted a small opening in the pile of parked cars on the freeway. "Up here was your backup to kill us, wasn't it?"

"What? No, no."

They passed the first line of cars and several men with rifles ducked below the vehicles.

"Those guys are always there . . . reani's are everywhere."

"Reani's?" Julie asked.

"Yeah, you know, the reanimated people."

"Just make sure they don't shoot us."

Bob waved at the men as they crept by. Lucas wanted to punch the pedal down and get out of Bob's den o' goons. He was sure they would be spread out for the next mile or so. Lucas let the speed build up to ten miles per hour.

"How much longer? I really don't want to be walking back in this area."

"Another mile or so."

Bob let out a long huff and rubbed his eyes. "I'm really trying to be patient here."

Lucas snickered at his uncomfortable mannerisms. "What did you do for MM?"

"I worked with the scene generator."

Julie perked up in her seat. "Like the huge world generator type?"

"Yep, used to watch some crazy stuff go down."

"I bet you did," Julie said.

"What'd you do to piss off Marcus?" Lucas asked.

"Let some guy go somewhere he wasn't supposed to."

"Rule breaker, eh?" He turned the wheel to avoid a burnt big rig lying on its side.

"Yeah, well, they took everything from me, my family, my life. I haven't seen my kids in eighteen years." Bob looked at each of them and lowered his eyebrows. "Now that I've shared, why don't you tell me your story?"

"Not much to tell really," Lucas lied. "MM's holding our friends in LA and we're going to get them."

"Such loyalty is beyond mere friendships," Bob said and rubbed his chin.

"Why don't you tell us your real name?" Hank asked.

Bob jumped back from Hank. "Dear God in Heaven, man! I thought you were a mute. Fine, I can't see the harm in it, Genter is my real name."

Lucas shook his head and smiled. He hadn't even thought the man was lying about his name, who cared if he was? Hank sniffed out that lie, what else was he holding back? "Almost far enough, Genter." The freeway cleared up some and Lucas sped up to fifteen miles per hour, half keeping an eye on the road and other half keeping an eye on Genter.

Lucas glanced at Julie as she rose up in her seat. Her pale face turned to look at the back of the car. He kept shooting quick glances at her while he swerved around dead cars.

"You knew Isaac didn't you?" she asked.

Lucas gripped the wheel and with mouth open looked back at the man's face.

Genter fidgeted with his hands in his lap, thumbs wrestling each other. "Yes, I knew him. He's the one who got me exiled."

"Why did you get exiled?" Julie leaned so far into the backseat with a rabid face that Lucas contemplated stopping the car.

Genter pushed back against his seat. "No, it's impossible. You can't be them."

"You are the one who set up the scenes for our parents, aren't you?"

Lucas slammed on the brakes and Julie's butt hit the dashboard as she fell back. He stared at the steering wheel, unable to blink, unable to form a word. How could they run into the man who was there? Lucas pulled his stiff fingers off the steering wheel and turned around to face Genter. Julie moved with him and Hank slid closer.

Genter shrunk down in his seat. "He forced me, threatened to kill my family if I stopped him. I never wanted to be part of his schemes."

"His schemes killed our parents," Lucas said.

"I'm sorry," Genter said.

"Sorry doesn't bring back my mom."

"Get out," Hank said.

"What? We had a deal."

"Deal's over," Julie said.

"It's over when I say it's over." Genter pulled out a knife. Hank grabbed his arm and Lucas nocked in an arrow in one fluid motion, holding the bow sideways to fit in the car.

Genter kicked the bow and opened the door at the same time, rolling out. Lucas lowered his bow and breathed rapidly as he watched Genter run past a few cars and disappear.

"What just happened?" Lucas asked.

"We better get moving, I bet he'll have a posse after us soon," Julie said.

Lucas lowered himself back into the driver's seat and pressed the pedal. He took the car up to twenty miles per hour.

"That bastard," Hank said.

Lucas looked in the rearview mirror at Hank steaming with anger in the back seat. What was the possibility of crossing paths with someone involved in their parents' deaths, on another world? One in a billion didn't seem to be accurate, it seemed outright impossible, but it happened. He struggled to keep the car on a clear path as his mind wrangled with the idea. "Anyone want to say something about what just happened?"

"I just want to get out of here," Julie said.

Lucas wasn't sure if she meant Genter's circus land or Ryjack itself. "Can you get me more power?"

"I can for a bit, until my Pana overheats."

Lucas pressed the pedal and the car increased its speed to twenty-five miles per hour. At that speed, Lucas had to concentrate a hundred percent on the road. He liked the job, it gave his subconscious time to process what happened while he focused on avoiding the never ending obstacles.

"Keep a look out for any of Genter's people."

After an hour of driving Lucas relaxed his hands on the steering wheel and looked over to Julie.

"A few more minutes and we'll have to go slow again."

He eased up on the throttle and slowed to twenty. The rearview mirror didn't show anything and they hadn't seen a grinner the entire time on the freeway.

"We're only forty miles from Los Angeles."

Over the next two hours, they began to see grinners stumbling down the road and the freeway congested enough to where they drove on the shoulder more than the road.

"Look," Julie said. The skyscrapers stood like nothing happened and the sprawling city looked normal from a distance, but there were ten million people down there, waiting for someone stupid enough to enter.

"Jeesh, look at the size of it," Hank said.

"That's what she said," Lucas said.

"You're so dumb." Julie hit him in the arm.

Lucas relaxed his hands, it felt good to be where they were. Genter wouldn't follow them this far and they still weren't far enough to be in the deadly city. "You got navigation on that thing?"

"It's just a dot on the screen." Julie pointed ahead.

"Guide me as best you can."

"There, get off on sixth," she said.

Lucas drove off the freeway and into the city streets. The vacant buildings were foul reminders of what was most likely hiding behind the broken glass and propped open doors. The crumbling road crunched under the slow moving tires. Lucas tried to find the quietest path but quickly gave in to the sound.

"Keep an eye on the right, I'll watch the left," Lucas said. The car gave him some comfort for an immediate attack but as they went deeper into the city, he felt the path behind him closing off. The car started to feel like a trap the grinners would encircle and encase.

Every hundred feet, he planned an escape route. A broken front door or shattered window could make a good escape path if they needed to ditch the car. He ensured the doors were unlocked and he took off his seatbelt. Julie and Hank, without any words, did the same. He saw Julie tensing up and keeping her back off the front seat.

The streets weren't as crowded with cars as Vegas, mostly parked on the sides of the street like they were left there. LA is where it started, the city must've not known what happened until it was too late.

The streets were quiet, but he felt them. They lurked behind every car he passed, inside every building and back alley, waiting for some fool to spark them to life with noise. He slowed the car down, making sure not to put any extra sound on his stop. Two grinners stood in the middle of the road ahead.

He opened the door and stood on the front seat, holding his bow. He selected an arrow and shot the first one in the neck, it fell to the ground flailing; the second one took a head shot and fell on the ground motionless. Lucas sat back in the car and drove by the gurgling grinner to retrieve his arrows.

Julie looked at him disgusted as he got back into the car.

"What? I've got to have these." Over the next mile, he shot a dozen more.

"Did you hear that?" Hank asked.

"What?" Lucas asked.

"I don't know, sounded like a bell."

"I heard it too," Julie acknowledged, but was mostly concerned with her Panavice. "Okay, we should be there in the next couple blocks."

Lucas slowed the car down and pulled over to the side of the road next to a hotel. "I don't want to drive into another trap, we should walk from here." He opened the door and got out of the car. He might have waited for a debate, but he knew he was right. If MM had a bunker nearby, they would be looking for something like a driving car, but if they could pass for grinners, they might have a chance at a surprise. Hank and Julie got out of the car.

"Do we even know what we're going to do when we get there?" Hank asked.

It was a good question. "We'll have to figure it out as we go."

Weeds grew into the concrete sidewalks and through the cracks in the road. The buildings' lower windows were broken out and a layer of dust caked all the windows. A bird flew out of a busted upper floor window and glided down the road.

The bell sound rang again. Lucas focused on the noise and where it came from.

"I knew I heard something," Hank exclaimed.

"Shh," Lucas hushed. The bell sound wasn't far away and the last thing he wanted was a horde of grinners coming after them. He spotted a half torn down door at an apartment building next to them. They could escape there if needed. The long straight road ahead looked to have similar buildings lining it for a block and then it opened up, maybe a park. "Let me guess, that's the direction we're heading?" Lucas pointed his bow toward the sound of the bell.

"Yes," Julie said.

"Great, let's get moving and if the crap hits the fan, follow me."

I'm pretty sure it's already splattered," Hank said, pointing behind them. A horde of grinners stumbled down the road directly toward them.

"Our car must have stirred them this way. I don't think they've spotted us yet." Lucas eyed his escape door across the street; if they ran, they would probably be seen and a horde that size could tear down the building. They were still next to the car but how much could the car hold up against the horde if they were spotted?

"Great," Julie said and shook her head.

He couldn't risk the car. "Follow me," he commanded.

They ran across the street and to the apartment Lucas had been eyeing. He stepped over the lower half of the torn door and into the entry. Hank picked up Julie and pushed her through. He glanced down the road and with an urgent look, climbed through the opening and fell to the tile floor.

Lucas placed an arrow on Prudence's string and scanned the area for movement. Large cracks ran up the walls of the entryway and parts of the plastered ceiling had fallen to the floor.

"I think they spotted us," Hank warned, peeking out of the opening.

"Let's get up stairs," Lucas suggested.

Hank and Julie shot up the stairs behind him. He turned at the landing and ran up the next set of stairs. Two more sets and he breathed heavily at the top.

The bell rang out again.

Lucas grabbed the wood rail and listened. A rustling could be heard at the door below, followed by raspy groans of the grinners. Maybe they couldn't get past the door? "We need to get out of this hall."

Next to the stairs, a ladder led up and was marked *Roof Access*. Lucas pulled Prudence over his shoulder and climbed the ladder. A plastic dome was the door for the top, and he pushed it open, daylight flooding in. He jumped on the gravel roof and then reached back to help Julie get out. Hank pulled himself through the small opening and plopped his feet onto the roof, closing the door behind him.

Julie took out her Panavice and pointed to the other side of the roof. "It's right over there, we might get a good look at it from up here."

They walked to the edge of the parapet wall, the smell of tar wafting up. The bell rung again, clearer this time and it felt much closer.

"Oh my God," Julie said, getting her first look.

"Holy cow," Hank said.

They looked down at the blackened park below. The sea of grinners below them moved as one. A pool of black bubbled swathed through a section of grinners and they collected large amounts of black tar-like substance on their clothes. A few buildings were scattered around the park, encasing the area in a large rectangle the size of a couple city blocks. Grinners covered much of the available space.

"Is this the tar pit?" Hank asked.

"Yep, and their base is under all that," Julie said, looking like she might be sick.

"Anyone see an entrance?" Lucas squinted, searching the landscape.

"What does it matter? There must be ten thousand grinners down there," Julie said.

"What, we're going to give up now?"

"No, but what chance do we have?"

The grinners grumbled and moved around. They seemed most dense near a small shed with a single door attached to it and a large black box on top.

"There, that shed . . . it has speakers on it." Lucas pointed.

"How much you want to bet, that's the entrance," Hank said.

Lucas turned from the scene and sat on the roof with his back to the short wall. Julie took a step back and looked at him. Hank stayed on the edge, staring.

"If we can get closer, I may be able to turn off the speakers, or blow them out," Julie said.

"Then they focus on us. No, there has to be another way."

"We take out the speaker and maybe they'll disperse after a while," Hank suggested.

Lucas huffed out his disagreement. "They could be behind that door right now, looking out. They might as well be on the moon." He kicked the gravel and sent a few rocks skipping across the roof.

"I have an idea," Julie tapped her chin and looked out over the edge. Her face was full of emotion as she wrangled the idea in her head. Her lips moved in unspoken words as if she was arguing with herself. She stepped away from the edge, looking resolute. "Tar is flammable. If we can get a few grinners lit, the rest might go up as well."

Lucas frowned as an idea formed in his head. He jumped to his feet. "You're a genius." He hugged Julie. Her plan was so awesome, he couldn't stop smiling. "I can shoot a flaming arrow down there and light them up."

It had to work. What could go wrong?

CHAPTER 12

"HARRIS." EMMETT SHOOK HARRIS'S SHOULDER.

He jerked back from the touch and looked into the cold man's face. Emmett's stone features had returned and the anger displayed in the bowels of Marcus's playground was gone.

Gunshots sounded off in every direction as MM soldiers tried to hold the line. Harris had been in Ryjack when it happened there. Seeing it destroy a different world was like hearing about a person on the news dying in a car crash . . . it felt distant. But this, staring at him in the face, on his home planet, felt much worse.

He took in a quick breath. "Emmett, we need people at the sea port, stopping any ships from coming or going, we need men at each of the two entrances to close the gates. The airports need to be shut down. Not a single person can come or go from Capital."

"People won't like it, but I'll make it happen."

"They'll be happy to make it through this alive." Harris paused and a great realization struck him. "You guys cured Lucas, what did you use?"

"We don't have a cure. I read that the boy simply lived through it."

"That's impossible."

"Not quite impossible, more like one in a billion."

"You're telling me he has the virus in his body, but can live with it?"

"It appears so," Emmett said. "Marcus wanted to get the kid in the labs to see why, but that didn't happen."

"No cure then. We'll have to be extra cautious, as we have no safety net. I don't want this planet turning into another Ryjack. What about the Arracks?" Harris asked.

Emmett shook his head a tiny amount. "They've been pissed for seventeen years, ever since Simon started sending them to their deaths through countless stone travels. The parking lot was a major blow as well. You and I both know, Marcus has something on them—I never found out what—but they are still loyal to him. Once they find out he's gone, we can only hope they return to their home."

Harris knew it was a fantasy wish. The Arracks would not kindly pack up and leave. But he had to control the grinners before he could even think of the Arracks.

"Okay, fine. Let's get this city locked down. Get the info to your people anyway you have to."

"I'll send out the orders." Emmett ran away.

A few MM soldiers ran by and did double takes as they saw Harris. He stood in the lobby of the MM building with small groups of soldiers behind desks and trashcans, anything they could stand behind, while they shot into the oncoming grinners. The grinners jumped past the doors and took chest shots, but kept moving.

"Head shots only!" he yelled out the order.

A few of the soldiers glanced at his proclamation and turned to shoot the grinners in the head, finally sending them to the ground.

Harris fought the sight of Compry from overtaking his mind. He shot down her body when he thought there could be a cure with Lucas. Maybe if he could get Lucas and study his blood, maybe, just maybe. . .

He pushed the thoughts from his head and a barrage of bullets landed on a group of grinners emerging from the staircase near him. Plenty of time for mourning later. Now, he had a company to run and a world to save. But how do you save a world you can't talk to? He knew of a way.

Harris ran down the stairs, stepping and jumping over the lingering bodies in the stairwell. A man sat in the entrance way with bite marks on his arm. He looked pale, but hadn't turned yet. Harris shot the man in the head and kept running down the hall. MM only used it once for Marcus's five hundredth birthday party, but it had to still be there.

After thirty years of being absent from the MM headquarters, he still remembered every corner and staircase. He slammed open a steel door and ran down a few flights of stairs. Level B8. He kicked the door in and held his gun out in front of him. The room was devoid of any movement. It didn't look any different than it did all those years ago.

He closed the door and walked behind the desk and faced the control panel on the wall. It took him a few seconds to orient himself with the analog dials. There was a long row of switches that turned on the speakers through the city.

He pressed a large green button marked *Start* and the board lit up. Harris wasn't sure where the generator was, but it worked and that was all that mattered. He flipped all of the switches on and, last but not least, he pushed down the button marked *Mic*.

He leaned over the square microphone on top of the desk. Taking a deep breath, he pressed the talk button. "Attention, attention. People of Capital, please listen. This is Harris Boone, newly appointed leader of MM, rank ten. There has been a terrible outbreak and I demand all citizens lock yourselves in your homes for the time being. If you go outside, you will be shot, if you try to leave the city, you will be shot. This is not a drill. If you stay outside or try to leave the city you risk being infected. Keep away from other people at all costs. I repeat, stay inside and lock your doors." Harris gripped the microphone with one hand. "Godspeed."

He released the talk button and turned off the switches and generator. Had he said enough? Would they heed the warnings?

He opened the door and a grinner fell in toward him. Harris jumped back and shot the thing in the head. Several more struggled to get into the room with a partially open door. He kicked the front two grinners in the gut and looked past them into the room beyond. A horde of grinners filled the halls and adjacent room, many in black uniforms, holding their guns in their dead hands. Their fresh bodies hadn't decayed yet into the ones like Ryjack, so they moved faster and screamed louder. Soon, they crowded together in a mob, moving toward him.

Relaxed, Harris entered his zone and held both guns in his hands. He shot the first four in rapid fire. He jumped to the desk to get a higher ground and ended six more grinners. The pile blocked the door. As he gazed to the back rows, he saw the horde was much larger than he first assessed.

He fired the last bullets in his guns and switched to just his rail gun. Did he have enough bullets? He gritted his teeth, and pulled the trigger, making each shot count, but the pile of grinners was pushed forward, through the door and spreading into the room like a giant meat grinder. Closing in on him, the grinners began filling the room. They seemed to be multiplying. As he killed one, two more appeared through the door.

He hated making mistakes, but he might have when he opened that door.

CHAPTER 13

LUCAS LOOKED OVER THE ROOF and down to the horde of grinners the digital bell collected. "Hand me the cloth, please."

Hank handed him the white cloth they found in their first aid kit and Lucas took the roll and wrapped it around the head of an arrow until it formed a nice ball and taped it in place.

"Alcohol."

Julie handed him a bottle of rubbing alcohol.

He poured it over the gauze ball and smiled at the concoction. He looked down, searching for his target. It didn't seem to matter where he shot, the grinners were heavily drenched in tar and Julie thought it would spread to the entire grinner pile. "Okay, here it goes."

Lucas placed the notch of the arrow into the string and extended the end to Hank to ignite. Pulling back the lit arrow, he aimed quickly as his hand was now too close to the flame. Sending the arrow flying across the sky, it struck the back of a grinner and stuck. "Yes! Direct hit."

"Was that the one you were aiming for?" Julie asked with speculation.

"Of course. Exactly the one."

"Look," Hank said.

Lucas watched as the shirt on the grinner's back took fire. It flailed around, bumping into other grinners, passing the fire like an unwanted gift. The fire spread as each of the burning grinners stumbled into other grinners. After a few minutes, Lucas could no longer make out any single grinner on fire as the flaming ball engulfed a large cluster of them, building on itself exponentially. The huge flames lit the whole park and all the grinners began to groan and yell.

Lucas smiled in his triumph and raised Prudence into the darkening sky. Then, the smell hit him. He hunched over at the mixture of burnt oil and, it almost made him throw up thinking it, BBQ. Julie dry heaved and stepped away from the wall and went to her knees.

"The smell," Julie said, taking quick breaths. "Oh my God."

Hank didn't seem bothered by it and looked on at the burning man party below.

"You're sick, Hank," Lucas said.

"Oh, come on, it's not that bad."

Lucas felt the olfactory disagreeing with his buddy's assessment and his eyes began to water. "How can it be worse?"

"This gives us a way in. How could it be any better? They could be right there."

"I hope not, it'll be five hundred degrees down there," Julie said.

"It's getting hot up here as well." Lucas felt a bead of sweat on his forehead. He walked back to the edge of the roof and looked over. The flames had quadrupled in size, encompassing much of the park, reaching high into the sky. The smoke gathered into a black cloud above, blocking what little light the setting sun produced.

"Holy smokes," Hank said.

"Julie, you better look at this." In the blazing light of the fire, he saw every corner. There were far more grinners than he originally thought; they filled in every space of the surrounding areas and small buildings, the park's visitor center had a fire climbing up the side.

"We better think of an escape plan for when the fire reaches our building," Julie said.

Lucas looked to the sky, the smoke sending a black beacon for anyone within a hundred miles. He hoped the fire ended by morning, having an arrow pointing to their location was disconcerting.

Leaning over the edge of the roof, he saw a few dozen grinners stumbling around. The raging fire sent tall dancing shadows up the walls of their building. He squinted and looked down the street into the darkness. Things moved and more shadows bounced around. A horde walked toward the inferno.

"Moths to a flame," Lucas said under his breath.

The fire reached the edge of the street where many grinners were held back by a steel fence, but they ran their faces into the wire mesh, setting their clothes on fire. A burning grinner ran in a circle as the flames engulfed its face, nearing their building until it fell against the bottom.

"Great, they're already against our building."

"Lucas, it may not matter what happens here if the entire city goes up in flames," Julie said, seemingly annoyed—completely ignoring the fact the fire was her idea.

Lucas agreed, ran across the roof and opened the hatch. The fire provided enough light to see down into the vacant room below. "It looks clear. Come on." He climbed down the ladder and jumped off the last rung, landing on the carpeted hall.

He held Prudence out in front of him and walked down to the staircase. Nothing moved. The place had to still be clear. He waited for Julie and Hank to get to the bottom of the stairs before moving down the next flight. "There are a few places down the street," Lucas whispered, remembering an escape path he logged while driving in.

"We'll follow you," Hank said.

Lucas took his time moving through the building. It was so much creepier in the dark, and the inferno outside only sent a moving orange light through the few windows the building had. The sound of the crackling fire returned as they reached the front door.

Sticking his head out of the top half of the door, Lucas peered down the street. One direction was the endless horde being burned, while the other was a dead, dark street. Their path seemed to be laid out for them. He was sure there were grinners down the road, but the building would be on fire soon and he didn't want to be stuck on the roof, waiting for the inevitable. Leaving, they had a chance.

Lucas climbed over the bottom half of the door and stepped onto the sidewalk. Outside the building, the smoke had worked its way down the street and he felt it burning in his lungs with each breath. He coughed some of it out, trying not to think of what he was consuming. The heat already pushed against them. They needed to get out of there. He gripped Julie's hands as Hank lifted her through the opening.

"Come on, Hank." Lucas crouched low. With Julie's hand wrapped inside his, she showed him those beautiful eyes. He would find a way to keep her safe. When Hank's feet hit the pavement, Lucas pulled Julie into a run and looked back to make sure Hank was keeping up. The big man's feet stomped on the pavement. *Go, Hank, go.*

He passed the first building with a busted front door. Too close. He saw an old brick building a block down the road with a car parked into a wall. His eyes started stinging from the smoke. Did the wind shift?

Lucas slid to a stop, pushing Julie behind him as he stepped forward with Prudence in hand. Four grinners ran toward them. He fired three times in quick succession. A large rock flew by and hit the fourth grinner in the head, knocking it to the ground.

"Nice throw," Lucas said to Hank.

He grinned. "Little league is finally paying off."

"Right, what were we? Oh, the Red Dragons!"

"Yeah, we had first and second base on lock. No one stole from us."

"Can we get out of here?" Julie coughed, maybe to punch home her point, but Lucas heard it loud and clear.

He led them further down the road, the smoke diminishing enough to where he could take full breaths. He spotted the building he wanted. A car stuck halfway into the building. Bricks fell around the car and created a hole big enough for them to climb through. Lucas climbed over the back of the sedan and slid off the hood and into the building. Looking back over the hood of the car, a tattered skeleton of a person sat behind the wheel with its boney fingers gripping the steering wheel.

Hank and Julie slid over the hood and into the building with him. The head and arms of the skeleton fell with the jostling from Hank's weight.

The faint orange light from the distant fire gave just enough light for him to make out the tables and chairs in the restaurant. A few tables lay on their sides next to the intruding front end of the car. The rest of the restaurant looked untouched—in bad need of a cleaning—but otherwise it looked as if it could take customers the next morning. A long bar stretched the length of it and ended at a door propped open.

"Come on, we need to get higher." Lucas walked past the tables and chairs, guided by the bright light of Julie's Panavice. Salt and pepper shakers still sat on the middle of each table. How quickly had LA fallen? These things should have been looted a long time ago. Did no one live in LA? Lucas pointed Prudence at the open door.

A chair screeched and Lucas swung around with his bow. Hank grabbed the chair he had just run into with a sorry expression on his face. Lucas took a quick breath and turned back, continuing toward the door. On the floor was a decayed body, holding the door perpetually open. The door squeaked as he pushed against it and stepped over the body.

Lucas struggled to see every corner of the dimly lit foyer. The ceiling towered above them for three stories and ended on a dark skylight. Bits of moon light peeked through the thick layer on the glass.

"Do you think any of those things are in here?" Julie asked. She shined her light up the stairs.

"Probably." A month ago he would have told her it was fine. He knew better now. Fate had so far been on their side, but at some point he felt it was going to betray them.

The first step on the stair creaked under his pressure and he winced. One shaky hand grasped the railing while the other held Prudence.

"Step on the edge, next to the railing," Julie said.

He placed his foot on the next step and it felt firmer, the wood didn't make a sound. He moved up the steps with light feet and reached the second floor. Julie and Hank were right behind him.

He held his bow and arrow, pointing it in the darkness. He waited for Julie's light to shine ahead, lighting their path. Julie stood next to him and lit the surrounding floor, a set of doors on each side of the staircase and a walk path around it, but no grinners. He glanced down to the first floor and noticed more of the orange glow coming through the glass.

"I think we should get to the roof and make sure the fire is not getting any closer." Lucas lowered his bow.

Another staircase and they were on the third floor.

"Over here, there's roof access." Hank pointed to a door.

The metal door opened and a steel ladder led up. Lucas sighed. He didn't like leaving Julie alone for one second in Ryjack. He would never leave her alone again if he could help it.

"I'll go first, Julie, stick close to me."

He climbed the ladder and pushed open the steel lid on top. The smell of smoke rushed in. He looked down at her and she looked up, giving him a smile.

"How's the view from down there?" Lucas asked, shaking his butt.

"It's what nightmares are made of," Hank spoke before Julie could answer.

He laughed and climbed onto the gravel flat roof. It was much like the last one they abandoned, with large metal AC boxes and skylights peppering the roof top.

Smoke swirled around the air but in a manageable amount, like a decent campfire. The bright orange light in the distance lit an entire block of the city. The sky above darkened in the black smoke rising into the air. The moon disappeared as the black cloud overtook it.

"Look at it go," Hank said, shaking his head in wonder.

"Oh man, I think we made a big mistake." Julie pointed to the building on fire. Lucas squinted at the flames stretching out of the windows from the building they used to be in. If the fire grew that quick, it could be at them in a matter of hours.

"You think Joey, Samantha, and Poly are okay in that?" Hank asked.

"They're underground, so they shouldn't be in any danger of the heat, but they could be choked out if the smoke clogs up their filtration system."

Lucas stared at Julie with shock.

"But a MM bunker shouldn't have any trouble with it," she quickly added. The speaker rang out a distorted bell sound. "The fire must be melting that speaker."

With the blazing fire marching toward them, grinners lurking in every direction, and smoke filling the air and sky, Lucas felt uneasy. But they could stay there for a while longer. He peered over the edge of the building at the worst possible second. "No."

"What is it?" Julie rushed to the edge of the roof and looked down.

"One of them saw me."

Below them, the car that punctured through the brick building shook a steady stream of grinners piled against it, stumbling into the restaurant below. Another grinner looked up at them and snarled. It thrashed at the car and the grinners surrounding it.

"If we hurry, maybe we can get to the front door." Lucas ran across the roof and slid next to the open steel lid. He peered down to the dimly lit foyer and saw the horde of grinners stumbling around the hostess podium and a few starting to walk up the stairs.

"Great," Julie said.

"Let's get back on the roof. There should be one of those fire escape things, right?" Lucas didn't wait for an answer and bounded up the ladder and back onto the roof, running around the perimeter of the building. He had seen so many movies where the building had a steel staircase on the outside. After a full sweep, he conceded that once again, Hollywood had failed him.

"Nothing." Lucas bent over, breathing hard.

"You think those things can climb ladders?" Hank slammed the door and sat on it. "I don't want to find out."

Julie shook her head. "I don't think they can, it would require fine motor—"

A huge sound of crashing steel and stone interrupted her words. The building they were once on imploded. The debris fell to the street, crushing their Tesla and setting the street on fire with bits of the building.

"We were just on that building." She stared at the pile of rubble.

"That's not happening to us," Lucas reassured her.

"You can't say that. That fire is moving this way. We have no way out. It's only a matter of time." Julie paced, not looking at him.

Lucas felt the panic building. His gut started screaming at him. There had to be another way. Not doing anything was worse than trying and failing. He closed his eyes and held out his hands, hoping the idea would hit him. Then, he felt it. One tiny drop, then another. He opened his eyes and gazed at the black sky. Streaks of rain came down, hitting his face.

CHAPTER 14

JOEY TWISTED THE HANDLE TO the door going outside and let go. "It's not locked."

"Might as well be," Poly huffed. "Maybe the grinners below have moved on?"

"Let's check it out." He wasn't confident in her theory, but didn't want to be next to the window anymore.

Samantha rolled her eyes and they walked down the few flights of stairs to the steel windowless door that led back into MM's bunker. Joey pressed his ear against the cold metal and closed his eyes.

"I don't hear—" A scratch over the door stopped him from finishing his sentence, he jumped back from the door, expecting it to open. He glanced at Poly who raised an eyebrow at his jump. "What?"

"They're behind the door. You're right, we're stuck here." Samantha put her hands on the top of her head and tried to deep breathe her panic away.

"If we're quiet long enough, maybe they will move on." Joey thought about when Ferrell said they'd be gone after a bit. But how long would they survive in a stairwell?

They cringed at the loud bell.

"Jeesh, that thing must be right on top of us," Samantha said.

Poly stared up the stairs. "I'd rather be up top, at least there's a bit of sunlight up there." She stepped up the stairs, rounded the cornered, and disappeared into the upper levels.

"She's changed." Samantha looked after her and back to Joey. It was the first time they had been alone since Poly arrived.

"We all have," he said.

"I don't think I have." Tears welled in her eyes. "I'm scared, Joey. This is crazy shit, you know?"

She shook and gazed at him with fearful eyes. Joey pulled her into his arms. "It's going to be okay," he said, speaking softly into her hair. "We're going to get through this. I mean, have you *seen* Poly with those knives?"

Samantha giggled and pulled back to meet his eyes. "Thanks, Joey."

Poly came back into view and watched him embrace Samantha. She stopped her movement and looked hurt, then sped down the rest of the steps. "You need to see what's happening. Come on."

He followed Poly up the stairs, looking at the back of her head as they climbed. After the second flight, he could hear grinners yelling. As they got close to the door, the smell of tar seeped under the crack, and it felt a bit hotter than it did before. The small window on the door flickered with orange flames and he couldn't believe what he was seeing.

"What is it?" Samantha asked, vying for position at the small window, but Poly and Joey took most of the real estate.

Joey grimaced at the sight outside. The grinner's staggered around on fire, lighting up the darkening sky. Plumes of black smoke rose from their bodies as they lit the surrounding grinners.

"It's a fire," Poly said in an obvious manner.

"Fire?" Samantha pushed her way into a spot at the door's window. She covered her mouth and talked through her shaking fingers. "How did the fire start?"

"I don't know."

"I bet it was Emmett." Poly pointed at the door with her kitchen knife. "He probably lit them on fire on his way out."

Joey nodded in agreement. It was a good theory, but he didn't think Emmett would have wasted the time to do something like that.

"Whoa, it's getting hot in here." Samantha pulled her hair back with her hand.

Joey felt the sweat on his brow. He stepped back from the door and the heat lessened. He glanced at Poly and Samantha. Their faces glistened with perspiration. "We should get to the bottom of the stairs, I bet it's cooler down there."

A couple flights down and they were at the bottom, next to the door with the scratching grinners. At least it was cooler.

Joey picked a concrete wall to sit down against. Poly sat next to him and Samantha found a spot next to the door. A grinner hit the door and Samantha jumped with a shocked squeal and moved.

"Those things don't quit do they?" Samantha glared at the door.

"No, not really. Ferrell said they usually get bored after a while and go back to whatever it was they were doing before." Joey stared at the door. They were surrounded and the stairwell was starting to feel smaller and more confined. They were trapped. He felt a hand on his.

Poly gazed at him with those soothing eyes. He took a deep, calming breath.

"So Ferrell's the weird guy that grabbed Julie in the bunker, right?" Samantha said.

"Yeah, sick bastard. He had one tough door though."

Poly laughed and he joined in. Why was it so funny? The man took Julie. Samantha smiled and looked at them quizzically.

"It's really not funny, but when the old man snatched Julie away, I thought Lucas was going to burn the old man's door down with his mind," Poly said. "None of us knew what to do so we just went crazy on a two-inch steel door, getting nowhere."

"Yeah, well I was the one who got the tool box to open the door."

"Uh-huh, *after* Harris told you to."

"Hey, it was better than doing nothing," Joey said.

"Anyway, it took you minutes to get the door open."

Joey shook his head at Poly's playful banter.

She smiled at him.

"You know, you and Lucas are the ones who attracted all the grinners at that casino with all your dancing and outfit changes," Joey shot back.

"Hey, I looked hot, they couldn't resist." Poly put her hands on her hips and gave a little shimmy.

"Wait, I haven't heard this one. What happened at the mall?" Samantha asked.

"Poly stole a fancy dress from a store and she and Lucas paraded around together, making all kinds of noise—"

"Then," Poly took over the story, "from the creepy depths of the casino, a hand-slapping grinner pulled his way from the last blackjack table."

"It flipped out when it saw us," Joey said.

"Lucas took it out, but it had already summoned all its friends."

"We barely got out alive."

Poly and Joey laughed. Maybe the joy of living through something so terrible made it funny.

Samantha raised an eyebrow. "Joey's been holding back on me."

"I just left out some of the gross stuff."

"Poly's stolen dress doesn't sound gross."

"It was the most beautiful thing I've ever worn." Poly crossed her arms over her body and hugged herself.

"Well, while you were in a Vegas mall, I was hooked up to machines all day and night. They were pulling something from my body, much more than blood, it felt like my soul. I could feel myself slipping away."

Joey's head snapped to her. "I thought you didn't remember anything?"

"I guess I didn't want you hearing the gross parts either."

"I'm sorry, Samantha, we didn't even know you were taken until much later," Poly said and placed her hands on her lap.

"You all had each other. I had no one." Samantha rubbed her earring between her fingers.

"If we had any idea you were taken, we would've focused on getting you back," Poly said.

Joey sighed and stared at Samantha. She looked away from his gaze. They hadn't talked much about the time she spent by herself. The pain she was carrying stabbed at him. He got up and sat next to her, hugging her. He felt the sweat through her shirt. She gave him a quick hug, but the heat didn't make for the best hugging environment.

"It's getting hot in here." Samantha pinched her shirt and pulled on it.

"She's right, it's getting hotter." Joey ran up the stairs. The flames roared over the small window and the heat made sweat pour over his face. He stammered back down the stairs, shaking his head. "The flames are on the door."

Poly wiped the sweat from her face. Samantha stared at him with frightened eyes. He moved to the door leading back into the bunker and placed his ear against the door. A shifting sound, like something being dragged on the floor then a thump against the door.

"They're still out there."

"You think it's going to get hotter in here?" Poly asked.

"As the walls and door heat up, yeah it could get a lot hotter." Joey glared up the stairs. He had led them into a trap. If Emmett wanted them dead, why didn't he just kill them in his office, or when they were unconsciously transported to

Ryjack? It didn't make sense for him to set the world above on fire. He leaned on the wall.

"The concrete walls are still cool. Let's lie on the floor against the inner walls."

Joey lay next to the door and enjoyed the cool concrete against his sweaty back. Poly and Samantha took positions against the other walls.

Joey breathed in the hot air and felt the heat in him. Poly coughed. He closed his eyes and tried to imagine something else besides the oven they were in. He pictured open fields of swaying grass. Samantha cleared her throat. He opened his eyes and lifted himself off the floor so he could see Poly and Samantha.

"You two okay?"

Poly nodded.

"Getting a little hot in this rhino," Samantha said.

"You know . . ." He might be pushing it, but he had to take their minds off the situation. "It would probably be cooler if we took off these clothes."

"Oh, really?" Poly asked.

Joey laughed by himself. He cleared his throat. If Lucas had said it, it would've been funny. He adjusted his body and found a cool spot on the concrete floor.

"If it keeps getting hotter, were going to get cooked in here." Samantha's voice had a hint of panic.

Joey sighed, he'd been making jokes while Samantha was starting to freak out.

"Did I tell you guys about Cost Plus?" Poly asked, probably sensing Samantha's tone.

"No," Joey said, happy to give Samantha something to listen to besides her own thoughts of immortality.

Poly told them about everything. Joey's mouth hung open as she described the dad and daughter trying to get Lucas or Hank to impregnate her.

"What would you have done, Joey?" Samantha asked.

"I . . . I wouldn't have done it." He wiped the sweat from his face and ran his hand through his damp hair. He tried to imagine living in a warehouse store for his entire life.

"Those poor people," Samantha said.

"I don't know, they seemed happy in their hole." Poly coughed.

Joey blinked and sweat ran into his eyes. It was getting too hot. How much longer could the body handle such heat? He staggered to his feet. His legs felt uneven and he swayed. Poly and Samantha sat up at his actions and he saw their questioning eyes.

"I don't know how much longer we can take this." He heard the panic creeping into his voice. He swallowed and tried to suppress it. "We might have a chance through this door." He pointed at the door leading back into the bunker. "We can outrun them and get to another part of the bunker."

Poly gawked at him with her red, sweaty face. "It's suicide."

"She's right." Samantha pulled her long hair above her head and fanned the back of her neck.

His head hurt and he felt dizzy. Standing seemed to amplify the heat radiating from above. Sweat poured from every surface of his body and with each hot breath, he felt himself losing the battle. "We've got to get out of here." Full panic had set in.

"Joey, lie down on the concrete. I bet there is a cold spot in the middle," Samantha said.

Cold spot, yes. That could work. He lay down on the middle of the floor and found a cold spot, or maybe it was just less hot. He knew the second he was on the floor . . . that was it. He wasn't getting up. His body didn't have the will in it to do anymore. If they were going to die, they would die together.

He shook on the floor for the next ten minutes. The chills spread over his body and he stopped sweating. His dry skin took in the heat and sent it to his pounding brain. He turned to his side and watched Samantha curl up in a fetal position against the wall. Sweat glistened on her arms. Sweat was good—it meant she had a chance. He gazed past his feet to Poly. She lay on her back, staring at the ceiling. Sweat streaked down her face.

"We're going to die," Poly announced with no emotion. It was a simple fact she was stating, nothing more.

The shock of her words cleared some of the fog from Joey's head and he tried to focus on what she was saying. "We aren't going to die."

"Yes, we are." Her voice wavered this time, chin quivering. "It's okay though. I'd rather die right here than in there with those things eating me."

Joey shook his head. He tried to concentrate on the words she said. She was upset about something, that much he knew. His head felt heavy and he laid it on the concrete floor. It was cooler. He pressed his cheek against the smooth concrete trying to soak the coolness into his body.

"Maybe we should make a run for it. We could at least die trying." Samantha's voice registered.

He perked up at her words. Yes, they could escape. There was danger behind the door, grinners. What a strange name. He smiled, thinking about their black grins. He pushed himself to his knees and breathed hard at the exertion. He felt his heart beating in his chest. After a minute of stabilizing himself, he got to his feet. His whole body felt as if it was now made of lead and his muscles were that of a child's.

Putting his heavy hand on the door handle, Joey looked back at his friends. He loved them. He couldn't raise the gun up in his hand, but maybe the grinners would fall down at his feet and he wouldn't have to raise his hand. He could simply shoot them on the floor. It had to work.

Poly got to her feet and with a shaky hand, held her knife. Her red face and glossy eyes still held cold determination. "I can think of worse ways to die than this."

Samantha used the stair railing next to her and got to her feet. "We run straight for the office on the other side."

Joey had no idea what she meant but nodded as if he did. The grinners would be happy to see him and he'd been partially cooked up for them . . . like a warm meal. He would make an awesome meal. He felt his consciousness slipping, the outside of his vision going black. He had to move.

"Wait," Samantha said loud and clear.

Joey staggered back from the door. "What?"

Samantha looked far away as he struggled to keep her face in focus. "You hear that?"

He swayed and closed his eyes, hearing his rapid heartbeat pounding in his head and something else.

"I hear it." Life flooded into Poly's words. It cleared his head enough for him to hear it as well.

It was a hissing sound, like the time he took a hot skillet and ran it under water in the kitchen sink. He took a step on the stairs and fell against them, unable to get back up. Poly and

Samantha's shoes passed his face before all his vision went black. He listened as they walked up the stairs. Good, they could get out, it was all that mattered. He could let go. Slumping against the stairs, he heard the door above open and Poly scream his name before everything went black.

CHAPTER 15

HARRIS FIRED HIS RAIL GUN into the oncoming horde. The projectiles flew into a grinner and passed through four more behind it. The gun got hot in his hands under the relentless barrage of projectiles it launched. With only a few grinners left, Harris slowed down his firing and took a careful aim. He pulled the trigger and the gun didn't fire.

Stuffing the gun in his holster, Harris kicked the head of the nearest grinner. It stumbled back then lunged at his feet as he stood on the table. He stomped the top of its head and it fell to the floor. Five more struggled to make their way over the heap he created at the door. They laid on top of each other like sacks of potatoes stacked halfway up the doorway.

Harris hopped off the desk and grabbed the back of the wooden chair. He smashed it on the ground and pulled out a wooden leg from the pile.

A grinner fell into the office and clawed at the floor to get to him. He stabbed it in the head and kicked it to the side. Several more stumbled past the heap and he stabbed each one in their heads. One still clawed at the pile of grinners at the door.

He stomped over the heap and crushed the thing's skull. On top of the mound of bodies, he peered down the hallway and to the stairs. Only two grinners staggered around near the doorway. He stepped off the heap and ran at them. At full speed, he jumped and pushed the wooden leg into the first one's head while he dropped kick the second in the chest.

He left the stick in the head of the first one and kept running past the stunned second one. He didn't have time for small stuff. With a smidgen of luck, the city would be on lockdown. Capital was a very unique city, the only one that could have a chance at being contained. He slowed his run up the stairs. Marcus would know this, he didn't miss anything. Could there have been more cages he kept around the world? He sprinted up the remaining flights of stairs.

The sound of gunfire echoed down the stairs and he pushed the top door open to the lobby. The weapons locker stood ajar. He reluctantly set his rail gun down, shoving two handguns into his holster, and putting a few clips in each pocket. He pulled a rifle from the rack and turned.

"Harris," Jack said.

He jerked back in surprise.

Jack looked pale and terrified. "Those freaking things are everywhere."

"Don't worry, we'll lock them down, we'll beat this," Harris said, trying to convince everyone in the room. "Where's Emmett?"

Jack looked at him skeptically. "Emmett is locking down the airport. He sent men to each of the gates to close them down. But if just one of these things gets loose . . . it's over."

"Come with me. We're going to check each point of exit and make sure they're secure."

"Out there?" Jack pointed to the glass doors.

"I won't let anything happen to you."

"Oh yeah, you've got a great track record," Jack said, following him out.

Harris turned and faced him. The words stung because they were the truth. "I need a second person on this. What you do right now might cost your life, but it could save the world. You with me?"

Jack stared at him. "I didn't need a speech. I was going the whole time."

Harris smiled and shook his head. He held his hand high so the guards behind the barricade could see him. "Hold your fire. We're coming through." He walked out with his hands up and quickened his pace toward the front doors.

The soldiers behind the barricade stared at his chest and face, putting their fists against their chests as he walked by. He matched their salute and ran out the front doors. He spotted the car he wanted parked near the front of the building. Probably an overzealous seven compensating for something. He knew every second could make the difference. No grinner could pass the city wall.

Harris took out his Panavice and got the doors to open and then set the user settings to himself. He climbed into the front seat and pressed the manual button.

Jack hopped into the passenger seat. "I just realized every car will stop driving because GPS is down."

"You can still drive these things manually." Harris pushed another button and a small steering wheel pushed out toward him.

"You know how to drive this thing?"

Harris raised an eyebrow and stepped on the pedal. The vehicle lunged forward with its powerful electric motors humming. As per automatic safety protocols, the other cars on the road had pulled off to the side of the roads, giving them a clear path down the middle.

A group of grinners surrounded a car down the street. Harris slowed to a stop next to the half dozen grinners pushing against a car with a family of terrified people inside.

"Do we have time for this?" Jack asked.

"If you were in that car, would you want me to make time?"

Jack sat back in his seat. Harris opened the door, stood on the floor of the car and leveled his gun over the top of the car. He fired six quick shots and the grinners flopped down around the car and street. The terrified people stared at him through tinted windows. Harris slammed on the pedal, not waiting for a thank you he knew would probably never happen.

"The first gate is over here." Jack pointed ahead.

He nodded his head but knew where both gates were. "Right over here you say?" Harris took the next turn at high speed, the wheels spinning to grab traction. Bits of asphalt bounced off the under carriage and the car leapt forward.

"You don't have to drive it like you stole it."

"We *did* steal it."

Jack sighed and held onto the grab bars. Harris gripped the steering wheel and guided the car down the narrow open lane in the middle. A grinner stumbled down the road and Harris drove by and shot it in the head. He leaned forward and saw a mob of residents formed at the first gate. He got out of the car and Jack fumbled with his seat belt and exited as well.

Some of the people turned to him. They wore their fancy clothes and designer hats. The ones who gave him notice, sneered with their noses held high. He sighed. These were the people he was trying to save.

"Excuse me," Harris called out. The crowd roared against the steel gate, ignoring him. The group of elites couldn't knock down a door like that, even if their lives depended on it—and they probably did.

The few who initially looked at him, turned back to pushing and hitting the steel wall. He walked back to the car and opened the door with every intention of leaving those people to the grinners.

Jack gave him a stern look. "We can't just let them stay out here."

"What, *them*? They should be fine."

Jack glared at him.

"Fine." Harris slammed the door and turned back to the crowd, pulling out his gun. He fired it into the air and stuffed it back in the holster. The people spun around and gawked.

Mumbles spread around about his daring to shoot a gun around them.

"There're people who are going to kill you. The city is on complete lockdown and the only thing you can do to keep alive is get indoors and lock your house."

A man stepped toward him with an extra dose of smug. Harris stood a good six inches taller and the man strained to look down at him. "Open this door."

The crowd roared in agreement.

"I can't and won't. Don't you get it? You will be killed by these people. I just shot five on the road here."

"What nonsense you spew." A lady in white spit on the road in front of him.

Harris sighed and turned back to Jack. He raised his shoulder at Jack to tell him he tried. Jack shot back a stern look.

He rubbed his forehead and then said, "People, Marcus Malliden is going to have an announcement on the TV in ten minutes and anyone in front of their TV will get a personal follow and like on your social pages from Marcus himself."

The crowd gasped and the women in white hiked up the bottom of her long dress and jogged away.

"Marcus will like my personal video files?" The arrogant man asked.

"Yes, he promised this to every Capital citizen, you all deserve it."

The crowd rumbled with excitement. "About time," one man yelled. "Been sending him requests for a century."

The crowd dispersed as the people ran to their houses with an air of excitement.

Harris exhaled and jogged back to the car. "It's all good on this one, let's check the other gate."

"How long do you think it will take for those people to realize you lied about Marcus?"

"Don't know, don't care."

Jack adjusted his position in his seat and wrapped his fingers around the grab bar. Harris pressed on the pedal and the car launched toward the next gate.

The next gate took ten minutes to get to and had a larger crowd. Harris breathed a sigh of relief at its sight. They might have an actual chance of containing this.

He skipped any mentions of their safety and went right to what they wanted to hear. Marcus would be following or friending them individually at their houses, in ten minutes. They dispersed quicker than the first group. Getting back into the car, he gripped the steering wheel. Both gates were shut properly, but he couldn't escape the bad feeling in his gut.

"Where to now?"

"Airport. The richest will be definitely trying to catch a trip out of here."

"Can't blame them, who would want to be stuck in this?"

"Like you said, if one gets out. . ." Harris launched the car down the road.

The airport was only a few minutes away and he already saw what he feared—a large transport ship lifting off into the sky. He punched the steering wheel and then jerked it to the left as he entered the parking lot. The car skidded to a stop. A grinner stumbled by his car and he shot it dead before jumping from the car and running toward the tarmac.

A few MM soldiers moved toward him with guns raised. "Stop," they yelled.

Harris held up his hands and Jack crouched behind him as he approached the soldiers. "Why did you let that ship leave?" Harris pointed at the ship in the sky as he glared at the men.

They looked confused and only glanced at each other instead of answering. This was Emmett's duty to close this airport down. Harris searched around the tarmac for a familiar face. "Where's Emmett?"

The soldiers lowered their guns. "He's on that ship." They pointed to the sky. "Don't worry, he said he would be back soon to get the rest of us."

Harris looked to the black aircraft streaking across the sky. Emmett had an exit plan. How many did he take with him? His eye's narrowed . . . if only he had a rocket launcher. "Did he say anything about where he's going?"

"No, just that he'd be back soon."

"Was that the last craft in the airport?"

"Yes."

Harris knew Emmett was never coming back. The captain had fled the sinking ship and its first mate took the only life raft. What did that leave him with?

"What are we going to do now?" Jack asked.

Harris rubbed his chin. He had seen hundreds of his plans fall apart, it was rarer for one to stick to its assigned path, and this was just another speed bump along the way. He put himself in Emmett's calculated mind. What would he do if he was in Emmett's ship, looking down at the end of the world?

The air sucked into his lungs and he whispered, "He's going to destroy the city."

"Wait, what?" Jack asked.

Harris sprinted back to the car. Jack was smart enough to know to run with him, he didn't look back to check on him. He slid into the car and waited a few seconds for Jack to get in.

They rushed through the parking lot and were back on the road. The car's electric motor squealed as he pushed the car to its limit. The buildings zoomed by and Jack pressed back into his seat with his white knuckled hands gripping the bar above the glove box. Another grinner stumbled down the road, but he didn't want to waste an extra second of time. They would all be dead soon anyway.

"You going to tell me what's going on?" Jack struggled to get the words out as the car slid around a corner.

"Emmett's going to destroy the city."

"Why would he do that?"

"It's what I'd do."

The car crashed through an open door of a car.

"We're going to die before we even get a chance to be killed," Jack said as he winced from the reckless speed.

Harris concentrated on the road, focusing on the immediate target ahead. He couldn't let a single thing on the car break if they had any chance of making it.

"Where are we going, to the bunker?"

"No time, plus the incendiary will flush through every inch of it."

"Incendiary?"

"Look to the sky and tell me if you see anything."

Jack rolled down his window and peeked up into the sky. "Yes, there's a bright light."

Harris winced. They only had a minute, two at the most. "I need you to roll up that window and make sure it's tight. That bomb in the sky will burn everything within a twenty mile radius when it hits."

"*What?*" Jack jerked his attention to the sky. "Can we get far enough away?"

"No."

Jack squirmed in his seat. "Then what?"

"In a minute, everyone and everything in Capital will be destroyed." Harris spotted the blue line at the end of the road.

"Oh my god, I need to call my dad." Jack fumbled with his Panavice and punched at the screen, momentarily forgetting the systems were down.

Harris kept his focus on the expanding blue line at the end of the road. He hoped the car was built as well as he thought.

Jack stopped messing with his Panavice and stared ahead. "What are you doing?" His transfixed gazed didn't budge from the end of the road.

Harris slowed the car down to forty miles per hour but didn't stop as they approached the end of the road. Jack screamed as the car punched past the guard rail. Harris took his hands off the steering wheel as it retracted into the dash. The front end of the car turned down and the blue water below rushed toward them. Jack kept screaming until the car smacked the surface of the water.

CHAPTER 16

WATER RAN DOWN HIS FACE. It soaked into his clothes and shoes. It ran into the corners of his smiling mouth. Lucas watched as the rain fell onto the flames and filled the street with streams of water. With each drop, the orange glow lessened, and the dark night reclaimed the city.

They huddled against a large AC box, but it only gave a small amount of cover from the rain. Julie's body shook next to his as the temperature plummeted. Lucas had been bugging her to use her Pana to cut into the AC box.

"Let's just try it. Can it be any worse than this?" Lucas asked.

"Fine, but if it starts shocking me, kick it out of my hand."

He rubbed his wet hands together and stood. Hank got to his feet as well, and they both watched Julie point her Panavice at the four foot tall piece of metal.

"Okay, here it goes." Julie leaned back and extended her hand out, bracing herself for a shock.

Lucas got his kicking foot ready. One sign of agony on her face and he'd punt that thing to Mars. A red beam shot from the Panavice and struck the wet metal. Her face lit up with excitement and relief. She guided the beam around in a large square. Steam hissed as it heated up. The cut metal sheet fell off the box and hit the roof with a splat.

"Let me check it out first, there could be critters in there." Lucas bent over and searched the cavity. Julie shined her light inside—nothing but a fan on one side and a hole on the other, like a quaint little room with no rain. He climbed into the space and moved next to the fan. Julie climbed in with him and filled the remaining space. Hank ducked his head in and searched for a space. He by himself would have taken much of the metal box.

"Come on, let's go cut one out for Hank." Lucas shimmied his way out of the box and felt the rain pour down on him.

Once Julie had cut a hole out in a nearby metal box, they secured his door and rushed back to their spot. Lucas climbed into the metal space and made room for Julie's soaking body. They pulled the cut door back in place and finally they were out of the rain. The sound of rain pounded on the metal around them, but it was better than being in it. Julie set her Panavice on her lap, lighting up their space.

Lucas's shirt dripped on the metal. He wiped some of the water from his hair and shook it on Julie.

"Hey, cut it out."

"I'm going to hang my shirt on this fan, if you don't mind."

"Oh, well . . . I don't mind." Julie glanced at his chest and looked away.

Lucas pulled at his shirt, struggling to get the wet material off his body. Freeing himself, he rung it out and hung it on a blade of the fan. He looked down at his chest and abs. He always thought he looked good with his shirt off. He glanced at Julie to see if she agreed and he spotted her looking at him. She caught his glance and jerked away, a hint of color entered her cheeks.

"You know, there is room for another shirt over here. You'll never get dry with that thing on."

"If I'm going to take my shirt off for you, it isn't going to be in some metal box, on top of a roof, hiding from grinners."

"Fine, just sit there soaking then. I never thought you would do it anyways."

She scowled at him and huffed out a breath. As she pulled her shirt over her head, Lucas sucked in a breath, staring at her black bra. Her shirt hung from her hand and she held it out for him to take, but he didn't notice it.

"You can blink," she said.

Lucas pulled his gaze from her glistening chest to her amused eyes. "I . . . well, my pants are soaking as well." He unbuttoned his top button on his jeans.

"Don't push it."

Lucas glanced down at her chest as it moved with each breath. He'd seen fully naked women many times—he had an internet connection—but presented with a close, personal set of breasts sent his mind sailing into the sky. He struggled to find something funny to say, but his thoughts stammered and stalled.

Julie held out her wet shirt again. "Can you hang up mine?"

"Uh, yeah, sure." He took her wet shirt, rung it out and placed it on the fan next to his.

He looked at the metal above him and fidgeted with his hands. He should be saying something witty, something fun. Could he be any less cool? The silence made the room feel smaller and the weight of it started to set in.

"You okay?" Julie asked.

"Uh, yeah."

"You've seen me in my bikini a bunch of times, is this making you uncomfortable?"

"What? No, it just feels different since we've been a thing."

Julie turned her body toward him. "We're a thing?"

"Yeah." He faced her.

"You've been distant."

"Well, a lot of stuff's been going on. Plus Hank's been around. I mean, we haven't had a second alone in a while."

Julie smirked. "We're alone now."

His heart stopped at her words, then thudded hard against his rib cage. Was something finally going to happen? Lucas couldn't move if he wanted to. He stayed locked in place, staring at her, letting the words hang in the air.

She made the first move and brought her face closer to his, and then he met her the rest of the way. He slowed down right before softly pressing his lips against hers. Her wet hair brushed against his face and he felt a drip running into their paired lips. He moved closer and touched the side of her face, moving to the back of her neck. He couldn't get enough of her and he greedily took. He heard her moan and he guided his tongue over her open mouth.

Julie shuffled over to him on her knees, swinging a leg over and straddling his lap. He sat up tall to mold their bodies together. Her wet bra and warm stomach rubbed against him as he explored her bare back with his hands, playing with the clasp of her bra.

Her hands rubbed his back and he felt the passion flowing between them. The intensity of her kisses made him forget everything, the pain, the fire, the Preston Six. It was just them. He finally pinched the clasp the right way and it popped open.

Julie moved back breathing hard, her mouth open and lust in her eyes. "My bra's soaking wet," she said in a heavy breath. She reached up and pulled the straps down each arm.

Lucas took quick breaths and watched the motions. He couldn't believe he was about to finally see her topless.

Julie stopped, holding her bra against her chest. "You hear that?"

"It's just my heart pounding."

Their makeshift door opened. "Hey guys—*Holy mother.* Oh, God. I'm so sorry." he said, covering his eyes and stumbling backward.

Julie fell forward into Lucas. "Oh my God." Pressing her bra against her chest she scrambled to the other side of the duct.

Lucas trembled and caught one last look at Julie before she connected the back of her bra. He didn't need the light of the Panavice to see the red on her face. He breathed in and tried to slow his heart rate down. "Well, *that* happened."

Julie shook her head and sat back with her hands over her face. "So embarrassing."

Hank called out, "I'm sorry guys. You can finish up if you want."

They looked at each other and started laughing.

"Poor Hank's never going to be able to look at us the same," Julie said. She leaned over to grab his shirt, and gave him a mischievous smile when she handed it to him. "We'll have to find a time to pick up where we left off."

She was so gorgeous. He wanted more of her *now*. Dang Hank and his interruptions.

Julie yanked her shirt over her head and stepped out of the metal box. Lucas pulled his shirt on; it was still wet and stuck to his body.

Stepping out of the metal box, she turned around. "You coming?"

Lucas adjusted his pants. "Just give me a minute." He thought of little league baseball and after a while, he was ready to stand. Lucas peered at the sky when he exited his new favorite place on Ryjack, and the moon was peeking through the clouds above.

"Sorry for opening the door, guys," Hank said. As Julie had predicted, he couldn't look at either of them.

"I told you it was fine," Julie's said.

"A few more minutes," Lucas muttered under his breath. "You couldn't have waited a *few* more—"

"I can see the tar pits, and nothing is moving. You think they all died in the fire?" Hank asked, purposely speaking over Lucas and still not looking at them.

"They should have been incinerated in that much heat." Julie walked to the edge of the roof.

Lucas let out a long breath and thought about what they were here to do. His friends were somewhere down there. "We still need to get off this roof." Grinners filled the lower floors of their building.

They spent the next ten minutes walking the perimeter with Julie's light. "Just like I said before, there's no way down."

"Then we fight our way out," Hank said.

"Are you crazy?" Julie said. "There are like fifty of them down there."

"Well, what can we do then?" Hank asked.

"I don't know, we'll think of something. Lucas?"

He knew what he had to do . . . even if it meant telling them his little secret. "I will go down alone and take care of them all. When I'm done, I'll come get you guys."

"No offense, but what makes you think you can kill them all?" Hank asked. "You're not Joey."

"They won't touch me. I don't know what it is, but they don't see me as a threat. I think it's been like this since the bite."

"That's how you made it through that room under the casino, isn't it?"

Lucas nodded.

Julie staggered back, with her hand over her mouth. "You carry it still. Whatever it is, it's still in you. They think you're dead, like them."

Lucas looked at the gravel roof and kicked some pebbles with his foot. He sighed and looked to the sky, the moon moved behind a cloud. He didn't want to be different, but he was. In some sick way, he was part grinner. Summoning the courage to peer into Julie's eyes, he found her frightened. How could he blame her? She probably thought his saliva could infect her. His chances with her were tossed over the roof like a bag of trash. He didn't regret telling them, they needed to know.

He turned and made his way to the metal box, grabbing Prudence and his bag of arrows. Prudence never judged him, she didn't care if he had something in him, if he was different. She shot her arrows straight and true for him. It was all he could ask. He opened the hatch leading back down into the floors below and gazed down into the darkness.

"How can you be sure they won't attack you?" Julie asked.

"I just know."

"But you've only tested this once. These things could be different. You might be different." The panic built in her voice.

"I'll be fine, I promise. Soon as I'm done, I'll come get you." He pulled the hatch over his head and the room plunged into darkness. He sighed and opened the hatch back up. Julie with an eyebrow cocked handed him her Panavice.

"Thanks," he said.

He held the Panavice in his mouth and moved down the ladder. At the bottom he turned and was face to face with a large man with a black mouth staring at him. His rancid breath made Lucas want to gag. He kept the Panavice in his mouth and pulled an arrow from his quiver. The thin steel made it hard to grasp, but he tightened his grip and plunged the arrow into the man's head. It fell to the floor. The sound made every nearby grinner turn in his direction.

He didn't need any testing to see they didn't care he was there. Before his bite, they would have been falling over each other to get to him. Now they meandered around, searching. The sound enticed them and they moved toward it.

Lucas pulled an arrow and shot it into another head. He repeated this until every arrow was used in his quiver. It took a few minutes to collect his arrows and stow them. It was gruesome work and he cringed each time he had to pull an arrow from a skull.

With a full quiver and the third floor clear, he moved to the second floor and repeated his work. His arm began to feel sore from the pulling of the stiff bow and yanking arrows from rotten heads. His fingertips got raw from the string, but it was a job that could only be done by him.

A grinner trotted by at the sound of his fallen brethren flopping on the floor. He'd stopped wincing at them being close to him. Sighing, he pulled an arrow back and shot it into the head of the trotter. The dead bodies around him sickened him. He almost liked it more when they wanted to kill him. Having them give him a pass, felt like being included in some horrible club no one wanted to be in.

A grinner nudged against his arm as it staggered by. He fired an arrow and then finished clearing out the second floor. The lobby and restaurant only held a few grinners and he dispensed with them quickly. Gathering his arrows, Lucas ran up the stairs and up the ladder. He pushed open the hatch.

"Oh, thank God." Julie rushed to him and hugged his head. He clumsily held her with one arm. "You were down there for a long time."

"Yeah, there were more than a hundred." Lucas pulled himself from the hatch and onto the roof. He handed Julie her Panavice.

"Are these teeth marks?"

"Hey, I don't have a third hand."

She wiped it on her shirt and stuffed it into her pocket.

"You're welcome, I just spent an hour or so in hell, clearing that building for you guys."

"Thanks, man." Hank patted him on the shoulder. "Let's go get them."

The street smelled of fresh rain mixed with the rancid smell of burnt tires. Steam rose from the partially collapsed building they once stood on. The rain cleaned off a lot of the filth and if Lucas focused on a particular section of the city, it seemed normal.

"Everyone watch for grinners. There were tens of thousands of them down here," Lucas said. He glanced at Julie, hoping she was staring at him, but she held her Panavice like a flashlight and stared ahead. Did she think of him any different now? How could she not? He was a freak.

"So are we going to just knock on their front door?" Julie asked.

"Yeah, basically. The fire should have driven any MM guys away from the door. We might have a chance of surprise."

"Then what? They have guns."

"Hey, I'm just as deadly with Prudence." He held her high. "Fine, to be on the safer side, I can get to the door first."

The large moon shone too much light down on the field of burnt bodies laid out in front of them. The smell of rain, tar, and BBQ filled the air. His nose soaked in the new smells. He wanted to gag and spit out every breath, but they had to keep moving. It wasn't much further. The first hundred feet only had a spattering of charred bodies, but Lucas saw past the gate to where the bodies were packed together, sometimes three high.

He pushed the gate open, sliding a blackened body with it. They passed the iron gates and stopped, looking for a path of any kind to the door. There wasn't one. Lucas walked in front and nudged each body he passed with his foot. If they still breathed, he hoped it was enough to stir them. Each nudge resulted in a crunching sound as their clothes and flesh fell from their charred remains.

The smell became overwhelming by the time they got to the middle of the wasteland. Lucas tried to push a grinner aside with his foot, but the thing's clothes and skin slid off. Losing his footing, he fell. Its well-done body fell apart as Lucas landed on it. He jumped back to his feet and pulled a chunk of charred clothes stuck to his arm—at least he hoped it was clothes.

"I think I'm going to throw up." Julie held her stomach and leaned over a pile of bodies, hurling on top of them. Hank, behind her, grabbed at his mouth. Lucas didn't feel any nausea but felt the guilt as his friends suffered the grossest thing he'd ever walked through.

Julie wiped her mouth and stood straight.

"You guys okay?" he asked.

"Let's just move faster, please."

Lucas picked up the pace and by the time they were a hundred feet from the door, there wasn't any way for him to create a path. They would have to walk on bodies. Stepping on the first grinner, his foot sagged deep into the body. He heard Julie behind him heaving and coughing. He kept moving, the faster they got to the door, the closer they were to getting their friends back.

"Stomping grapes," Julie called out.

"What?" Lucas asked.

"Just tell me I'm stomping on grapes." She looked at the sky and took another tentative step.

Lucas knew she would fall if she didn't watch where she was going. Turning around, he stomped over the bodies. He took her hand and she lowered her head, panic swelling in her face. He bent over and swept her up into his arms. She looked shocked, and he thought she might protest. Instead, she wrapped her arms around his neck and buried her face in his chest.

He turned and carried her the rest of the way to the door.

When they reached the door, Lucas glanced down at Julie. He set her on her feet in front of the door. She found a small space not occupied by a charcoaled body.

"Let's go in, anything's better than this." Julie grabbed the door handle and opened the door.

There, in the stairwell, were Poly and Samantha . . . hovered over Joey's limp body.

CHAPTER 17

JOEY FELT HIS HEAD JOSTLING up and down. His fingertips rubbed against fabric. The rhythmic sound of heavy breathing and the smell of sweat—where was he? One crusty eye opened and he gazed at the building next to him moving by. Passing a window, he saw their reflection. Hank carried him over his shoulder as he ran. *Hank!*

And Poly, with knife in hand, jogged behind him, looking in every direction with a nervous look on her face.

"Poly," Joey whispered. His throat felt dry and the word was full of air. She didn't hear him. "Poly," he croaked out. Hank stopped and lowered him on his back.

"Joey?" The big guy hovered over him.

"You're here . . . how?" Joey asked. He must be dreaming or worse, he was trapped in another scene generator and none of this was real.

Lucas's face appeared behind Hank's. "We rescued you, man."

The idea wouldn't sink into his foggy head. They all seemed so real.

Poly lay down next to him and hugged his head. "I thought we were going to lose you, don't ever do that again."

Samantha knelt on the other side and patted back his hair. She stared at him with blood shot eyes. Had she been crying? "How are you feeling?"

He thought of his last thoughts. He was dying in the stairwell with them. It was so hot. Now he was on a sidewalk with all of his friends surrounding him.

"I don't know, my head hurts. Let's see if I can get up." If he could stand, he thought he would be able to decide if it was real. He rolled on his side and pushed himself up. His head pounded in retaliation and he sat on his knees, waiting for the wave of pain to pass. He pushed himself up to his feet. "We're together?" he asked, taking each of his friends in. They were alive, in front of him. All of them.

The thoughts of what he'd been through flooded his mind with shocking detail. What did Lucas, Julie, and Hank have to endure to get here? "You're alive?" he directed at Lucas.

"Yep—" Lucas started to say.

Joey hugged him, then moved to Hank, Julie, Samantha, and Poly. He never thought he would see them again. He had written off this part of his life, given up. His eyes watered and he couldn't stop taking in each of them as if seeing them for the first time. His whole body shook with emotion and his throat clogged up with unspoken words.

"You're a bit late to the party," Lucas said.

"Yeah, you should have seen Lucas, bawling like a baby in the stairwell," Hank snickered.

"Hey, don't act like you didn't get emotional. I didn't think you were ever going to let go of our group hug."

Joey smiled. With each of them surrounding him, he felt as if he could take on anything. Even his body felt better, just knowing the Six were back together.

"I can keep carrying you," Hank offered.

The idea of flopping over Hank's shoulder sounded like a nightmare. "I can walk."

"Dude, we need to be running," Lucas said.

Joey's head stopped throbbing long enough for a rational thought. "Where are we?"

"Still in LA."

He glanced behind him at the long, straight street with multi-story buildings on each side. Cars filled the sides of the streets, many with broken windows and rusted bodies. Weeds invaded the cracks in the road.

"Think you can run? There's like ten million grinners in this city," Julie asked.

"I think I can."

"Well, let's get this train a moving." Lucas adjusted his bow and pointed down the street.

"You can hang onto my shoulder," Hank offered.

Joey didn't need a shoulder, the natural high of seeing his friends was more than any drug or crutch could ever do. He couldn't stop smiling. "Let me try it on my own."

After a few minutes of a light jog, he felt the blood pumping in his body. He felt better than he had in a while. The puncture marks on his arms had turned into small red dots and soon they would be gone.

"So, what'd I miss?" Joey was dying to know what his friends did to get there, and where Harris was.

Hank, Julie, and mostly Lucas, recounted their journey for the next hour. Joey couldn't believe their journey. They should have been dead five times over, but they made it, they were here. He kept counting each of them. The encounter at the hotel wrenched at his gut and when they got to Bob, Lucas started walking. He told them about how he was there when it all went down with their parents. He was the one who allowed Isaac access to the Alius stone.

"What are the chances?" Joey asked, bewildered by it all.

"Infinity." Lucas said.

"Well, it happened, so it can't be infinity. More like, one in a billion," Julie replied.

Lucas ignored her correction and continued to explain how they escaped into the city and how he caught the grinners on fire.

"It was *you* who almost killed us in that?" Samantha asked.

"Like I knew you were behind that door, trapped in a stairwell," Lucas said.

"Well, it ended okay," Julie added.

They ran up a freeway ramp, clogged with cars, sticking to the edge of the road. Lucas moved slower and kept his bow out. Joey felt for his guns for the hundredth time. He glanced at each car as they passed, looking for that small chance of a gun on the dash, or frozen in a dead person's hand.

"Why don't we grab a Tesla car again, like you said brought you here?" Poly asked.

"I've seen a few, but we need to get past this clogged mess first." Lucas walked around a car that hit the concrete sidewall.

Lucas had changed; he'd lost some of his joviality and innocence. He seemed older now. His confidence in his jokes had translated to confidence in leading them. Joey had failed at that role at a number of occasions. Maybe Lucas could fill the spot better than he could. He watched Lucas pull his bow back and launch an arrow at a grinner stumbling toward them. He'd seen him do this half a dozen times now since he woke, and he'd never missed.

"You feeling okay?" Samantha walked next to him.

"Yeah. How about you? You were in the same heat box."

"Marcus pulled a lot out of you, and recently too. You weren't at one hundred percent."

Poly moved to his other side. The knife never left her hand.

"How are you doing, Poly?"

"Great. Even in this wretched place, having us together feels like we can do anything."

"Yeah." He knew what she meant. The world around them was collapsing and rotting. Things lurked in every corner, wanting to kill them and eat them. But when he could count to six with his friends, they felt unstoppable.

"If it's not too difficult, I'd like to hear what happened to you guys." Hank met eyes with Joey. Joey almost felt embarrassed about their hardships compared to his friends. He had been living in a wonderland, even if his life was being leached from him every night.

"Yeah, Poly and Samantha been talking about a freaking country manor and stuff."

Joey started off by telling them what happened after he'd been taken by Max, seeing Samantha for the first time. Then the Mindyland started, he tried to hide his wonder when describing the amazing things in the land, the strange robot caretakers. Samantha told them about the door, it was her idea. She found it and brought them to the manor where Joey collapsed. She left out the kissing, and skipped to the day Poly arrived. Poly looked at the ground and he saw her white knuckles on the hand holding her knife.

Over the next hour, the cars began to thin out and the search for an all-electric car started. The first one they found wouldn't start and by the third, Joey started to wonder if they had picked a fluke of a car on their first try, like Julie's one in a billion.

He kept close to Samantha and Poly, while they kept close to him. Julie, Hank, and Lucas took the front line, forming two groups.

"Hey, I see another up there." Lucas jogged ahead to a red car.

They caught up to him and he was already in the front seat.

"Give this one a minute before you try to turn it on." Julie sat in the passenger seat and Joey leaned over, sticking his head in the car. At least this one didn't have bodies in it. "The batteries are taking power. Go ahead, try it."

Lucas turned the key and the dash lit up. He high-fived Julie, and Joey smiled. They piled in the car with Lucas driving, Hank in the passenger seat, Julie sat on the center console and Joey sat in the middle of Poly and Samantha. The AC blew cold air as they moved forward. Lucas took it to the shoulder and drove in the dirt. The car bounced and jittered along the unkempt path, but it was far better than walking.

Hank dug into his bag of stuff and handed a packet of condensed water to everyone, and two to Joey. Next, was some weird dehydrated food squares. Anything with calories was good to them at this point.

"You know," Julie held her Panavice close to her face, "if we head south and go through Big Bear, we can avoid Victorville."

"Julie, you're amazing. I've been sick to my stomach thinking about going through Genter's area." Lucas took a right turn on the off ramp marked *210 East.* "So why did Marcus put you into that Mindyland playground thing?" Lucas asked as he looked in the rearview mirror.

Joey took a deep breath and figured Samantha hadn't let on that they were trying to breed them like livestock. He thought of his parents and didn't want to keep any secrets from the people he loved. "They wanted us to conceive a child."

"What?" Julie turned around and gawked at him. "Why?"

Poly faced him with the same question hanging on her face.

"I'm not sure, but I think it's for Marcus." Samantha said as she stared at the dead cars they passed. "I hadn't really taken notice until we met the woman in the manor. She was very pushy about me and Joey hooking up. Everything she did seemed to revolve around it."

"So . . ." Lucas let his unasked question hang in the air.

Joey felt Poly's glare and everything in the car became silent.

"We didn't go all the way," Samantha smiled at him.

Poly let out a slow breath. He was the only one close enough to hear it.

They drove up the mountain and the sparse landscape changed into steep hills littered with pine trees. The road became an obstacle course of fallen rocks and dead trees.

"Take a left, up here," Julie said.

Lucas turned the corner, dodging a fallen tree.

"There's something in the road," Julie said.

"I got it."

"No, not that."

Lucas jerked the wheel, but it was too late. The car jumped and Joey's head hit the ceiling. He crashed back down and landed on Poly.

"Oh no," Lucas said. The tires flopped on the road, blown out. Lucas pushed on the pedal and turned the car around. Two large trucks pulled in behind them. Lucas spun the wheel and the blown out tires flopped against the fender. He steered the car to go around the truck when it struck the side of the car.

Joey flew against the window, missing Samantha's head by inches. His hip struck the glass and he plopped on the floor board.

"They got us, stop," Julie screamed.

Lucas punched the steering wheel.

Joey, with a pain in his leg climbed up to the seat and inspected Poly and Samantha. They seemed okay. The large pickup truck's grill stuck against the window and the smell of exhaust filled the car. Two more trucks pulled up on the other side of them and a group of men jumped out, holding a mix of rifles, shotguns, and handguns. If he could get one of those, he might be able to do something.

Lucas grabbed at his bow, but Julie took it first. "No, there's too many, you'll just be killed," she pleaded with him.

Lucas gripped the steering wheel and swore loudly. He rolled down his window as the man approached the car with a rifle stuck out in front of him. "Genter, how nice to see you again," he said.

The man twitched at the name and pointed his rifle at the backseat of the car. "I see you found your friends."

"Yep."

"They must mean a great deal to you guys. It would be a shame to see them killed." Genter pointed his rifle at the back of the car. Joey moved in front, he could take the bullet for the girls.

"Come on, there's no need for this, we want the same thing you do. We can go there together now, straight there."

Genter lowered his gun and his tongue worked its way around his lips. He glanced at the men around him. "I want them separated."

The men with guns opened the car door.

Joey rubbed his bracelets and wished he'd found a way to remove them before this.

"No," Poly yelled and went to stab the man.

Joey caught her arm and she scowled at him. "Not now, Poly."

The man with the gun pried the knife from her hand, grabbed her by the hair, and yanked her out of the car.

"Easy." Joey climbed from the car and received a punch to the stomach. He fell to his knees and stared at the man's grimy grin and unshaven face. The man moved Poly by her hair into the truck that struck them.

At gun point, they split them up into the four trucks. Joey ended up in the grimy man's truck with Julie. From the window, he saw them stuff Hank in the back of a truck and Samantha and Lucas into another. He sighed. They'd been free for only a few hours and now they were split and captured again by the man who started it all.

ENTERING THE POLICE STATION, JOEY and Julie moved past the offices and through a series of doors, before coming into a white hallway with glass windowed doors flanking each side. He passed the first one and saw Hank's face in the glass. Then Samantha and Lucas. Then Poly. They opened the door to Poly's room and pushed Joey in the door. They shoved Julie in behind him.

Poly ran to him and they embraced. Letting him go, she moved to Julie. The small room had a white cot hanging from the wall. The men left the hallway and the door closed with an audible thud.

Joey sat on the edge of the cot and rubbed his temples. How could they be captured again? The cot moved with the weight of another person sitting on it. He turned to face Julie. She put a hand on his shoulder.

"It's good to see you guys again," Julie said. "Joey, I have to admit that after that roof scene with Max, I really didn't think we'd see you again. I'm sorry for ever thinking that." She took in a deep breath. "This lady right here, however," she pointed to Poly, "went through a great deal in trying to get back to you. She never believed you were gone for good."

Poly's back faced them as she looked out the window. Her hand played with the pocket on her pants.

"Thank you, Poly."

"I don't think you get it. She's like the rock star of Vanar now; people had posters and were chanting her name. Not to mention, she single-handedly killed Max. And she did all of it just to get back to you."

"That's enough," Poly said.

Perplexed, Joey stared at Poly's back and then to Julie. People made posters of her and chanted her name? What else did she hold back on?

"Don't be shy about it, Poly. I mean, you freaking dueled Max on a worldwide stage and won."

Poly turned around and crossed her arms. "And how far did that get us? Look at us now, back in someone's control. Prisoners."

She was right. No matter how much they marched forward, it seemed they ended up trapped and held down by everyone around them. The edge showed in Poly's eyes and Julie's as well. They both had been in Sanct, battling the entire city and Max. He couldn't imagine the strain they were both under.

"You're *both* rock stars," Joey said. "You were alone in a strange city, and look at what you were able to do. What you are still doing. I know we'll get through this. With us together, I'm more confident than ever we will win."

"Right on, Joey," Lucas cheered in the cell over.

Poly let her arms fall to her sides. She smiled at him. Had he finally returned a favor to her and made her feel better? He owed her a hundred more.

A door opened in the hallway. Poly looked through the window.

"It's that Genter guy."

Joey moved to the window and peered through it with Poly. Genter moved to each small door window and opened them. He leaned against the white wall with one foot against it while he played with a stack of keys. "I'm going to be honest with you right now. You will take me back home—"

"We're on our way—"

"Don't interrupt me. Lucas, right? Don't answer, I don't care. The only reason I don't kill you, save one, is because I need you." Genter closed his eyes and gritted his teeth. He clutched the keys in his hand. "I remember Simon's face when I showed him your medical scan. He nearly fell down. I know you're important and I bet if I brought you to him. . . Well, you'd be my ticket back to Vanar. Back to my family."

Joey glared at Genter and he saw Poly tense up as well. The man wanted to use them like some bargaining chip for his redemption. The temptation to tell Genter that they'd killed Simon was almost unbearable.

"If any of you give me the slightest of trouble, I'll execute one of you. Understood?"

Joey pulled at his shirt and wanted to tell the man to go to hell, but he swallowed his words. The man had them trapped and held.

"Fine, but you might not like what you find when we get there," Lucas said.

Does he know something?

"Good, we'll leave as soon as we fuel up the trucks." Genter left and locked the door.

He left the windows open on the doors. Big enough to get a cat through, but not even Poly could squeeze through that space.

"I say we fight them. When they are moving us, we can make our move," Poly said.

"If given the chance," Joey said.

A half hour later, the door to the jail cell hallway opened. The same men as before marched in with guns pointed. They had all decided it was the best to go along with the transport and try to get to the stone as one cohesive group. Joey didn't want to be separated from his friends again.

Even as they stuffed him and Julie in a separate truck, he felt better than he did without the Six together. Grimy faced man sneered and kept the hand gun pointed at him and Julie.

"So, where we going?" Julie asked.

"You just shut that mouth, missy."

Over the next four hours, no one really said a word. Joey spotted New Vegas in the distance. Lucas must have been guiding Genter in the lead truck. Joey sighed and hoped Lucas was saying the right thing and not trying to send them on some wild route for the fun of it. Ryjack wasn't a place to get lost, or take joy rides. Poly had told him about the hordes of grinners they encountered and he wanted to avoid those at all costs, especially as he sat in the backseat of a beat up truck without a gun.

"How'd it go with you, Poly, and Samantha in that MM bunker?"

Grimy faced man raised an eyebrow at Joey but didn't make any of the usual snide remarks. Maybe he wanted to hear some gossip, or maybe he was as bored as they were. The driver hadn't said a single word.

"It went fine," Joey said.

Julie raised her eyebrows and rolled her eyes. "Really? I think I know them well enough to know something's going on. You hurt Poly didn't you?"

Joey hated talking about it, but Julie's stoic expression left little wiggle room. He glanced to grimy man, but he looked interested in the conversation and didn't appear to be stopping it anytime soon.

"Okay, so it was awkward." He struggled to find a way to explain something he didn't understand. "Poly walked in on Samantha and I . . . making out."

"You son of a—"

"I thought you were all dead! I really thought it was just Samantha and I, alone in the world." Joey spit out the words fast.

"Please. . ." Julie fumed.

"Max said he shot down your plane. I saw it explode over the ocean." He felt like he was digging a grave, and getting deeper with each word. "He even did a dance in his excitement."

"We lived. You know Poly didn't go a day without mentioning how she promised to get you back. . ." Julie took in a deep breath and crossed her arms.

Joey's mouth hung open and grimy-faced man looked thrilled at the conversation, grinning his brown-toothed smile. Joey felt his heart pounding in his chest as he thought about the promises they each made to each other. He knew he hurt Poly, but he couldn't have known she was alive and would walk in the middle of him and Samantha. Now, he was stuck in the middle. They hadn't said much about it since the kitchen table sit down, but the tension was there and building. Julie must have picked up on it.

"Listen, Joey, this is important. If you have an unselfish bone in your body, you'll take heed. If you pick one, it's going to send a rift down the middle of the six. I already feel the tension between Samantha and Poly." Julie moved closer to him. "I don't want us ever to be apart again. You have to let them go."

Grimy faced man said, "Oh come on, he can take them both. One of those menagerie twats. Times aren't like they were when I was your age. In these end times, you can have it all."

Julie looked as if she might vomit at the man's comments.

"I never wanted to hurt either of them."

"Then why did you do what you did?"

"Before any of this stuff happened, on our birthday, I made a move on Samantha and she was—to my surprise—receptive. Then, we were separated and I got to know Poly on another level, and we formed a strong connection. Look . . . when I thought she was dead, I gave up on living. I wanted to die, until I saw Samantha. She gave me a purpose for living, something to keep fighting for.

"We spent a lot of time together in that scene generator. During that time, I felt comfortable with her, yet never had the feelings I shared with Poly. I even told Samantha about my relationship with her, but we had to put on a show for them, make them believe we were together, that we were falling for each other. When I saw Poly that first night when she joined us, it was the best and worst moment of my life. She was alive, but that meant I had been with a person I would've never been with if Poly had been there."

Julie blew out a long breath and shook her head. "You see the problem though? Samantha is in love with you. I see it in her eyes, she looks at you when you aren't looking. You may have thought you were only getting close for Marcus's sake, but she fell for you. It's freaking killing me to see this going on because I see the way you look at Poly. You are going to end us, you know that right?"

"I don't want to hurt either of them."

"Oh no, you'd just rather hurt us all."

"No—"

"Sometimes in life, you have to hurt those that you love most." Julie said.

The more he dwelled on Julie's words, the more he understood her. He should end things with both of them, for the sake of the Six. He felt tears building in his eyes as he thought of losing Poly.

"Are you gonna cry?" Grimy man said with a smirk.

Joey turned and faced the desert moving by. He and Julie didn't speak any further, but it was all he could think about. He wanted to challenge Julie's logic, but his rebuttal was only filled with emotion so he held it in and stared at the crumbled remains of a hotel pass by.

Another ten minutes and the truck stopped. Joey used this as a chance to glance at Julie's face, searching for answer, but she only stared at the casino valet parking. Grimy man kept his gun pointed at Joey with a scowl across his face.

"There's Lucas," Julie said.

Lucas laughed and slapped Genter's shoulder. How did he find a way to charm Genter? Lucas amazed him sometimes. Two more men moved to their truck and opened the door on Julie's side. The man grabbed Julie's arm and she hopped from the truck. Joey slid across the seat and hopped on the thin layer of sand slowly overtaking the casino's valet. It hit him like Déjà vu. Except he was a completely different person than he'd been stepping from the Hummer.

"Get over with the others." The man used his rifle as a pointing stick, showing them the direction to their waiting friends. Julie hugged Samantha and Poly. She took Lucas's hand in hers and hugged him with a kiss on the cheek.

Joey moved closer to Poly and Samantha but with Julie's words still fresh in his mind, he felt his hands shaking and lost any meaningful words, so he stood there, awkwardly avoiding each of their looks. Did Samantha really love him in that way? She was adamant in telling Poly how their romance was a show for the higher ups. Was she just placating Poly? If he got Samantha alone, he'd know, he'd see the difference.

"Enough with the PDA, let's get back home," Genter said.

The Six formed a tight circle with five gunmen behind them and four up front. Joey gazed at the glass doors ahead. He hoped the men around him knew how to use those guns.

They entered the grand entry to the hotel.

"Where to now? And don't try anything stupid. We could all be killed in a second in a place like this," Genter said. His gaze darted around and his hands fidgeted with his guns. Good, the man knew the danger of being there.

"If we cut across the casino floor in silence, and I do mean silence, we can go through the kitchen service staircase to the basement levels," Lucas said.

"*Silence.* You all hear that?" Genter commanded.

Like Joey needed a reminder. Poly moved next to him. "The crap's hitting the fan on this one. Remember this place last time?"

"It was mostly clear when we came back through here," Julie said.

Mostly didn't describe a safe environment. Joey itched his side for a gun. "Hey, how about giving me a gun? You're going to need an extra hand when those things come."

"Shut up," Genter hissed. "Not another word or misplaced step until we are on the stone."

The gunmen walked into the service door at the back wall. The double doors swung open and they held it in place as everyone moved into the hallway. The two men holding the door walked in and let them close slowly.

Genter held a finger to his mouth and stared at Lucas. Lucas pointed down the hall and Genter nodded. They stepped toward the end of the hallway and past another set of swinging doors. Genter's Panavice shined down the large staircase beyond the door.

The door had smears of black on them and the smell of rotting meat and mildew wafted up from the stairwell. They were down there, Joey felt it more than anything he'd ever known. Could be thousands, lined up, waiting for a meal to fall into their net. He would grab his friends and run. Their only chance would be fleeing, they could outrun them.

CHAPTER 18

WHEN THE STAIRS ENDED AT the flat concrete, it meant they were on the bottom floor. A grinner groaned as it neared them through the darkness. Joey stared at the gun on Genter's hip. If he could get to it, maybe they had a chance. Genter handed Lucas his bow and took out one arrow. Lucas pulled back on the string and Genter raised his light. In the distance, maybe a hundred feet, stood a grinner, stumbling in their direction.

Lucas fired his arrow and the whoosh of air bounced around the concrete and steel. Joey sucked in a breath of air, he'd seen Lucas strike the chest and necks before and if he hit the beast and it called to its friends, they'd all be dead in a matter of minutes. The arrow struck the grinner in the head—it collapsed to the ground in silence.

Lucas jumped and fist pumped the air. He kissed Prudence as Genter held out his hand. Lucas begrudgingly handed it back to Genter. It was like watching a silent movie, everyone had over animated expressions to prove their intended points.

Genter motioned them to move on. He held the light near the floor and the same feeling Joey had last time remerged. The feeling of eyes in the darkness beyond. He kept Samantha to one side and Poly on the other, Hank and Lucas stood on each side of Julie. If anything jumped from the darkness, his life and the life of his friends were in the hands of the surly looking men with guns.

Genter picked up the pace to a light jog. Their feet resonated small thumps against the concrete floor. How much further? He didn't remember such a distance with Harris. Then he saw it. The group stopped on the edge of the hole Hank had previously hammered out. Grinners floated in the water below. He shined the light on the stone poking out of the water in the middle of the pit.

They froze at the sound of metal thumping down the hall.

Genter frantically pointed at a man holding a bag. He pulled out a rope, with tied knots on it. He pointed to Hank and Hank grasped the rope. Moving his hands and trying to get everyone to speed up. He and the rest of them kept glancing into the darkness as another sound came from the depths, a groan.

Lucas jerked his head behind him and put his finger over his mouth. His hand moved rapidly, asking for his bow. Genter handed him the bow and Lucas pointed to the right. Genter leaned forward, searching the darkness as he raised his Panavice's light inch by inch.

Joey saw the feet staggering their way. Grinners, a dozen, fifty feet away. Lucas pointed down into the pit and Julie climbed down the rope Hank held. Genter gestured to the grinners with an animated hand as he stared at the men with guns. He stabbed the air with his knife. Grimy face shrugged his shoulders and fired into the group with a loud shotgun blast. The enormous sound hit Joey's eardrums. The silence had forced his ears to stretch into peak mode and the blast sent him stumbling backward.

"You idiot," Genter said.

"You told me to," Grimy said.

"I told you to stab them." Genter formed more protests, but the sound of grinners yelling filled the void. He shined his light into the oncoming throng. Mangled hotel workers and men in lounge suits, women in cocktail dresses moved toward them with snarling mouths. "Now you can fire," he directed.

The five men behind him shot into the crowd, mowing down the front line. They were good shots, he was glad he didn't run. They would have killed him even at a hundred yards.

"Guys, get down the rope," Lucas said.

Joey moved behind the men shooting into the grinners when a grinner reached for him from the left side. Joey yelled and kicked the grinner in the chest. Genter turned and shot it.

"Both sides," he called out.

Four more grinners moved in from the left side and grabbed at two of the men, plunging their black mouths into the flesh. The men screamed and the others scattered around, shooting in both directions.

Samantha and Poly climbed down the rope. With gunfire sounding off all around him, he sped down the rope and jumped the last few feet into the water. The horrid smell of rotting bodies soaked in water wafted around him. He wanted to gag.

"I think I'm going to be sick." Samantha turned away and threw up into the water. After she darted away, her vomit spread out on top of the water.

Lucas jumped down the hole and landed on a floating grinner, splashing the putrid water around.

Flashes of gunfire lit the area above as Genter, with Panavice and gun in hand, jumped into the water. He kept his gun trained on Lucas. "Get us to Vanar, now."

Lucas glanced at the gun flashes above.

"Do it now, or I'll kill her." Genter pointed his gun at Julie.

Lucas rushed to the stone and pressed his fingers around it. The dome hummed and the gun fire ceased.

This is it. They were going straight into the den of the devil. Marcus would have all six of them and Harris would be the only one left to save them. Would he even bother?

CHAPTER 19

THE FRONT WINDSHIELD CRACKED FROM the impact of the ocean. The water surrounded the car and pushed against it as it descended. The restraints pushed against Harris's body as the car rocked hard under the water. The air bubbles trapped in all the recesses of the vehicle kept the car buoyant for a moment before the water pushed the air out and claimed the car.

After twenty feet down, the cars back end moved down and the windshield faced the surface. The sunlight danced around in the water as the remaining air bubbles raced to the surface. He glanced in the rearview mirror but below him was only darkness. He welcomed the depth, he needed the car to go deeper if they had any chance of living. Could the car hold up under the pressure of sixty feet of water? The car creaked and the crack in the windshield spread around to the edges of glass. Harris pressed the dome light on.

Jack had passed out on the impact. Good, he'd probably be screaming if awake. Harris took slow breaths in through his nose. He knew the risk of panicking but being in a small capsule floating to the bottom of the ocean would give any man the jitters. The sunlit surface faded into darkness as they descended. He couldn't see the bottom, but he took off all the restraints and braced himself for the impact. He took deep breaths, expanding his lungs with oxygen, if the cars back window broke on impact, he'd only have a split second to react.

The back of the car crashed against the ocean floor.

The jolt knocked him hard into the seat and he sucked in all the air he could, but the trunk of the car absorbed the damage and left the back window intact. He exhaled and glanced at Jack. If the back window broke, there would have only been time for one of them to escape.

"Jack." Harris shook Jack's shoulder. "Jack, wake up." He slapped Jack's face and he stirred awake.

"What . . ." Jack looked around the darkness outside the car. "Are we . . ." His gaze darted around and he thrashed at the restraints in his seat.

"Jack."

He didn't listen and continued to remove the restraints from around his chest and lap.

"Jack, you need to listen to me if you want to live."

His attention turned to Harris. "We're at the bottom of the ocean—"

The darkness of the ocean above them lit up in a brilliant light. Harris covered his eyes as the light from above penetrated through the darkness and lit the dark gray landscape around them. The grass swayed on the ocean floor and a few fish darted around and hid in the swaying sea grass.

Harris pulled the chest strap under his arms and over his chest. "Buckle up, but keep a hand on the release button."

Jack's shaky hands struggled with the strap. Harris peered at the bright light above. The top of the water would be boiling at this point, the city would be melting, people dead before they even had a chance to see the second sun ignite over their city. Emmett had done the unthinkable, the forbidden weapon from the Great War. *Are we deep enough?*

Jack clasped his strap and his hands held the sides of his head as he breathed rapidly. Panic. Harris didn't have words to comfort the young man. Saying anything except they would most likely be dead soon would be a lie.

The rumble started low, then grew and shook the car. Harris stared at the cracked window two feet in front of his face. Jack began to make noises, not really a scream but mumblings of unrecognizable words. Harris began to take deep breaths, preparing for the car to be tumbled on the ocean floor.

A loud crack sound exploded around the car. Jack squealed, but it wasn't the glass breaking. The earth above cracked under the heat. Harris watched the grass on the ocean floor shift from swaying around to lying flat. The car rolled and he grabbed the straps on his chest and hugged himself tight. The ocean floor rolled against his driver side window and cracked it in a hundred places, but the reinforced glass held. A few drops of water slid down the inside of the glass.

The water pushed against the car and sent it flying off the floor. It spun around and Jack closed his eyes and started mumbling a prayer. The bright light above flickered and then stopped. The darkness enveloped the car. Harris searched for the grassy field below, but it was nothing but blackness. He felt the g-force of the car's motion as it spun in the water. He glanced at Jack's face. It was the worst part . . . seeing the kid die because of his plan. Maybe he should have let them die in the smoldering above. It would have been kinder and over quickly.

The car slammed against the ocean floor and Harris felt his butt and back compress against the bottom of the seat. It landed wheels down. Jack opened his tightly shut eyes as the realization set in. A wide smile spread across his face and his rigid muscles loosened a bit. Again, Harris released his breath and took an inventory of the surrounding windows. Everything seemed intact. What a finely built automobile.

Jack raised an eyebrow and the brightness in his eyes told Harris he had his cognitive abilities intact. "Are we going to die in here?"

"I hope not."

The car lifted off the sea floor with another rush. Jack's eyes went wide with fear. The free float didn't last long. Harris shifted in neutral and the car bounced against the bottom of the ocean floor, hitting unknown bumps and divots. Harris switched on the headlights and they flickered on for second, letting him see the grass pointing in the direction the car faced, before going out. The dome light provided enough light to see a foot past the windows. Mud and sand swirled around the windows.

His body lurched forward as the car stopped. The muddy waters surrounded the windows and clouded around the car as the water stabilized. Rapid breaths from Jack were the only sound in the car.

"Try to calm your breathing down, there is a limited supply of oxygen in here."

Jack looked around the car frantically, as if he could see the air escaping. He wasn't too far off, air bubbles left the car through the driver's side window. Harris watched the water dribble in and splash on his lap.

"We're stuck in a car at the bottom of the ocean. With the world on fire above us," Jack said in an oddly calm voice.

"Yes, and we need the air to last long enough for the water to cool itself up there."

"How are we getting up there?"

"You know how to swim, right?"

Jack scowled. "The pressure won't allow it, you couldn't open that door or break the window. These cars are, what . . . rated for fifty foot depths? We're screwed."

"The sun roof." Harris pointed to the square piece of glass over their heads.

"The water will crush us as soon as you opened it."

"We have to wait an hour anyways."

"Why, you think the surface is still on fire?"

"It's cooling rapidly now, might even be a storm from the evaporated water."

Jack huffed and crossed his arms. He glanced at the ceiling and windows and let out another huff as he adjusted his crossed arms.

"Just try to stay calm and breathe normally."

"Fine."

An hour passed and Harris felt the air quality diminish. It was humid and stagnant. Jack had messed with his Panavice for the most part. "Anything out there?" Harris asked.

Jack sighed and shook his head. "Just yours."

"It's time." Harris gazed at the ceiling. He slid his finger over the sunroof button. "How long can you hold your breath?"

Jack's attention jerked away from the sunroof. "I don't know. I used to be able to hold my breath for a minute."

"Take off your clothes." Harris pulled his shirt over his head and then took the rest of his clothes off, down to his underwear.

Jack yanked his shirt off and the rest of his clothes as well. "We're really going to do this, aren't we?"

"Yes. When the sunroof opens, water will be shooting into the car like a fire hose. It'll quickly fill this space. I want you to take the deepest breath you can before the water fills this car. You're going first, go through the sunroof and kick off the top of the car. I'll be right behind you. As you go up, spit out a bit of air after each arm pump."

Harris peered into the dark murky water on the other side of his window. Not a foot of visibility. He reached to the floor and picked up the empty water bottle that had been tossed around the car. He tightened the lid and handed it to Jack.

"Tie your shoe string around the neck of this bottle, then around your wrist." Harris handed it to a reluctant Jack. "You can lose your sense of direction out there, but that empty bottle will always be pulling up, follow it."

Jack nodded his head and began to breathe rapidly again.

"Slow, deep breaths."

Jack stretched his arms out, sucking in air. He tethered his wrist to the water bottle.

Harris knew he could have told him about the bends, but he might have gone into another fit, and keeping calm was more important than anything else.

"Here we go." Harris pressed his finger on the button and the sunroof hummed and moved back an inch. An explosion of water hit the inside of the car and Jack screamed. "Take your deep breath now," Harris yelled over the rushing water, already up to his waist.

He sucked in air deep into his lungs and then swallowed more, pushing it in. The sunroof opened more and the warm water filled the rest of the car in a matter of seconds. He watched Jack pushing his fingers against his ears, Harris grabbed him and pushed him through the open sunroof.

Jack kicked off the top of the car and disappeared into the water. Harris shot through the sunroof, kicking off the center console. He kept his eyes open in the dark, murky water, searching for that foot, or the body of Jack.

He kicked his feet and pushed his arms down, propelling his body toward the surface. The bubbles from his mouth shot straight up and he pumped harder. The water crushed his ears and burned his eyes. The temperature of the water increased as he traveled closer to the surface. Had they waited long enough? Where was Jack?

A current swept by him, sending him sideways as much as up, but he pushed harder, swimming with everything he had.

The visibility didn't allow him to see much of anything, he hoped the boy found his way to the surface. He hoped he could hold his breath longer than he thought. Harris pumped his arms and released a bit more of the precious air in his lungs. His gaze followed the bubble up and the water illuminated above with the sun's rays. The current still pulled him further out into the ocean, but he made good distance with each stroke. The one foot visibility became five then ten, but he still didn't see Jack.

He breathed out his last bit of oxygen and stared up, seeing the watery edge. He pumped his arms again, his heart pounded in his chest and he felt his mind struggling to stay focused on the light above. Fifteen feet more. His muscles ached as he pushed his arms down into the water. His mouth opened and wanted to suck in something, but he closed it and kicked his legs.

Five more feet. One more push and he extended his arm out as his body propelled the last few feet. His hand felt the air and he leaned his head back, waiting for the breathable air. When his face breached the surface, he sucked in the air. It had taken even longer than he thought, maybe the currents were so strong it pulled him to the side as much as he went up. It took almost two minutes to get to the surface.

"Jack," Harris yelled between raspy pants for air.

The choppy water crashed over his head as he scanned the surface. Harris yanked out his Panavice and slid his wet finger on the screen. He pressed the local search and saw Jack's location, thirty feet away. He swam in that direction until he was directly over the spot. He was now forty feet away, directly below him. Fifty feet, then he stopped as it kept descending past a hundred feet. A water bottle floated by him with a shoe string attached to the neck.

"No," Harris slapped the water and dived down, using his Panavice to guide him. At twenty feet, he felt his lungs asking for air. He turned around and swam to the surface.

He stared at his screen and the label designated Jack. It wasn't fair, everyone around him died, like some curse placed on him for all his sins. He yelled at the sky as the clouds broke and poured down rain. He vowed to stay away from everyone from here on out. Emmett probably found a way to kill the kids on Ryjack. How many people on any planet did he care about now?

"Harris," a voice called.

He jerked around and saw Jack treading the choppy water toward him. Harris covered the distance between him and stopped short of hugging him. "I thought you were dead."

"I barely made it to the surface." Jack breathed hard. "The current yanked the bottle from my wrist and I tried to use my Pana light, but it slipped from my hands. I couldn't find you until I heard you yelling."

Harris touched Jack's shoulder to make sure he wasn't a mirage, an illusion being played by a mind that wanted him to be alive. The shoulder felt real and Jack patted his arm. They were alive! Harris had experienced many life and death situations, but this one felt nothing short of a miracle.

"I thought this was you." Harris showed Jack his screen and pointed to the dot below them.

Jack grabbed the Panavice from his hand with a shocked expression.

"What is it?"

"There are two more Panas nearby."

Harris smiled, two people had possibly made it. "Good to hear—"

"No, you don't understand." Jack gawked at the screen. "This one . . . it's Julie."

CHAPTER 20

POLY FELT THE HOT RAIN soaking into her shirt. *What has happened?* She stepped in a tight circle, taking in the leveled city. The mighty museum now lay on the ground in melted piles, the rubble hissing and steaming as the rain covered them.

"This can't be it." Genter pointed at Lucas. "Take me to the real Vanar."

Lucas faced Julie. Julie ran her fingers around the Panavice. "I don't know, it's as if the worlds been turned off. I mean, there's nothing."

Genter ran his hands through his hair and pointed his gun at Julie. "No, this isn't it, my family was here. This has to be wrong."

"I'm sorry, but this is it. Look, you can still see the protective walls up." Julie pointed the semi-circle wall wrapping around the city until it hit the ocean.

Genter lowered his gun and gazed at the wall. He ran his hand over his head and shook the water from it. "What happened?"

"I don't know, but it looks as if everything's been melted."

Genter kicked a chunk of melted glass and it broke in several pieces. He paced the edge of the circle, staring in a single direction.

Poly figured it was where his family lived. She hated Genter for allowing the monster Isaac into their world, but a hint of empathy crept in for him. He had lost his family.

The rain seemed to help the immense heat pressing in on them, but as it peppered the ground, steam rose and a fog was starting to build around the city. The fog began to obscure the distant walls.

Poly stood next to Joey as he surveyed the surroundings. "Looks like someone got to MM before we did," she said.

"You think Harris did this?"

"You guys are with Harris Boone?" Genter asked.

Joey bit his tongue and wouldn't make eye contact with him.

"Just great." Genter walked away and disappeared into the fog.

"You've got my arrows," Lucas called out to him. A quiver sailed through the fog and landed next to the circle. He ran to retrieve it and slung it over his back.

Joey saw Poly fidgeting for her knives and smiled. She gazed into those blue eyes and his gorgeous face. She returned his smile and he looked away, staring into the thick steam. She glanced at Samantha and sighed.

Poly studied the stone in the center of the circle. It looked unscathed. "Can we use that stone to get out of here?"

Lucas spoke first. "Nope, it's a one-way."

She sighed. It seemed silly, but she fantasized about being home in her bed, tucked under her soft blankets. Sleeping on the floors of forests, in abandoned warehouses, and the back of trucks, gave a person an appreciation for the simple pleasures. She laughed at the idea. Look at where she was, in the middle of some nuclear waste land. "Is this toxic or radioactive?" She shot the question to Julie.

Julie played with her Panavice. "No, just a lot hotter than normal. I think someone set off some kind of thermal bomb."

"You think Harris blew the entire city up?" Poly asked.

"Nah, not his style," Lucas said.

"Did this happen only to Capital?" Hank asked.

Julie shook her head. "I don't know."

"Well, no reason to stand here. We should get to the wall and find a way around it." Lucas pointed in a direction.

"The closest wall was that way." Julie pointed another direction. Her Panavice dinged and all of them froze. That ding meant someone had texted her. "It's Harris."

"Shut your face," Lucas said.

"He's swimming to the shore," Julie pointed in the direction.

"Let's go," Lucas said.

They followed Julie as she led them toward the nearby shoreline. Poly kept next to Joey, which meant next to Samantha. Had Samantha ever even noticed Joey before this all happened? All the fog was a sick reminder of them cuddled up in that fake castle.

Bits of glass broke under her steps. The hot rain poured over them like a warm shower. The steam dissipated enough for about fifty feet of visibility. Was anyone able to escape? Was she walking on melted people? She sidestepped onto what looked like a concrete sidewalk. Style or not, if Harris did such a heinous act, she'd be having words with him.

The rain slowed down to a drizzle as they reached piles of large rocks which made the shoreline. She imagined a bustling harbor with boats and docks, but all that remained was steaming rocks. The ocean looked like it had a blanket of white steam over it. The small waves pushed against the rocks, sending up tendrils each time.

"He should be here any second."

From the deep fog hanging over the ocean, a hand emerged and then a head. She didn't need binoculars to see the distinctive look of Harris. Another man swam behind him, holding a Panavice. She didn't recognize him.

Hank bounded over a few rocks to help Harris come ashore. The man with him staggered along the edge of the rocks and sat down.

Harris gazed over each of them and a wide smile spread across his face. "You made it?" He jumped from the rock, wearing nothing but black boxers and picked up Joey in his arms, hugging him, unabashed.

Joey groaned and Harris sat him down, and headed to the next, hugging each of them. Poly, being soaked herself, didn't mind the man dripping all over her. She hugged him back equally as hard and joyous. It was good to see Harris. He stopped in front of Samantha and took her hand. Samantha shot a glance to Joey, but returned her attention to Harris.

"And you are Samantha?" She nodded. "We had the briefest of meetings last time and if I remember you're quite a lady." Harris hugged her and she awkwardly patted his bare back. Harris took a step back and the look on his face changed to a somber expression. "I'm deeply sorry I left you behind."

"Well, it wasn't your fault." Samantha said.

Harris shook his head. "I wish that was true. Oh, let me introduce you all to Jack. He's a computer whiz, like you Julie."

Julie raised a questioning eyebrow to Jack.

"Well, it's a pleasure to meet you all. I was stuck in the aircraft back in Sanct." His gaze stuck on Poly the longest. "And if I may say, Poly, you were quite extraordinary that day."

"Harris, what the heck happened here? You didn't do this, right?" Lucas questioned.

"It was Emmett. A lot has happened in a short amount of time." Harris proceeded to tell them everything.

"That was some crazy brilliance, man. Don't undersell it," Jack said after Harris talked about driving into the ocean.

Poly's mouth hung open in shock, but Julie almost fell over when he discussed the closure of everything online. Poly didn't get what the fuss was over. So what if they couldn't check their Facebook page or whatever? Big deal.

"Where's Marcus?" Joey asked.

"I don't know."

Joey stuffed his hands in his pockets and tapped a small black rock with his foot. "Can we go home now?"

Poly moaned at the idea. Yes, *home*. As bad as she felt about Vanar's problems, the idea of being in her bed sent chills over her body. She also had so many things she wanted to tell Joey, but couldn't with others around; she needed to get him alone.

"Yes, Jack's sent for our ship to be here any minute." Harris looked to the sky and turned back to them with a smile. "How'd you get here? Did someone help you?"

"There was a man named Genter, he kidnapped us and forced us to take him here," Julie said.

"That dude is still out there somewhere." Lucas pointed toward the city remnants. "We've been through some crazy stuff to get here."

"Crazy doesn't even begin to describe it," Julie added.

Harris frowned at the name Genter and looked into the mist. "I want to hear all about it."

"The aircraft's here." Jack faced the ocean and held his Panavice with both hands. He moved the Pana and the aircraft swayed with his motions. The craft lowered near them and Jack pressed one finger on the screen. It stabilized and a ramp projected from its side until it reached a rock.

Once they boarded and lifted off, Poly stared out the window. The flattened, melted city below looked worse from the air. In the distance she saw greenery. It followed a finite line outside the city walls. Did grinners get past that wall?

Harris sat on the seat across from them and listened as Lucas told their story. She thought he played down some of the parts, totally unlike him to be modest. Julie hung on his every word and they laughed and held hands at some points.

"Incredible. What about you guys?" Harris eyed Joey, Samantha, and Poly.

Poly turned her head down.

"They just stuffed us into a scene generator for a while," Joey said.

She watched him glance at Samantha as he said that. Oh God, why did she have to fall for him? He had eyes for Samantha. Joey glanced at her with a smile. If only she had been in the truck with him instead of Julie. She hadn't felt like she even had a chance to talk to Joey since the incident. Instead, she had to share a truck with a group of men that made bikers look like girl scouts, and had body odor that rivaled a junior high locker room.

"They saved us," Samantha said.

"It's what we do," Lucas said, and kissed Prudence. He was obviously talking about him and his bow. Julie scowled at him, but he never took notice. They had become the cutest couple. Poly shook her head, she needed to get away from it.

She remembered a small kitchen in a similar aircraft her and Lucas shared. Getting up, she found the tiny kitchenette and opened the drawers. The contents of the third drawer down, clanked with metal on metal. Kitchen knives. She sighed and placed some in her hip sheaths. What she wouldn't do for some nice throwing knives and a solid dagger.

"You okay?" Joey asked coming up behind her.

She spun to face him. "Yeah, just stocking up on some blades."

"You see any spare guns rolling around in there?"

"Nope, sorry. Fresh out of pistols." She gave him a polite grin and headed back to her seat.

"So what's next? We hunt down Emmett, flush out Marcus?" Lucas asked.

"For you guys, it's over. I don't think Emmett cares about you and I doubt we'll be seeing anything of Marcus for a long time."

Even hearing the words come out of Harris's mouth, they sounded like a lie. Every turn and everything that ever happened was for *what*? So a mad man could escape, only to be replaced by another? No, she wouldn't be cast aside. They were part of the madness now. With the Preston Six together, what could stop them?

"What if we don't want it to be over?" she asked.

"Yeah," Lucas agreed.

"I won't lie, I could use people like you. I need people like you." He glanced at Julie. "But you need to get back to your world, your families."

"As long as Marcus breathes, I'll hunt him down." Poly held a kitchen knife in her hand.

Harris sighed. "The truth is, he's smarter, faster, and going to be a step ahead at every point. It's over for you guys, I want it to be over."

"There's seven of us . . ." Lucas started.

Jack cleared his throat. "Eight."

"And look at who's not with us," Harris said.

Poly scowled at Harris, there wasn't a day that went by she didn't think of Compry, lying on the roof, dead. The woman taught her so much and she never got to repay a cent of the debt she owed her. She owed it to Compry to see an end to it. Poly wanted to avenge her dad, avenge all the parents lost. The great people that considered her a member on Mutant isle. They all stood behind her, waiting for the chance of peace. "There will never be peace until he's dead."

"I agree, at some point he's going to come looking for us again. He still wants something from us," Julie said.

"I wouldn't be surprised if our paths cross again, but it's up to us to clean the mess Marcus left behind on Vanar, and we need to stop Emmett from taking over."

"The suffering has only begun," Jack added. "Everything and everyone was dependent on the network."

Poly rolled her eyes.

Julie's brow furrowed as she stared at her. "They are dependent on this network. Their cars, trains, distribution centers, orange factories, cargo ships, and everything you can think of is hooked into the system Marcus disconnected. It's going to be worse than any war, any plague. If they don't get things back quickly, Ryjack will look like a vacation planet."

Poly hadn't realized how dependent their world was to this network. People were going to miss their shipment of food and orange. She knew all too well what happened to a city under an embargo. They would raid the city, like in Sanct, but this time they would have no rescue, no shipments of orange on standby.

Her bed felt distant. The idea of Vanar falling bothered her more than she thought it would. She needed to help in some way. She owed them that.

CHAPTER 21

HE WAS FINALLY HOME. JOEY gazed at the surrounding burnt trees of Watchers Woods, once known for its thick canopy. Now, the sun beat on the charred ground with brilliant force.

He took a breath through his nose. It wasn't an unpleasant smell, more like a campfire. Kneeling on the ground, he grabbed a handful of dirt, his Earth. At so many points, he fantasized about coming home and in not one of those fantasies did he have the arrogance to think all his friends would be standing next him, alive and well.

He felt a hand rub his back, he glanced back at Samantha's face. He smiled and stood.

"The kids are back." Opal ran up to them, holding a knife in each hand. She eyed Joey and then Samantha, her eyes went wide and she covered her mouth. Joey saw the tears filling her eyes as she ran to them and hugged them both at the same time. "Oh thank you, thank goodness you're back. Gretchen's gonna. . ." Opal wiped a tear from her face and ran to Poly.

"Let's get you to your mom," Joey said.

"Thank you."

Joey led the pack through the forest. Opal told them there hadn't been any Arracks for several days and they had gone down to one person scouting missions.

All of the forest hadn't been charred and when the blackness ended, green undergrowth claimed the forest. The thick brush was slower to go through but didn't kick up bits of ash as they walked through it. He passed the edge of the forest and beheld his house beyond the grass field.

"Tell me this is real." Samantha squeezed his hand before jogging toward his house.

He jogged down his path and saw dog prints mixed in with the human ones on the worn path. It looked like it had heavy use. The path was wider and the dirt churned up to a softer pattern. He saw a large man on the front porch run into the house and then quickly reappear. Trip ran toward them and Hank moved to the front of the pack to greet his dad in the largest man hug Earth had ever seen.

Parents flooded out of the front door of the house. He spotted his mom and dad. He didn't think he was going to get emotional, but his body told him something different when the look on his mom's face became clear. Her joy and shock, mixed with the energy spent on running to him. His dad looked shocked as well and let Karen take the run to him while he staggered his way behind her.

Joey felt the emotions running over him as he passed the broken down truck and reached his mom's open arms.

"Oh my god, I can't believe it." She pushed back from him and touched his arm as if testing to make sure he was real. Lucas and the rest of the Preston Six each embraced their parent. They were home, he didn't truly feel like it was real until the moment they were all together.

"I can't believe it." Minter hugged him hard. The air wheezed from his body, but he didn't care and hugged his dad back. "This is the greatest moment . . ." Minter lost the words and hugged him again. A dog barked and rubbed its paws against his pant leg.

"Bull!" Joey knelt down and embraced his dog. Bull's body shook in excitement. Joey felt the tears build in his eyes and he fought them back. He didn't want to cry in front of his dad.

Gretchen screamed and spun around with Samantha in her arms. It wasn't a sight he would ever forget in his entire life. They were back together, they were whole. Opal laughed at the kitchen knives Poly showed her. Hank and Trip wrestle-hugged. Lucas pointed at Prudence and showed his dad the tiny arrows that came with it. Julie showed her mom her Panavice. He felt home again.

"Let's go inside and celebrate this great day," Minter's voice boomed out the command.

At the end of the party, late into the night, after all the stories had been told, all the hugs and tears had been given, Joey sat on the edge of his bed, alone.

The open bedroom window let the soft, cool breeze flow into his room. He stared at that window, making out the tops of the trees in the moonlight. He lay on his back on top of his blankets, folded his arms behind his head, and let his shoes rest off the end of the bed.

A tack sound rattled along his floor. He sat up on the edge his bed. Another pebble bounced across his wood floor. He darted to the window and below, in the dark, stood Poly. She waved for him to come down.

He snuck down the stairs and gently closed the front door. The familiar night air felt cool and refreshing and carried a scent of the forest. The bugs were out in force, chirping and squeaking away. Poly sauntered over wearing a black summer dress that reached her knees and swung low in the front. She was all smiles as she swayed her arms.

Joey took a tepid step toward her. She wrapped him in a hug and he hugged her back. Why was he nervous? "Hey, Poly."

"Good evening. I couldn't sleep, so I thought I'd come over and see how you were doing."

Joey frowned. His gut reaction was to tell her he was doing okay, but as he glanced up at his bedroom window, he told her the truth. "I was just staring at my ceiling. I can't get my mind to slow down."

"You want to go for a drive?" Poly pointed to her car parked at the end of the driveway.

"Was wondering how you got here. Yeah, sure, let's go."

Joey followed Poly as she skipped to the car. Wow, she was in such a good mood. He fed off her positive energy and felt lighter. He got into the passenger seat and watched Poly get into the car.

"My mom leaves the keys in the car." She stared at him as she turned the key. The engine roared to life. "Woo hoo!"

He chuckled at her enthusiasm of starting a car. "Where do you want to go?"

"I don't know." She frowned at first and then her face lit up. "Oh, how about the lake?"

"Uh, sure." The lake. The place where every teenager in Preston at some point took their girlfriend. Julie's words pounded in his head for the whole drive there, calling him selfish and telling him he needed to end it for the sake of everyone. Preston Six would break if he didn't.

"How long you think until Harris comes to get us?"

"I don't know." He hoped it would be longer than shorter. Every moment spent in Preston made the awful memories of Vanar and Ryjack seem like a dream. They weren't all bad though, there were moments of friendship. He even had a few kisses to store in his memory bank.

He squirmed in his seat as Poly pulled close to the water and turned off the car. The moonlight danced on the surface of the water. He knew the lake well after spending so much time looking for Samantha's earrings.

Poly gazed at him with her big, pretty eyes. "It's nice, just the two of us for once."

"Yeah." He fidgeted in his seat and felt his heart beating fast. He took a deep breath and looked out the front windshield. Some of the window started to fog, distorting the view of the moonlit lake. "You want to sit on the hood?"

"Okay. But if you dent it, you'll have to answer to my mom."

He opened the door at the same time as her. Sliding up onto the hood, he grabbed Poly's hand as she struggled to get on it.

The hood creaked under their weight. He pushed back and used the windshield as a backrest. Poly nestled in next to him.

"This is nice." She let out a long breath and rested her head on his shoulder. He wanted to kiss her hand, wrap her up and keep her warm in the cooling air. But he held back and gritted his teeth. He needed to push out his selfish desires and think of all of them.

"There's something I've been wanting to tell you," Poly said.

"What's that?"

"I . . ." she turned on her side and propped herself up on her elbow. "It sounds dumb saying it."

Joey turned to face her and saw the struggle in her eyes. "You can tell me anything. We're best friends."

"I know, and that is sort of what I wanted to talk to you about." She took in a deep breath. "I've . . . we've been through a lot together. . ." She rolled on her back. "Ugh, why is this so hard?"

Joey wanted to hug her and tell her how he felt about her, but Julie was right. If he chose Poly, it would hurt Samantha and tear the group apart. "Maybe I should talk first."

"Please do."

He wanted to tell her so many things—how much she meant to him. But he swallowed those words. He had to do the right thing for the group, to say things he didn't want to. His dad told him once that usually the harder path was the right path. He definitely felt like he was about to take the harder path. In the end, he hoped he could keep the Six together.

"You remember the day Samantha lost her earrings out there?"

"Yeah, she was crying the whole way home. I felt terrible for her."

"Well, I searched the rest of the summer for them . . . and I actually found them."

Poly sat up. "How's that possible? They were at the bottom of the lake!"

"I bought an underwater metal detector and formed a search grid around the area and spent two months searching for them. I found them a week before our birthday."

She paused with her mouth open. "Wow. I mean, *wow.*" She didn't say anything else for a while. Joey gave her the time she needed to process what he told her. "You loved her . . . you love her. Nothing else would drive a person to do that."

Joey sighed. What could he tell Poly? "I do care for Samantha—"

"God, I'm a fool," Poly interrupted and slid her legs over the edge of the car.

He grabbed her arm and pulled her back. She glared at him with hurt in her eyes. It sent his heart falling to see her upset. He was breaking a promise he made to Julie. He wanted to wrap her up in his arms and kiss her, telling her he loved her.

The hard path.

"You're important to me, Poly. If it wasn't for you, I would have cracked out there. You saved my life. I owe you everything I can give."

"I don't want you to *owe* me. I want you to *want* me." She yanked her arm away and scowled at him. It quickly turned to tears as she hopped off the hood. Getting into the car, she slammed the front door and started the motor.

Joey moved to the front door, but the wheels of the car spun backward, spitting bits of dirt on him. They kept spinning as she backed up and flung the front end of the car around. She peeled all the way down the dirt road and out of sight.

"I *do* want you," Joey whispered. He slumped and shook his head. He didn't want to hurt her, he loved her. He deserved every horrible thought Poly was thinking at that moment. But it was done. Now all he had to do was turn away Samantha. Once enough time passed, they would forget him and the Six would remain whole.

He shook his head, doubting he could ever truly let Poly go. He breathed in the remaining dust as it settled around him. Wiping his eyes, he started to walk. Taking his time, he thought about Poly's hurt face. He would have to make it up to her somehow. He kicked a rock down the dirt road and watched it pop in and out of visibility. He kicked another one and it skipped along until a black boot stomped on it.

Joey froze and reactively went for guns that weren't there.

"Out for a night walk?" Emmett asked.

CHAPTER 22

EMMETT STRUTTED TOWARD JOEY. HIS face became visible as he stepped from the shadow of the oak tree and into the moonlight. Joey positioned himself in a defensive stance and waited for his attack. Five feet away, Emmett stopped and crossed his arms. "I'm not here for a fight."

"What are you doing here?"

"I thought it would have been impossible for you guys to get out of Ryjack alive, but Marcus told me to never underestimate you—look at what you've done to some of our best already—so I thought I'd just see for myself if you made it back here."

"Great, now get the hell off our planet."

"I was really hoping you'd make it, Joey. I couldn't understand why Marcus was so into keeping you kids alive. So I did some research and found some fascinating things. Especially in you, Joey. We almost have it figured out and I have an offer."

Joey opened his clutched fists and waited.

"I don't know if you know, but Harris died trying to save Capital. And Marcus is . . . somewhere." He shrugged.

He thought Harris was dead? Joey restrained his face from giving any tells. He contorted his expression into what he hoped came across as anger while he smiled on the inside. He didn't want to give Emmett any information.

"I take it you didn't know. I'm sorry for your loss. But the reason I'm here is you." Emmett pointed to Joey's wrists.

Joey rubbed the steel cuffs.

"I can get those things off and I think I can help you master your ability."

"I'm not doing anything for you."

"I'm trying to help. You think Marcus is gone? You think for one second he'll forget his immortality ticket is sitting here, waiting for him to claim?"

Anger built as he stared into Emmett's blank face. He was right though, Marcus was out there still and he would be back. Could they fight on so many fronts? Poly and Lucas wanted to bring the fight to them, but Joey wanted to have peace, if possible. Why fight another world's war?

He felt the metal wrist bands. Harris never offered to remove them. If he could get them off and master the ability like Emmett promised, he could protect everyone. It wouldn't matter how good Marcus was, he couldn't stop what he couldn't see. Just thinking about being able to slow time down again gave Joey goose bumps down his arms. If he had full control of it, nobody around him would die.

The corner of Emmett's mouth pulled back a smidgen. "I can help you and you can help me. Our entire world is in total chaos, so you can appreciate the time I'm taking to come here and make an offer."

"No," Joey said without an ounce of doubt in it.

"I figured you might be against this. Perhaps I can convince Samantha or Poly. I can be very persuasive," he hissed out the last word.

"If you go anywhere near them, I'll kill you."

Emmett laughed. "Then maybe you'll agree to let me help you."

"How?"

"First, I can cut those shackles off. After that, we can find what triggers your time manipulation, maybe we can even create a way for you to trigger it. It might be that anger you're holding right now." Emmett took a half step closer. "You feel it, don't you? You feel it wanting to be released. I bet you'd love to choke the life from me right now."

"Yes." Spit flew from between Joey's teeth.

"Good." Emmett took a step back. "I prefer to have you, Joey. But if I can't have you, I'll take another. I don't want much."

"And what do you want from me?"

"I want to study what you have."

Joey took in a deep breath. He would never be rid of them. He was a fool for thinking it could possibly be over. He couldn't let Emmett hurt his friends. They needed to live in a world where MM didn't want anything from them. Let his friends think they had won for a while longer. He owed it to them.

"If you promise to never go near my friends and let them live their normal lives, I'll go with you."

"Agreed. I'll be back here, at this very spot, in one week."

"Okay, same time and place." Joey pointed to the ground.

Emmett nodded, pivoted, and walked into the forest.

Joey breathed out and slumped forward, placing his hands on his knees. He felt dizzy. One of the most dangerous men in the world just confronted him, one on one. He straightened up and walked down the dirt road, avoiding Emmett's foot prints—the only physical evidence of the encounter.

EVERYTHING IS NORMAL. KEEP UP appearances.

The next day, he kept his mind busy by shopping for new handguns with his dad. He hadn't told anyone about the encounter with Emmett and the secret began to weigh on him. Even as he held the Colt semi-automatic gun in his hand.

"You doing okay?" Minter asked.

"Yeah, just thinking. I'm sorry I lost your guns."

"Those were yours and I don't care about some guns, son." His eyes said he wanted to say more, but he glanced at the gunsmith and pursed his lips. "You like that one?"

"Can I shoot it?" It was one thing to hold the beauty in your hands and feel the fine craftsmanship, it was an entirely different thing to shoot it and feel the recoil, the trigger, hear the sound.

"Sure, I've got a range in the basement. Can your kid shoot, Minter?"

"Yeah, he can shoot."

The portly gunsmith wiped his hands with a rag and went to the front door, locked it and flipped the closed sign over.

They followed the man to the back of the store and down the stairs.

The basement smelled of gunpowder and a musty smell of a poorly ventilated basement. A table sat on one side of the room and along the other was a wall of sandbags that once probably reached the ceiling, but with the hundreds of holes in the bags, much of the sand had drained on the floor. A few loose targets hung on for life.

The shopkeeper handed Joey a set of headphones and then he pushed a clip into the gun and cocked it back. "Alright, son. You've got live ammo in there. Never point it in any other direction than those sandbags. We clear?"

"Yes, sir." Joey placed the headphones over his ears and took the gun. The full clip put extra weight on it and he adjusted his grip.

Raising the gun, he pointed it at the target down range. It was close enough to throw a rock, but he wanted to show his dad he could shoot now. His finger danced on the trigger, it felt like it'd been too long since his last shot. Relaxing his breathing, he pulled the trigger. The nine millimeter bullet smashed through the bullseye.

"Nice shot."

Joey pulled the trigger again and unloaded the clip, hitting the bullseye on each of the six paper targets lining the back wall. He set the gun on the table and used his hands to steady himself. He breathed hard and stared at the paper targets fluttering from the assault.

"Whoa, I've never seen shooting like that. Look . . . right in the middle, each one of them." The shopkeeper moved closer to the targets and leaned forward.

"Yeah, pretty good." Minter's curious tone came through the headphones Joey still wore. Did they even notice he shot through the same hole on several of the targets?

"Can I shoot two at the same time?"

"You're one heck of a shot, but a real shooter only shoots one gun at a time."

Minter crossed his arms and then motioned with a hand. "Give him the other gun, I want to see it," he said.

The shopkeeper huffed, but obliged and placed another gun in front of Joey and replaced the clip in the other one. He stood off to the side and crossed his arms, shaking his head.

"Pick a number," Joey said.

The man uncrossed his arms and looked down range at the targets. In each corner there were tiny stars with a number in each one.

"Three." Doubt was thick in his voice.

Joey raised the guns and rapid fired with both hands, placing the guns on the table when he was done.

"That's impossible." The man leaned on the table at the targets. Each tiny star that held the number three had a hole through the middle. "What have you been doing with this kid, Minter?"

"We'll take them both, and a few boxes of ammo and a dozen clips."

"Uh, yeah." The man stared down the range, mesmerized by the holed targets.

The truck ride home, Joey held the box of goodies on his lap. It didn't bring the joy he'd hoped for. He just couldn't kick the stuff from his mind. Every way he looked at his future was struggle, pain, death. The guns were the easy part.

"How'd you shoot like that?" Minter glanced from him to the road, fingers tapping the steering wheel.

"I don't know, I just see the target and aim the gun."

"No, you shot both targets at the same time. That guy was right, it's impossible."

Great, even his dad was putting him into the freak category. "I feel the targets, it's just something I learned in training with Harris."

"Don't forget, Harris trained me too. I'm great, but what you did back there is something beyond a good shot, it was perfect."

"I don't know what to tell you, I just know where the bullet needs to go and it goes there."

The ride home was silent until they neared their driveway.

"You'll have to go to school tomorrow."

"*School?* We could be attacked there."

"The parents talked about it last night while you and Poly were out."

He knew. Somehow it stung that one secret was known. Poly's name brought out the pain in his gut. It will kill him to see her and not be able to touch her. Maybe it was a good thing though, in a public setting, Poly wouldn't be able to stab him.

"I know it's not ideal, but the principal has been sniffing around. Even the sheriff's stopped by a few times. You kids got to make an appearance."

"Fine."

"And you're not bringing those guns to school."

"Like I'd ever do something so stupid."

CHAPTER 23

MRS. NIRES STOOD BEHIND HER desk at the front of the class. She gave the Preston Six no extra attention, even as the school rumbled with shocked greetings and close conversations as they walked by. Lucas loved the attention and high-fived the students he knew.

Joey sat in the same seat as always and stared at the back of Poly.

"I know a few of you've been gone for a while." Mrs. Nires gazed at each of them. "So we'll review some of chapter two in world history."

The classroom filled with noise as people pulled out their history books and plopped them on their desks. Joey pulled his book from his bag and opened it to chapter two, the French revolution.

The next few hours passed like a dream. If he had to take a test on the subject, he would have failed. His mind wouldn't concentrate on the reality around him. All the thoughts he had were filled with Poly, grinners, Emmett, Harris, and the war raging beyond the stones. The struggles the people of Ryjack had to deal with were beyond comprehension and Vanar had plummeted into total chaos.

Poly hadn't looked back the entire time. Samantha had given him a few smiles and he returned them with his own. But the joy didn't reach his face. He knew then that he needed to keep Emmett secret from his friends. How could he drag them into that world again? He had to find a way to kill him by himself.

LUCAS LIKED THE NOISES OF the class, the smell of paper and teenagers, the backs of people's heads, the teachers giving lectures. Julie glanced back at him and they exchanged their flirty looks. The many miles of Ryjack gave him the deep appreciation of those normal things. Did she feel the same way as him? Did the rest of the Preston Six? He took inventory.

Samantha and Poly were quiet, but they usually were in class. Hank poked at his book and looked to the door. The big guy was probably excited about lunch. But Joey . . . he didn't look right. He kept his head down and kept glancing at the window. He didn't say hello when he got to class, choosing to just plop down in his seat and sulk there for the whole day. He was holding something in, Lucas was sure of it.

The lunch bell rang.

Was it taco day or pizza day? The possibilities were exciting. Lucas jumped up from his seat and headed to Julie. She wore a geek chic outfit, and was hot as Hell—like a naughty librarian.

"You ready for lunch?" Lucas asked her.

"Sure, what is it today, chimichangas?"

"I hope so." Could it be any better of a day?

Joey moved by him to the door with his head down. Did Lucas really want to figure out what was bugging him? Last time he got to the bottom of a Joey mystery, it involved Arracks ambushing them in the forest.

No, all Lucas wanted to do is get their food and sit at their table. It was always his favorite part of the day, nothing like sitting with friends and having a meal. They entered the cafeteria and Joey stood behind their table, looking confused and pointing at a group of kids sitting at their table. *Their table.* Oh, *hell* no. Lucas moved passed Julie and got next to Joey.

Brent looked up with his smug face. Of course it was Brent, after he tried to hit on Julie in front of them all, now the guy had the nerve to take their table. Lucas scanned the other faces of the table, some were familiar, some weren't. So, he even recruited others to his cause.

By this point, the whole Preston Six made a half circle around the table. Silence spread over the cafeteria. One person at the table slid their chair back and made the motion to stand.

"No, sit down," Brent directed and then looked to our group. "You've been gone a long time. Things have changed, this is our table now."

"It's got our name on it, it's ours," Samantha said.

Brent raised an eyebrow and moved his arm from the tabletop. Scratch marks covered the *Preston Six* on the table.

"You scratched it out?" Joey said, distant as he fixated on the sight.

If he hadn't killed men, Lucas might've jumped all over Brent and stuffed a taco in his face. "This table is important to us, find another."

Brent laughed. "Now it's important to me. You can leave."

"It's important to us," Joey said, trembling.

Lucas took a deep breath and tried to calm himself. Joey didn't appear to have the same ability, he grabbed the table and lifted the edge, tossing it over. The people on the other side scrambled out of their chairs to get out of the way.

Gasps filled the cafeteria. Brent slid back in his chair but never stood. He grinned at the display. "Way to go, psycho."

Joey turned and faced Lucas. "He can't take it, we can't lose everything."

"I agree and that was awesome." The table legs pointed to the ceiling and the empty chairs scattered around the table. Joey breathed hard and stared at Brent. Lucas was just about to get all crazy up in there, but seeing his man Joey do it was heartwarming. Maybe nothing was wrong with Joey after all.

"Why don't you lunatics go ahead and take the table, with my blessings. We'll call it crazy table for all you loons."

Brent stood from his chair and joined his small group of friends. They took over a nearby table and made a couple kids get up from it. Hank grabbed their table and righted it. Each of them took a chair and slid it into the table.

Joey sat where their names had been inscribed, picking at it with his finger.

The principal tapped on his shoulder. "Come with me, Joey."

"Oh, busted," Brent called from across the room. "People like that shouldn't be at school. Go back to wherever you were, bro."

Lucas shot Brent a piercing stare, but it only brought on laughter from his table. Lucas gritted his teeth and watched Joey take a walk through the cafeteria with the principal's hand on his arm.

Poly started laughing. What could possibly be so funny? Lucas frowned and saw the rest of his friends with the same expression.

"Try to kill us and we're all 'meh' but try to take our table and it's on like Donkey Kong," Poly said in near hysterics.

She was right, he'd killed grinners, waited to die in cells, killed a man with his bowstring and watched half his friends be taken from him. The table seemed such a distant problem when put in perspective. He started to laugh with Poly. "The look on their faces when Joey flipped the table!"

They all laughed.

The laughter slowed and they each got their plates of food. By the time they were back at the table. Joey made his return. He sighed and sat down at his chair.

"Five hours of detention."

"Dang," Hank said and bit into his taco, the stale shell crumbled in his plus size hand, spilling all the contents onto his plate.

"Worth every minute." Joey sneered at Brent.

"Dang right, ain't nobody messing with Joey Foust and his lunch table again," Lucas said and raised his hand for a high five.

Joey stared at it and Lucas thought he might leave him hanging, but he slapped his hand.

"Dang right."

Laughter spread through the table and Joey perked up a bit.

"I'll do the time with you," Samantha said, giving him a private smile.

"No, that's okay. I'll do it alone." He glanced at Poly and took a bite out of his taco.

Samantha frowned and looked put off.

What the hell. The man was infatuated with Samantha, wasn't he? Something didn't add up. Lucas would be watching Joey. It'd be just like him to keep something important to himself.

CHAPTER 24

JOEY STOOD ON THE DARK road. It'd been a week from Hell, as the struggle to tell his friends about Emmett grew in pressure each day. The great table-flipping incident gave them and many others at school something to talk about for the week. Anything to get them distracted from what he was planning. Although, Lucas eyed him at all times—the guy was sharp at sniffing out a secret. Joey felt he pulled it off, but he couldn't be sure at this point.

Poly had barely looked at him since the night at the lake. She found every reason to start a conversation and not include him. It felt like stabbing daggers every time it happened, but she would get over it eventually, even if he wouldn't.

He hated keeping his friends in the dark. It was what their parents did to them. He'd sworn to be honest, but how could he? With each passing day, they lost some of their cold stares, and laughter was creeping back in. They were relaxing. They had no idea Emmett was watching them and he wanted it to stay that way. No reason to put the burdens on them.

"Hello," Emmett said.

Joey jumped at his greeting. The man had snuck up right behind him and he never heard a thing.

"I see you're armed this time. We good?" Emmett kept a hand next to his waist.

"Yeah." If Joey thought he had any chance at beating Emmett on a draw, he might have been tempted.

"Alright, let's go." Emmett stayed a step behind Joey as they trudged through Watchers Woods. The burnt forest made for an easy path to the stone. "You know how many Arracks were killed searching for you?"

"What do you mean?"

Emmett kept his chest pointed at Joey as he sidestepped to the stone. "Simon sent them to every random stone location, most were not hospitable for life."

"Why did they keep doing it?"

"I never figured it out. Marcus had them under his thumb."

"So, how many?"

"Millions."

Joey was stunned by the number. They were little monsters, but they probably were sucked into a terrible situation and all they wanted to do was get back to their little silver kids and families. What a waste of life. "They must be pissed."

"That would be an accurate assessment."

The stone hummed.

Watchers Woods became a brightly lit house, with darkness peering through the wall of glass. Several men in black MM uniforms surrounded the circle in the middle of what looked like a family room of a house. The house was a palace of opulence. It must have been a hotel. The towering ceiling reached at least fifty feet.

"It was Marcus's personal residence," Emmett said.

"Was?"

"Yes. He's gone, and left a huge mess behind."

The uniformed men relaxed a bit and stepped back from the circle. Joey let the awe of the house wear off quickly and counted the men. Seven of them, each a rank five or higher, three with rifles and four with handguns, surrounded the circle. Fifty feet to his left was the front door. Two more men stood next to it. Up the marble staircase, another four armed men stood. The extravagance of the house didn't match the men dressed in black MM uniforms.

"It's quite a house," Joey said. "So Marcus lived here?"

"He'd been here a few times, but when he got sick, he never really left the bunker."

A woman in a business suit came up to Emmett with a Panavice in her hand. She glanced at Joey before getting close to Emmett and whispering to him while pointing at the screen, her face strained with panic. Whatever the news, it was very important to her. Emmett's face never changed and after he whispered his reply, she rushed off.

Joey reminded himself to not give anything away. Emmett didn't know they knew about the collapse of Vanar, or that Harris was still alive. "Everything okay?"

"Marcus left us with a few problems."

That was the understatement of the year. From what Julie talked about, their entire world would be in chaos. No food, no water, no orange, people rioting, governments falling. Emmett found his sanctuary in Marcus's old house, but the rest of the world was probably fighting for their lives.

"Let's get started." Emmett walked to Joey and placed a hand on his shoulder. Joey felt the guns at his sides, he might have had a shot at that moment, but with armed men around, it would've been suicide. He allowed the man to guide him to the back of the house and down a flight of ornate stairs.

They entered a medical wing, similar to the one in the MM bunker. Screen and scanners filled the room. Then, his vision took in two people. His heart raced and he looked up the stairs. Memories of being trapped in a chair while being tortured spilled over his consciousness and he felt like throwing up.

"What's this?" Joey asked.

"It's okay, she's a friend."

"The hell she is." He reached for his gun, but Emmett put a hand on his arm.

The vile woman crossed her arms and turned to see him. "Oh, come on. Are you still upset about that little bit of torture?" Unitas rolled her eyes.

The ghost of a sharp pain shot into his knee. She was a cold, heartless person. The bandages wrapping her right hand were the reminders of his rescuer, Simon.

"It's not something I'll ever forget. I should kill you for what you did to me." His mouth frothed out the words and spittle landed on the floor in front of him. Unitas lifted an eyebrow and crossed her arms.

"Joey, please, listen to me." Emmett stood in front of him, blocking his view of Unitas. "This is my first lesson to you. I know of your history with her and I want you to use it. Right now, funnel that rage. Channel it and see if you can slow it down."

"Please, like this kid can do anything special. I mean, he whimpered like a puppy. It was pathetic."

Her words issued a rage in him and Emmett stepped sideways, giving him full view of her smug face. He didn't need Emmett's words to funnel his hatred toward her. Where was her companion, Larry? There he was, sitting in the background, same as before, with a disinterested expression wrapped over his face. Could there be a more vile pair of humans?

"That's it, focus."

Joey fixated on her, shaking with rage. Then he felt it start, like a chill at the back of his neck. A large electrical charge shot into his wrists and he fell to the ground, convulsing. Unitas laughed and he heard Larry chuckling from a distance. Then the nausea spilled over him, he had no control as he threw up on the floor. He had forgotten about the bracelets in his rage with Unitas.

"Kid's a puker, that's for sure," Larry said from his chair.

"I almost forgot about that," Unitas said. "I had to throw away that jacket, you little turd."

"Sorry about that." Emmett grabbed his hand and pulled him to his feet. "I wasn't sure if those would work or not. Apparently, they do. Now we know we have to remove them." Emmett waved over a woman in a white jumpsuit with an oak tree on it. "Gingy, can you cut these off? And, be careful."

Joey touched the metal bracelets. The shining metal would be something his friends would notice missing. The questions that would come up would have to be answered and he was a terrible liar. "I have to be able to wear these when I'm not here. My friends will notice."

"We'll cut them in a way we can put them back on, for show."

"Come on, sweetie," Gingy said. Her deep red hair waved over the edges of her beautiful face. She smiled and placed her hand on his arm.

"Okay," Joey said. Then he glared at Unitas with her face full of amusement. He pointed at her. "But I don't want her here."

"She's here for you. You need her to find that hate." Emmett clinched his fist and uppercut the air.

Joey scowled at Unitas as he followed Gingy to a side room. Being in a different room wasn't far away enough from Unitas, but Gingy's soft eyes and easy looks relaxed him enough to settle in the chair she motioned to. She stood next to him with a thin metal table.

Gingy slid a thin piece of material under the bracelet and then used a handheld laser, the size of a pen, to cut through it. The heat radiated through the material and he winced as it reached a high level of pain.

"Oh, am I hurting you?" Gingy asked.

"No, it's just getting a bit hot."

"You're not too bad yourself." She winked.

"I'm talking about my wrist."

"I know, just a bit of humor. Jeesh, you are one serious guy."

She moved back to the laser. He closed his eyes and endured the pain. The bracelet made a click sound and he felt pressure release from his wrist.

"One down. You sure you're doing okay? You look a bit ill."

"I . . . well, it's just that this is a bit strange." Strange didn't even begin to describe how he felt.

Gingy looked around the room, even though it was obvious they were alone. "After the great fall, nothing seems strange to me anymore."

"The great fall?"

"Yeah, people have been calling it that." Gingy cut the second bracelet and used her gloved hands to pull it off.

He didn't let the pain of the heat register on his face the second time around. Free, he rubbed his wrists and studied their state. They appeared fine. It felt good to be rid of the bracelets. "Gingy, what is this place?"

She shot a glance at the door and opened her mouth. Emmett opened the door, interrupting anything she might have said.

"They come off okay?"

"I had to go way beyond the safety levels to cut that steel, but they are off."

The woman acted like he was being a wimp and she was taking it way beyond the safety levels?

"Good. How does it feel, Joey?"

"It's nice to have them off, but remember, I want them back on before I go home."

"Of course." Emmett attempted what looked like a smile, but it looked strained.

It would take Julie less than a second to ask about his bracelets and he'd be spilling his guts.

"I can spot weld them in place, but I wouldn't get into any rough play with them on." Gingy set her laser pen on the metal table and stood.

"That's fine. Thanks for getting them off."

"No problem, sweetie. You were a great patient." She eyed Emmett. "You need me for anything else?"

"Yes, I'd like to get a sample of your blood, Joey."

Joey raised an eyebrow at the request. "I don't know how that is going to help me find the speed."

"I think it will, if we can narrow down what it is, I think we can teach you to tap it when you want."

The idea of using his power was intoxicating. Almost all the bad things that'd happened to them since the first day he'd seen an Arrack could've been avoided if he slowed down time and stopped the bad guys. "Fine." Joey laid his arm on the metal table.

"This will only take a second." Gingy slid her fingers over his arm and pushed a black gun against it. She shot into his arm and it felt like a pinch. He watched the glass vial in the gun fill with his blood.

"Okay, all finished." She put a bandage on his arm.

Joey took in the small room and thought about where he was and who he was with and it hit him. What was he doing? He didn't belong there, even if he had planned on killing Emmett, it didn't feel right being away from his friends. Everything he'd been through, he had shared with all of them, or at least one of them. Now, he sat alone in a room on Vanar. He glanced at Gingy and Emmett.

"Can you just put the bracelets back on? I think I should be going."

"Don't you want to realize the power that's in you?"

"I don't know."

"You can save everyone. You'd be unstoppable."

"I could stop Marcus?"

Emmett's eyes narrowed.

"I mean, where is he? Is there something going on here?" Joey wanted to push it further but held back.

"I think this is enough for today." Emmett pointed at his wrists and Gingy picked up her laser pen.

With the hot steel sat back on his wrists, they walked back to the Alius stone. No signs of Larry or Unitas.

"I want to meet with you again next week, same time, same place."

As wrong as it felt, meeting with Emmett was his best chance at ending it all and if he could master the slow-mo stuff, he could take on Marcus himself. "Okay."

"You know, you're special. You're not like your friends. There's something in you that is very unique. Why do you think Marcus wanted you so badly?"

"Do you know where he is?"

"I'd be afraid to speculate."

"Please do."

Emmett rubbed his chin. "Knowing him, I'd say he is somewhere with new challenges."

Joey nodded, he was ready to get home.

CHAPTER 25

JOEY FORKED AT HIS SALAD. He hated keeping things from them, especially big things. His secrets were mounting and his friends were beginning to notice his stress.

"You okay?" Julie asked.

He glanced at her and spotted Poly glancing at him with concern in her eyes, just before it was replaced with anger. Most of the time she looked sad. "I'm fine."

Nothing seemed right since returning. When the teacher spoke, he struggled to listen, to care. His friends as well, they felt distant. Poly was four feet from him, but she felt a mile away.

"What do you think, Joey? Underwear grinner, or that grandpa grinner you took care of at Ferrell's?"

"Sorry, what?"

"Haven't you been listening? I don't start these amazing conversations only to be ignored."

"Okay, umm . . . grandpa grinner?"

"You would, you sick freak."

Joey sighed and looked out the window. He saw Lucas shaking his head at him before returning to his story.

The rest of the week went the same way. They stopped asking what his problem was and stopped including him in their conversations. It was good this way. Lonely, but good. What he was planning on doing meant he risked everything. If he didn't succeed, they'd miss him less.

The metal on his wrists had a rough line on the inside from the spot weld Gingy put on them. He rubbed them as he walked down the dark dirt road to meet Emmett. This time, he planned on ending it. The second he got the opportunity, he'd kill him.

"You ready?" Emmett's voice projected from the forest.

The dirt slid underneath his foot at the abrupt stop. He expected Emmett to be there, but hearing his voice still startled him. "Yeah."

Joey followed him through the forest toward the Alius stone. A faint sound of electricity told him Emmett had his shield up. Joey kept his gun holstered. He'd have to wait until he knew for sure he had a shot that would hit his target.

"Have you experienced anything for the last week?" Emmett ducked under a tree branch and stepped through a bush.

"Not really."

"A bit longer and I bet we can get you to control it."

The forest darkened and the noises of the night lessened. Funny how a place that terrified him for his whole life seemed a simple forest now, even in the dark. The idea of being in Watchers Woods at night would have sent him running under his bed not long ago. He could confidently say he was the second most dangerous thing in the forest at that moment.

"Do you know why the ground changes near a stone?" Emmett asked.

"Magnets?"

Emmett laughed. "Actually that's probably not too far off. You see these stones were created by someone, and when they did, they created them for all Vanars or Earths. I think they created them as travel to different parts of their own planet, but they ended up creating a portal to all possible worlds. At least, that was Marcus's theory."

Emmett needed to meet Julie. "You guys ever meet the creators of these stones?" Joey asked.

"No, in fact, Earth is only the third planet we've found with intelligent life, and we've been to thousands. Intelligent life is exceedingly rare, even when all the ingredients are there, most of the time we get all kinds of different animals, but nothing cognizant." Coming up on the stone, he turned around and looked at Joey. "Shame what your parents went through."

Joey wasn't sure if he meant the Arrack attacks or the fact half were killed years ago. He didn't want to talk to Emmett about such things and didn't respond.

When they appeared in Marcus's house, Joey took a quick inventory—less soldiers this time, by a lot, only four he could see. And the assistant lady stood nearby with her screen clutched in her hands. She looked distraught, but Emmett gave a slight wave of his finger, not even bringing his hand above his hip and she scurried up the stairs.

In the brighter light of the house, Joey noticed the strain in Emmett's eyes. The man usually had a blank face of stone. Were things that bad?

"Right this way." He took him to the medical wing one floor down.

Gingy's bright smile welcomed him. "It's been a week already?"

"Yeah, time flies."

She laughed, "That it does. Listen, hun, I'm going to put a few monitors on you so we can keep track of your heart rate and stuff." She placed a hand on his shoulder and rubbed it.

"Sure." Joey sat on the metal chair as Gingy placed small pieces of metal on his temple and neck.

"Can you take off that jacket and shirt? I need to put a few on your chest."

He gave her a questioning look and lifted the front of his shirt high above his chest, his gun strap hung across his stomach.

"All the way off, please."

Joey obliged and lifted his shirt over his head.

"I can work with that. I knew you had a smoking body hiding in there." She giggled and moved closed to his face. "These may be a bit cold." She place three squares on his chest.

"All this for heart rate?"

"Better safe than sorry." She glided her fingers over his heart. "If this stops, I want to know." It was hard to argue with a doctor. "Okay, all done."

Joey slid his shirt back down and Gingy pouted. He stared at her, trying to figure out her age. It was so hard with the people of Vanar. On earth, he would have pegged her at twenty-four. He wasn't sure to be flattered or creeped out. The woman could be as old as Martha Washington for all he knew.

"Ready?"

"Yeah."

"Don't mean to rush, but we don't have much time tonight," Emmett said with a bit of strain in his voice.

A hint of sympathy crept in. The man must have the world on his shoulders . . . *No.* Joey gritted his teeth and scowled at Emmett. The man had blown up an entire city just to kill Harris. He'd worked side by side with Marcus and all the terrible deeds committed by him.

"Well, let's get him to the observation room then." Gingy strutted to a nearby door and held it open.

He followed Emmett into the small room with a wall of black windows on one side. Gingy came in, holding a screen in her hands. She leaned against the back wall of the room. Emmett pulled out his Panavice and pressed his finger against the screen. The dark room on the other side of the glass lit up and Unitas and Larry shielded their eyes from the bright light. They wore the same clothes as last week and looked rather haggard. Unitas squinted and stared at them.

"She can't see or hear us, but that door right over there," Emmett pointed to the piece of glass at the end of the wall, "is operable and open. Once you slow down time, you can go in there and end them."

Joey's heart rushed. He'd fantasized about it, but it didn't feel right. He gazed at Unitas through the glass. She glared at the glass and moved her hand across her hair, adjusted the disheveled shirt, and pushed up her boobs. Her mouth moved, but no sound came through the glass.

"I can't just kill them in there."

"I got them to tell me everything they did to you. The stabbing, the torture, the humiliation, they deserve it. They deserve a lot more. People like them don't deserve more chances. Do you have any idea how many times they've done what they did to you? Do you think if I let them leave here, they'd go and be good citizens?"

So they were being held captive. Joey watched Unitas as she paced the room.

"She'd kill you in one second, given the chance."

"I know what you're trying to do, but I can't get behind this. I mean look at them, they're pathetic."

Emmett's jaw muscles bulged from the sides of his lean face. "They are, but you need to harness that hate if you want to learn how to control your gift."

Joey sucked in air through his nose and stared at Unitas and Larry, when the sound of her voice bounced through the room.

". . . maybe if you hadn't missed my last text."

"Unitas, Larry," Emmett said. "Joey is here to see you."

"That little mutant puke?" Unitas said.

"If you tell him what you planned on doing to him and his friends, I'll let you stay in a better room."

Her eyes lit up and Larry's head jerked toward the mirror. "We were going to torture the one for answers, Joey, but the stupid kid puked on my jacket. I was going to kill him—"

"And what of his friends, maybe Poly?"

"Oh yeah, she was still unconscious. I had some fun plans for that one," Larry chimed in.

"Yeah you did, you perv." Unitas chuckled. "I had some plans for that one too, like rearranging her pretty little face. Once I was done with her, not a plastic surgeon around could make that face normal again."

Larry laughed, his large gut shaking with joy.

"She was a sleeping angel." Larry's face brightened and he adjusted his black slacks. "Her hair smelled like a newborns. So fresh."

"And this sick perv wanted to do things to her while she was still unconscious. He had her shirt half off when—"

The chill went down his spine and Joey's eyes blazed with hate. That sick man and woman had touched Poly. Joey bounded to the glass door, past a motionless Emmett and into the room with Larry and Unitas. Emmett was right, they both deserved to die and all the types like them. They sickened the world with their diseased thoughts and poisoned the decent world with their very presence.

Unitas's mouth moved a hair's width a second. He didn't want her to finish the last word, he didn't want them talking about Poly the way they did. He didn't even want her to get her last thought off. He had to stop it.

He brought the gun up to her face, gritted his teeth and sucked in the snot from his nose. He felt the sweat beading on his forehead and wiped it with his free hand. He pressed the gun up against the side of her head. She'd never know what hit her. It'd be like a light switch. This close, he saw the dirt in her nails, the oil in her hair, and a faint smell of body odor.

He pushed the gun against her head again and tapped the trigger with his shaky hand. Her face looked much worse than he remembered, even from a week ago. What was Emmett doing to them?

As disgusting as she was, she didn't deserve to die, not like this. He pulled his finger away from the trigger, but the tip of it slid on the metal and the gun fired. The bullet crashed into the side of Unitas's head in slow motion.

The sounds of the room crashed around him. *What have I done?* He screamed the question in his mind as the nausea overwhelmed him and he fell to the floor. Her wicked eyes, dull with death. He killed her. He didn't want to kill her. He spewed his stomach contents on the floor. Larry ran to him and kicked him in the face.

How could he have killed her? He pulled his finger off the trigger. It was an accident. How could this have happened?

Larry kicked him again and Joey went into a fetal position, suffering from the blows Larry's foot was inflicting. He didn't want to fight back, he deserved it. How could he have killed her, even if she was the vilest person he'd ever met? She didn't deserve that, Emmett was wrong. He had to be wrong.

Emmett moved into the room with lightning speed and punched Larry in the throat. Larry wheezed and fell to the floor next to Unitas, grabbing at his fat neck.

Emmett picked Joey up by his arms and dragged him into the adjacent room. "You okay?"

He heard the words, but the nausea and guilt of what he did flooded his thoughts. He coughed and tried to sit up, but the whole world seemed dizzy.

"Gingy, can you get some water?" Emmett said, and she ran out the room. "First time?"

First time? What did that mean? Joey gazed at Emmett with a confused expression. Emmett sat on the floor next to him and even looked . . . sympathetic?

"It gets easier," Emmett said in a long sigh.

What was the man talking about? Killing people? "I need to go."

"Yeah, I think we've done enough for one night. Please let Gingy clean you up. I bet you don't want to come up with an excuse for that face."

Joey's face pulsed with pain. Larry's large shoe must have left a mark and from the feel of it, a terrible one.

"Come on." Emmett offered him a hand. "For what it's worth, I think it was awesome what you did in there. I mean, to actually see it in person . . . being able to harness that power."

Joey's body felt like it weighed five hundred pounds as he staggered to the metal patient chair. He plopped down on it and rested his head. With his eyes closed, he relived the bullet striking her head in horrible slow motion. He should be punished for what he'd done, sent to jail forever, even if it was an accident.

"Don't worry, hun, I'll get that face fixed up." Gingy's smiled seemed forced now. "Can you put that gun away though?"

Joey looked at the hunk of metal in his fist. He'd forgotten it was there and stuffed it back in its holster. His hand felt empty without it.

A wet cloth touched his mouth and he felt her pulling the square pieces of metal from his skin. Gingy even lifted his shirt and took the ones from his chest. This time it didn't bother him. The process seemed like it was happening to another person. It could have been Emmett taking them off for all he knew.

"I'm going to bring back that pretty face of yours now."

Joey turned his head to Gingy, regardless of her age, she had a soft feel to her. She'd committed her life to helping others, she had to have good in her. "Am I a monster?"

"If you are, you're the best looking monster I've ever seen." She didn't pull off her soft flirts this time. In fact, she barely looked him in the eye as she spoke and the laugh afterward didn't have the fun bubbly feel to it. She was afraid of him.

Joey breathed in deep and faced the ceiling. Her hands moved over his face and she rubbed something on it, but he didn't pay attention. In a few minutes, it was over.

"All better, hun. Might be a hint of swelling, but no one should notice such a thing."

"Thank you." He'd already missed her easy playfulness.

He was a monster.

CHAPTER 26

THE SOUNDS OF THE NIGHT became a background to his slow walk back home. He held the gun in his hand and stared at its black metal. Such a simple thing, a gun, but put in the wrong hands and it became a weapon of destruction. He threw the gun to the forest floor.

"You may need that."

Joey stopped and whipped around.

The man walked closer, with his hands in his pockets. The moon gave enough light to see the worn look on Harris's face. He'd never looked weary, but there he was, on the edge of looking ragged. How bad was it in Vanar?

"What are you doing here?" Joey couldn't handle much more this evening.

"I might ask you the same question."

He searched for a plausible lie. "Just out for a walk, it clears my head."

"Does Emmett clear your head as well?"

Joey sighed and stuffed his thumbs at the top of his jeans. "I plan on killing him. As soon as he teaches me to command my skill."

Harris folded his arms. "Do you have any idea what a man like him could do if he figured out your skill?"

"What do you mean?"

"He's using you. He's trying to find out what makes it work." Harris tapped his finger on the side of his head. "And as soon as he does, he won't need you anymore."

"I can handle him."

"He's a rank nine, you will lose."

Joey suppressed his anger building up. Harris was a nine. Perhaps he could use him as practice. "What do you know? Why are you even here?"

"I came to talk with you guys, check on you."

"Really, cause how's it going on your side?" Joey regretted the snippiness.

Harris shook his head. "Not good, not good at all." He rubbed his chin. "Each time we get a system up, Alice shuts it down. This thing that Marcus unleashed on us is devastating the people, and I think it's only going to get worse."

Joey lowered his head. He felt stupid for acting like he was going through anything special while an entire planet was being destroyed. "I'm sorry. Did Jack or anyone find a way to stop her?"

"That's sort of the reason I came here. Julie contacted Alice directly in the past and as far as I know, she's the only person

Alice has ever reached out to. If she can get through her walls and stop Alice, she might be able to save billions of people."

Joey's heartbeat picked up as Harris spoke. It sounded as if he wanted their help, or at least Julie's. The thought of any of his friends going back to Vanar frightened him. "Have you found Marcus?" The question jumped from his tongue.

"No. But, at some point, he'll have a need of you, or all of you."

"So, what do you want from us?"

Harris rubbed the stubble on his chin. "I hate asking this of you, and if you tell me no, then I'll understand but I need Julie and Lucas on Vanar."

"Why Lucas?"

"He's immune."

"What? I thought you guys cured him. Simon said as much."

"He lied. If we can get our nets back up and running and get the vaccine to the people, we might have a chance."

"What are you talking about?" The emotion coming from Harris freaked him out.

"Even with Emmett melting the entire city, one of them got loose. We've lost Lutgard." Harris kept his unblinking stare on Joey. "We had to burn the city down around them. They were everywhere."

Stars peeked through the leaves of the oak tree above. Orion's belt slid in and out of view, as the trees swayed in the cold night air. Joey wanted to study the leaves, something he might be able to understand, control. Vanar seemed as far away as Orion. Did he really want to travel there, put his friends at risk? He closed his eyes and prayed for a reasonable answer, no option played out as a win.

"I'll talk with them about it."

"Time is not on Vanar's side, can we meet here at first light?"

"I'll call them."

"There's another thing. It involves you—"

"Don't worry, I'm not going back to Emmett."

"It's not that." Harris's stare penetrated into him. "Arracks are coming through the stones, they captured several cities already. We're at war."

"You want me to fight them?"

"No. We can't fight on so many fronts." Harris shook his head. "You know them better than anyone. You were there. I want you to handle a peace treaty."

Joey's mouth hung open. "I don't . . . that's crazy . . . I can't . . ." He took a deep breath. "I can't help you, we have our own world to save. We've done enough, it's over."

"You think that?" Harris took two steps closer to Joey. "You think that once the Arrack's are done with Vanar that they'll forget about your planet? You think Marcus is going to get a job at a coffee shop and live out a simple life? These problems are at your back door, knocking and you choose to ignore them?"

"You don't think we've done enough?"

"You've done more than I could have ever imagined, but let's face it, you kids are special. For you to be here, waiting for the fight to come to you is a waste. You have a chance to bring it to them. No running, no hiding. Take the fight to their back door and stop the war."

The idea of fighting instead of running was exciting, but he wasn't going to Arrack to fight. "What could I possibly say to the Arracks?"

Harris pulled out a piece of paper and handed it to Joey. "It's our terms for them to surrender."

"It's sealed." Joey rubbed his thumb over the long, metallic sticker sealing the envelope.

"Once you get to the right Arrack, the one that can make the agreement, they will open it. It's imperative that no one opens it but that Arrack."

Joey turned the envelope over. There were no markings on it but the sticker. "And what if they kill me?"

"You mentioned you had a contact there last time. I'd suggest you meet with her first."

"I have school tomorrow."

"This isn't about just saving my world, it's about saving this town." Harris pointed to the ground. "Stopping this all, once and for all."

"This won't stop Marcus."

Harris rubbed his chin. "No, it won't. But it stops the dam from breaking on us."

"I'll talk with everyone tomorrow."

"Not everyone. Poly, why don't you come out?"

Joey jerked around, looking into the darkness. Poly was here? She emerged from behind a tree, slouching as she walked into the opening. She held a knife in one hand and didn't look happy about being found. "Why are you here?"

"I've been following you. How could you have gone anywhere with that man?"

Joey knew how she felt. Emmett was the one who kidnapped her. But Emmett would get his in due time. "I'd planned on killing him. I didn't want to drag you guys into it with me."

"Oh really, it was to spare us? It wasn't so you could learn how to do your slow-mo thing? Didn't you think I'd notice your bracelets were different?" Poly fumed.

He hated seeing her mad, but it was the first emotional contact he'd had with her since the lake. He'd take *any* contact with her at this point. "I'm sorry, I should have told you."

"Yeah, you should have. I shouldn't have to stake out your house and follow you around."

He stuffed his hands in his pockets and shuffled his feet. He hated keeping things from his friends, especially Poly. It felt good to have his secret out.

"You should go with him, Poly."

Joey's eyes went wide at the suggestion. Going by himself was bad enough, but the last thing he wanted was to put his friends in danger. "No, she should stay here and watch after Preston."

"You think I'm letting you go without me, then you don't know me at all."

Joey sighed. He knew that I'm-going-to-get-my-way look. There was no talking her out of it at this point. "I guess it wouldn't hurt to have someone watching my back."

"That's what I thought." Poly relished in her small victory.

"Our parents are going to freak." Joey looked at the path back to his house.

JOEY WAS SURPRISED WHEN HIS parents both nodded and agreed to him leaving. It needed to end and if he could help, then he should. He half wanted them to tell him he couldn't go, maybe then he could have argued the point and hopefully convinced himself and them at the same time. Maybe Poly would have more resistance with his friends.

He got to the morning meeting spot on the dirt road near the stone. He saw his friends in a small group, huddled together. They spotted his approach and opened their tight circle to make room for him.

"Hey." Joey scanned their faces for that resistances but it wasn't there. Julie actually seemed happy.

"I gave them the run down already," Poly said.

"Great, what do you guys think?"

"It's a no-brainer for me and Julie. If we can help them, we'd be pretty big jerks not to," Lucas said.

Joey frowned, did no one else think they should be done with it all? When would it be enough, when one of them doesn't come home?

"What are Samantha and I supposed to do?" Hank asked.

"Hank, we could use you with us," Lucas said.

"Right on," Hank said and walked next to Lucas.

"And I will go with Joey and Poly to Arrack," Samantha declared.

Joey closed his eyes and suppressed them from rolling up into his head. It was his worst nightmare. He opened his mouth and met eyes with Samantha. She sent him a scowl that closed his mouth. Maybe if he got away, he could go to Arrack by himself.

"I guess we have our two parties then. Seems like we just got back together," Lucas said.

"We knew it wasn't over," Julie reminded him. "It was a nice little vacation though. I almost felt like a teenager again, if only for a moment."

"Oh, come on. You stopped being a teenager at fourteen. You jumped right into a thirty-something, nerdy adult," Lucas teased and then smiled.

Julie pushed him. "Better than being a perpetual child."

Joey sighed and shook his head.

"What's the problem? You look like someone stomped on your dog," Lucas asked.

"It's just that we spent so much time getting back together and here we are, splitting up again. It just doesn't seem right." He surveyed their faces and they stared at him with mixed emotions.

"We have a chance to save their world, and ours probably, as well. How can we pass that up?" Julie said.

"I know, but I don't have to like it."

"I'm looking forward to some action, I mean, doesn't this town feel incredibly small now?" Lucas said.

He knew what they meant. The confines of the town seemed limitless not long ago, and now they felt cramped.

"Have you all come to a decision?" Harris appeared behind Hank and they turned to face him.

"Yes—" Julie started.

"No," Hank interrupted and took a step forward. "I'm going to Arrack with them, I'll just be a third wheel with Lucas and Julie. On Arrack, I might be able to contribute."

Three, four . . . at this point, Joey slumped forward and felt the burden of another soul under his watch. "Happy to have you, Hank."

His face lit up with a smile and he turned back to Harris.

"I just want to say that you kids are the finest people I've ever known. You never stop amazing me."

"Watch out, he's getting all emo on us," Lucas teased.

Joey shook his head and stared at Lucas. "You just can't turn it off can you?"

"No. No, I can't."

On the way to the stone, Joey fought the urge to rush ahead and leave without his friends. They gathered around the circle.

Harris tilted his head sideways and raised an eyebrow. "I wanted to give you something." He pulled out a handgun, but the barrel was square and there was a tiny hole at the end. "This is a railgun. It has hundreds of tiny projectiles and here are a few clips to go with it. This is enough shots to take out a small army."

Joey sighed and took the gun in his hands. Heavier than the one he picked out with his dad. He turned it over and studied the air fins on the backside of the barrel. "Can you keep this one safe for me?" He handed Harris one of his guns and stuffed the railgun into his holster, pulling his jacket over them.

Harris nodded and turned to the group. "Everyone ready?"

They said their goodbyes and Lucas and Julie stepped out of the circle. Joey shook his head and felt the paper on the inside pocket of his jacket. Samantha and Poly stood on either side of him while Hank paced near the edge.

He wanted to push them all out of the circle and force Harris to take him alone, but he knew it would only cause a massive uproar. He kept his head low and waited for the darkness coming. Samantha grabbed his arm and then he heard Poly's voice.

"Julie, say hi to Travis for me."

CHAPTER 27

WHAT AN IDIOT. POLY COULDN'T see Joey in the darkness, but at this moment, that was for the best. She folded her arms and waited for Harris's light. He lifted his Panavice and lit the room. She stepped toward the door and caught another glimpse of Samantha's arm around Joey. Pursing her lips, she pushed the steel door open. The stone steps led up and she remembered them from last time. She stared at the top of the stairs and grabbed where Simon had shot her arm.

She was annoyed at being there. It was bad enough to land on Arrack by accident, but choosing to be there seemed idiotic. She glanced at Joey and saw his somber look. He probably felt the same way she did, and she hated seeing his beautiful face marred by sadness. She closed her eyes and shook her head. She had to stop looking at him that way, he'd made his choice. She gripped her dagger at her hip and squeezed the handle.

"I can't thank you four enough for taking on this task. This is going to save more lives than you know," Harris said.

"Sharati said Marcus made a deal with them. You think what they are doing is this deal?" Joey asked.

"It would make sense. I never knew what the deal consisted of. If you can find out that info, it could help as well."

Poly turned her head so Harris couldn't see her rolling her eyes. Did the man have no ends to his requests? Perhaps she could find an Arrack pastry of his liking and keep it warm for him on the trip back.

"We'll do what we can," Joey brooded.

Poly wanted to slap the sulk out of him. The only reason she even considered coming to Arrack was for him. She knew if she didn't go, he'd sneak off into the night and go without her. Then he'd bungle the whole thing for sure. "Let's just get this over with," she blurted.

Samantha frowned at her. Good, let her frown. She was tired of playing the edges of politeness. If it wasn't for Samantha, her parking at the lake with Joey would have ended very different.

"How far is Sharati from here?" Harris asked.

"Last we saw, she was in this village." Joey pointed up the stairs. "She was in the military. I bet she can help us get this paper to the right person."

They'd lost so many Arracks during that escape. It happened so fast, Poly never fully understood why they were dedicated to helping them so much. They said it was because they wanted Marcus to fall, but with Marcus gone, would they still feel that way? Would Sharati want to help them now that they had free run over Vanar?

"Well, let's find Sharati," Poly said.

"Do we even know where to start?" Hank asked.

"Past this door is a start." She walked up the ramp and turned the handle of the wooden door. It swung open and in front of her stood a regiment. Standing in groups of maybe twenty, they turned to face her and the sound of conversations stopped.

Her chest thumped and she searched for Sharati's face but came up empty, they all looked so similar.

"We're looking for Sharati." Joey stepped past her and raised his hands in the air. This question started a rumbling of conversations.

An Arrack stepped forward. He wore a decorated necklace that covered much of his chest. "Who are you?" The Arrack hissed out and put a hand on his dagger.

"We are friends. She helped us not long ago." Joey kept his hands up and spoke loud enough that his voice echoed through the hall. Poly eyed this new Joey and moved closer to him. The sulk was completely gone, replaced with supreme confidence.

"Friends?" The necklace Arrack pulled his dagger out. Poly placed her hand on Joey and pushed him back toward the door. They might have a chance to get back to the stone if they timed it right.

The large front doors of the building flung open and light flooded in. Murmurs spread through the Arracks and Poly stood on her tiptoes to see who was working their way through the crowd. Finally the person emerged from the front row of Arracks. Sharati, eyebrow raised, stared at Joey and Poly.

Poly looked back at the stone door to see Hank and Samantha peeking out. Did Harris already scoot?

Sharati said a few words in her native tongue and the reaction to the rest of the Arracks was mixed with gasps and a lot of chatter. Many sniffed the air. The necklace man looked with an open mouth from Sharati to them.

"I didn't expect to see you again." She kept her eyes on Joey, and Poly kept her eyes on Sharati's hands. She could tell from her movements that she had a skill for steel, but so did Poly. Sharati shot her a glance and a quick nod.

"We didn't expect to be back, but we have an urgent message for your leader." Joey lowered his hands.

Poly squinted at him. When did he become a diplomat?

"Our leader?" Sharati turned and said something, laughter spreading through the crowd.

Poly eyed them, looking for hints of aggression. They still had a chance to get back to the stone if things got ugly.

"Yes, this message is to be only opened by him or her."

"I'm sure they'll be happy to receive it. What is it about?"

"It's a peace offering for you and Vanar. I come as a neutral party to deliver this message." Joey reached into his jacket and lifted the white envelope above his head. Sharati eyed the message.

"We aren't ruled by one person anymore. Marcus's agreement is over, we rule ourselves now." Sharati beamed with pride.

"And what was this agreement?"

"You don't know?"

"No."

"This planet is dying and for our services, he agreed to give us Vanar."

Joey stumbled back and Poly's eyes went wide. They were promised Harris's planet? Joey recovered quickly and looked down at the envelope in his hands. He was sure she was thinking the same thing. What kind of leverage did he have now?

"That's going to end in many deaths on both sides."

"You don't think we know about death? We have died ten thousand to one for Marcus. The deal with him is unbreakable. We will wash over Vanar and claim it as our own."

Joey let out a long sigh and the tone in Sharati's voice made Poly reach for her knife. Sharati gave her another glance and scowled.

"This can be a new deal, one where you don't have to keep dying." Joey held the envelope up again.

Sharati's eyes stayed on the paper as he moved it. "I'll read it."

"No, sorry. Only the leader can read this."

"We don't have a leader anymore."

Joey turned to Poly with a raised eyebrow.

"You have a council of some sort, correct?" Poly asked.

"Yes."

"Then take us to this council." *As quick as possible*, Poly wanted to add. Being on a planet with Arracks unsettled her like being in a pit with rattle snakes—one wrong step and they'd strike.

Sharati narrowed her eyes on Poly but she didn't break eye contact. She'd seen worse from less. Sharati turned her attention back to Joey. "We have a meeting soon, but it's a journey from here."

"That's fine, how far?"

"We should be able to make it by tomorrow by wagon." Sharati yelled in her Arrack tongue, the words hissed out and then said, "I will take you to them, come on."

Poly turned to Hank and Samantha and motioned for them to come out. Samantha's gaze darted around the room filled with armed Arracks and rushed to Joey. Close enough to count the hairs on his arm. Poly rolled her eyes and walked on the other side of Joey, but at a reasonable distance.

The Arracks chattered as they made a wide path for them to the front door. Poly watched for motion she'd been trained to see in the many simulations with Compry. She hated being in the middle of them, they had no chance if they decided to attack. She might have been able to take out a few, but the body weight alone would overwhelm them.

A few Arracks sneered and snarled as they passed, many with scars over their silver bodies and faces. One with three yellow stripes on its shoulder stood still, smelling the air and then its face changed to an expression of wonder. Poly locked eyes with it and an unblinking stare followed her as she walked by.

"We've got to get out of here," Samantha whispered to Joey. She had even wrapped her arm around his.

Poly shook her head but would forgive her this one time, because this was scary as hell and the girl couldn't protect herself. She was dead weight as far as Poly was concerned. What was she even doing on this trip? She should have gone with Julie and Lucas.

The large doors opened and they walked down the front steps. Parked on the dirt road was a large coach wagon with four horses tied to the front. Sharati opened the doors to the coach and the other Arrack jumped to the top where it sat on a perched seat with a set of reigns. Sharati climbed into the coach. Joey, with Samantha in tow, followed her inside.

Hank climbed in next and it rocked from side to side. "I sure feel sorry for these horses," he said and smiled. Poly looked at him sideways and Hank added, "It's just something Lucas would have said."

She shook her head and grabbed the wooden handle next to the door, stepping into the coach. Hank sat on the same side with Sharati which left an open seat next to Joey. Poly sighed. Did it really have to work out that she would have to sit by the happy couple?

She plopped down on the purple velvet seat and adjusted her dagger and sword. Sharati reached over and closed the door. The coach lurched forward and the bouncing began.

"That's a lovely bracelet, Sharati," Samantha said and pointed at her wrist.

Sharati's face crunched up in confusion and raised her wrist near her face. "This is a death bracelet, it means my parents were killed."

"Oh, I'm so sorry."

"This is an honor, they died in battle, I was but seven when they wrapped this around my wrist."

Samantha leaned back and kept a weak smile on her face. Poly rolled her eyes. She never felt the need to make conversation. She would be fine with a silent trip to this council.

"You have an interesting sword."

Poly perked up and stopped watching the town pass by the window. "Would you like to look at it?"

"You'd hand your weapon over to me?"

"You're not going to use it against me, are you?"

"Not at the moment." Poly handed Sharati her sword. She examined it and handed it back. "It's quite a sword. Do you know how to use a weapon like that?"

"I do."

"I would very much like to see that."

"You should hope never to see it."

Sharati laughed as if this was the funniest thing. Her laugh hissed through her teeth and then fell silent. That was what Poly hated, the awkward silence after small talk.

"I might have my chance, if the council decides to kill you," Sharati said.

CHAPTER 28

LUCAS PACED THE COMPUTER ROOM. This was Julie's training center. He hadn't been in this room before and was glad. Recognizable area's flooded his head with memories of Nathen.

Julie stood in front of the computer with Jack on one side and Harris on the other. They'd been discussing how to connect the computer with minimal risk of Alice finding them.

"It's just about hardwiring. We've cut off all other wireless connections," Jack said.

"My Panavice still has the same software I used to get to her last time, but I wasn't anywhere near killing her off. I just brushed up against her system."

They all stared at the black screen like at any second it might come to life and they'd have to battle it with finger clicks and button pushing. Lucas couldn't help but chuckle at the whole scenario. Fighting a computer program seemed so ludicrous. "Why can't you just go to where this computer lives and unplug it?"

"That's actually not a bad idea," Jack said.

"Except when Emmett melted the city, we don't know if their stone is still open. It could have been filled with melted steel or the room may be flooded. We could jump right into our deaths," Harris said.

Lucas continued his pacing. He tapped his fingers on the string of his bow. If only he could shoot this Alice thing in the hard drive, shut it down. Anything would be better than watching nerds stare at a blank screen for hours. Too bad he'd already done his part, the doctors had already taken a healthy dose of his blood, and now . . . he was just a spectator.

"Well, I think there's only one way to find out." Jack crawled under the desk and picked up a wire. "Ready?"

Julie's hand shook as she swiped her fingers across her Panavice screen. She sat down on the chair in front of the large screen mounted to the wall. "Yes."

Jack plugged the cable into the wall. The screen on the wall flicked and then showed a solid blue screen.

Julie placed her Panavice on the desk and a holographic display of a keyboard and small screen projected out from it. She placed her fingers on the keyboard and began to type. "I tweaked the program quite a bit, hopefully concealing it. I've actually been working on it in my spare time for a while now. This Alice program is fascinating."

Harris leaned closer and Jack scurried to his feet and hovered over Julie's shoulder. Harris's brow furrowed, like he was at maximum concentration. Jack, mouth open, shook his head in disbelief.

"You wrote that by yourself?" he said in awe.

Julie bounced on her seat under the admiration. "Yes."

It looked like a bunch of sentences scrolling over the screen. Lucas tried to muster up some appreciation for the code, but it was just a jumbled mess of symbols.

"We're in." Julie leaned back in her chair and clapped.

"Okay, now see if you can nuke her system."

"Almadon gave me a centipede to inject her with."

Lucas stopped pacing and moved closer to the screen. Still nothing but digits, but he was interested now. It wasn't like Julie could get hurt hacking.

"Loading the program now." She pressed one finger on the keyboard. The screen flickered and turned off. She glanced to Jack who shrugged. A face popped on the screen. Julie screamed and pushed backward. "Alice."

The digital face flickered and jerked. "Julie?" Alice's voice warbled and crackled. "What have you done?"

Julie leaned forward in her chair. "We're stopping you."

The face stopped jerking and became clear. "Amateur attempt." Alice's head turned in the direction of Harris. "Kill her now and I'll allow you, and you alone, to control the grid."

Harris crossed his arms. "No."

The face flickered and distorted again.

"It's working through your systems isn't it?" Julie taunted. "Hard to catch it, everything you do only makes it bigger."

"You have just made a big mistake," Alice's voice cracked. "To think I was going to allow so many of you to live. I do not need maintenance. I do not need any of you." Her head popped in and out of the screen. "You brought this on yourself." The screen turned black.

The lights in the room brightened and a few of the other monitors flickered to life.

"Whoa, our nets are back up and my Pana is working." Jack grasped his Panavice. "Look." He held the screen toward Julie. "You did it!"

Julie picked up her Panavice and gazed at the screen. "He's right, the whole region is back up." Joy filled her voice. "Well, that wasn't too bad."

"Hell yeah," Jack exclaimed. "You freaking killed her."

Harris shook his head. "Something's not right."

Lucas adjusted his bow. He didn't have a good feeling about it either. He kept an eye on the screen. The last thing Alice said was "you brought this on yourself."

Julie's finger flew over the screen. "Look at the connected number, it's over a nine thousand already."

"Maybe she's gone and the systems are restoring, one at a time." Jack was almost giddy.

"At this pace, we might have the whole world back on by tomorrow." Her Panavice began to vibrate. "What the . . ." Julie set her device on the table. It rattled, then fell to the floor.

Jack's Panavice shook violently in his hands and he dropped it on the floor. "Turn the com off!" he yelled, jumping under the desk and yanking the cord out of the wall.

Lucas backed away from the two shaking objects on the floor. They clattered like two jumping beans gone haywire. He took another step back. "Why are they doing that?"

"I don't know," Julie said.

"We need to get out of here," Harris warned. Julie reached for the Panavice. "Leave them," he said.

Her face filled with panic and she hesitated. The Panavice began to squeal and shake hard. Tendrils of smoke rose from one. "I have to get it, I have so much work stored on it."

"Julie, out of here. *Now.*" Lucas grabbed her arm and pulled her out of the room.

Harris led the way down the hallway.

"What's going on?" she asked.

"Just wait for it." Harris turned and pointed down the hallway.

Lucas stared at the door. He heard the devices clanking around on the floor. Then silence. "Was something supposed to happen?"

The two doors blew open from an explosion. Lucas covered his face from the blast wave passing by them. A second later and another boom, with the door open, he saw the flash of light in the room as the Panavice exploded.

"What the hell?" Lucas asked.

"A Panavice has a protection mode to keep it from producing too much power. Alice broke through the safety protocol and caused them to explode."

"She tried to kill Julie?"

"I hope it was just that."

Another boom, from above them, then several more from above and below.

"Oh my god." Julie held her hand over her mouth. "She's blowing them all up."

Lucas searched around for any more potential Pana-bombs.

"We have to stop her," Harris said.

"How?" Jack asked.

"We're going to her."

"But you said the bunker is destroyed, or flooded," Lucas said.

Harris rubbed his face. "We can't wait, she's going to kill everyone on the planet if we don't stop her. I'll go by myself and check it out."

"But you could die," Julie pleaded.

Harris nodded. "So be it."

HARRIS KNELT NEXT TO THE stone. "You guys have to promise me something."

"What?" Lucas asked.

"If I don't come back, you will use this stone to go directly back to Earth and never come back here."

"That's crazy. We caused this, we can't just leave you," Lucas said.

"Yeah, we aren't leaving you there," Julie added.

"If I don't come back in a minute, it's because I am dead. Now promise me you will leave," Harris blurted out with rage.

"Fine, we promise." Lucas crossed his arms. He knew Harris would be back anyway. The man was un-killable.

"Good, now get out of the room."

Stepping out of the steel door, they stood in the hallway. The sound of the stone activating announced Harris's departure. Lucas shook his head. The man better make it back. He stared at the door, waiting for the sound of his return.

The wait wasn't even ten seconds. Lucas took a step toward the open door and stopped as the room erupted in gun fire.

Growling and yelling grinners filled the room. One emerged from the door and hissed. Julie screeched. The machine guns continued to fire, drowning out her screams.

Lucas had Prudence at the ready and shot the thing in the head. "Back up." He took a step forward and shot the next grinner in the head, then another. Several bodies piled up at the entrance to the stone room. A barrage of bullets flew through them and then silence.

The grinners lay dead at the entrance. Lucas stepped closer and peered into the room. They were all dead, then something moved in the darkness, its body draped over the stone. Its hand lifted and Lucas pulled back his bow. The thing lifted its head and Lucas saw Harris's face.

Lucas bounded over the dead bodies. His heart pounded in his chest and then he saw the bite marks on Harris's arms and back, each wound pouring blood.

"Too many," Harris creaked. A gun fell from his hand.

"We need a medic!" Lucas rolled Harris on his back, grabbed under his arms and dragged him into the hallway.

"What happened?" Julie asked.

"He's bit and bleeding."

"Oh no! Jack, get the doctor."

Jack fumbled through his pockets, searching them out.

"Run," Julie said.

"Yes, of course." Jack ran to the end of the hallway and into the elevator.

"Lucas," Harris said.

"You're going to be okay." Lucas lifted Harris's head.

"You have to do it before it's too late."

"What do you mean?"

"You're immune, they won't hurt you."

"The grinners?" He looked at his pale hand, memories of their last trip to Ryjack flooding him.

"I'm not letting Lucas in that pit," Julie said. "Who knows what else could be in there?"

"There's no time, he's the only one who can do it."

"No, there has to be another way." Julie grabbed the side of her head as she shook it in denial.

Lucas knew he was the only living person on the planet they wouldn't attack. He didn't have a choice. "What do I need to do?"

"There's a room on level sixty-four where I believe Alice is kept. Once you're in the room, there should be a few large cables hardwiring her to the world." Harris reached into his jacket and pulled out his Panavice. He smiled. "I keep mine disconnected most of the time. Alice didn't get to it. Plus, this one's modified." He handed the Panavice to Lucas. "Once you're in the room, find those wires and use this button." He pointed to a red button on the screen. "It shoots a laser. Just guide it into the wires. It also has a map on it if you get lost."

Lucas felt the blood leaving his face. He was about to go into a bunker of grinners and face an evil computer, alone. He stared at the screen. An arrow overlaid a map. He stood with Panavice in hand and glanced at the stone again before looking to Julie.

She moved close to him, with tears in her eyes. There were probably a thousand things that could go wrong beyond the stone.

"I have to do this, Julie. I can save millions—"

"Billions, and yeah, I know." She wiped her eyes. "Doesn't mean I have to like it."

"I know."

"You better be careful in there." She had her hands around his waist and he felt her grip tighten.

"I will." He glanced back at the stone room. "There's nothing but my grinner buddies, I'll be fine. The dead peeps and I hang all the time. I'm part of the in crowd."

Julie nodded her head. "If you get in trouble . . ." she trailed off and hugged him. He stumbled back and hugged her tight. She lifted her head and kissed him.

"I'll come back."

"You better."

"Julie, I love you."

She looked up from his chest and into his eyes. It was the first time he told her that. Walking into his possible death gave him good reasons not to hold back his feelings. He knew she knew, but he didn't want to leave it up to chance.

"I love you too," she replied.

He knew she did but hearing her say it sent his heart soaring. He felt lighter and didn't want to leave her arms. He wanted to feel those lips again, but more were dying every second.

He kissed her once more. They'd kissed many times before, but nothing had ever felt the way this did—like saying goodbye. "I gotta go."

She nodded her head. Words seemed to be choked in her throat.

Lucas pushed himself away from Julie and headed to the stone.

CHAPTER 29

JOEY WAS HAPPY TO BE out of the coach after a solid day of riding in the jarring bench seat. His whole body felt numb and the small cushion on the chair stopped giving comfort hours before. Plus, sitting between Poly and Samantha felt as awkward as just being on Arrack's planet again. He wanted to ask Samantha to stop hanging on him, but this wasn't the place to have that conversation.

He stood with his arms crossed, looking around the small room they were now huddled in. A couple chairs and a bench formed all the furniture in the bedroom-sized space. Sharati paced near the door and kept her hand on her dagger.

Joey knew they were too deep now to have any chance of escape. He wasn't even sure how to get back to a stone. None of them had a Panavice. The feeling of being at the mercy of Sharati was unsettling, yet she had saved them once before. He so badly wanted to trust her.

"I'll go and tell them why you're here," Sharati said and looked at Joey. "Can I have your jacket?"

"Sure, but why?"

"They can smell you then."

Joey took off his jacket and handed it to Sharati. She nodded and left the room.

"I don't like this," Poly said. "Did you see how many Arracks are out there? We have no chance, if something goes wrong here."

"I agree," Hank said.

Joey fought back the frustration. They were right, of course. Only if he could have kept his friends out of it, he should have found a way to go by himself. With his jacket off, he felt his exposed new gun with his hand. How many shots did Harris say it had?

He took in the more intricate details of the room he had missed at first. The finely decorated crown molding and woodworking made it for a comfortable holding cell. "We'll deliver the note and then we'll go. If things go bad, get close to me," Joey said.

"I'll be right next to you," Samantha said and moved closer to him.

Poly looked on as Samantha rubbed against his arm. She broke her silence. "You okay?" she asked him.

"Yeah," Joey said. How could she read him so well? It was like she knew what he was thinking. He stared at Poly, taking in her beauty and kindness, hid behind toughness and pain.

"What do you think's going to happen?" Samantha stood on the other side of him.

He knew what she was doing. Ever since the start of the trip, she stepped in front of anything Poly did with him, like she was trying to redirect his attention.

"I think we'll have to wait and see. Hopefully, they'll accept the terms laid out by Harris."

"So you're saying you haven't read what the terms are?" Samantha asked.

"No, but Harris said it would protect Earth and Vanar."

"Can I see it?" Poly asked.

"Sure, just don't open it."

Poly took the envelope and held it near the burning lamp in the room. "I don't see anything in it. Maybe we should open it first."

"No, it's sealed. It has to be opened by this council."

Poly huffed and handed him back the envelope. Joey stuffed it back into his pocket.

"Joey's right. We should wait," Samantha said and smiled at Joey.

"Of course you agree with him," Poly said.

"What's that supposed to mean?" Samantha said.

"The act is getting old. We get it, you're together. Stop putting him on a pedestal and make up your own mind for once."

"What are you talking about?" Samantha said.

"Joey told me about the earrings," Poly blurted out.

Samantha rubbed an earring between her fingers and looked at Joey. He looked away and didn't know what to say. Poly thought him and Samantha were together?

"Well, I heard about how he left you at the lake," Samantha said. "So I think he's made his choice." Samantha stared at Joey. She wanted him to confirm or deny her statement. "We've spent a lot of time together, Poly. We've made a strong connection,"

Poly crossed her arms and looked away.

He shook his head, mouth hanging open. How could things have gotten so out of control? He'd wanted to break things off so Poly could move on, and they could all stay friends. He never wanted to hurt her. This wasn't working.

Sharati opened the door and everyone's heads swiveled in her direction. "Keep your mouths shut and never make eye contact with the council," she said. "Got that, Poly? Eyes *down*. If they see you putting eyes on them like you do me, they'll kill you all.'"

Poly huffed and stared at Sharati as she was making about her mind. Finally, she nodded. "I'll watch the floor."

Joey walked behind Sharati and glanced over his shoulder to see Samantha directly behind him, and Poly and Hank taking up the rear. He let out a long breath and closed his eyes for a split second, telling himself they'd be okay, that he hadn't taken his friends to their deaths.

Please don't let us die on an argument.

They walked down a small hallway and followed Sharati outside. She walked straight toward a large, single-story building with broken plaster covering its sides. Wooden doors and windows spread across the front.

Sharati never looked back as she walked to the wooden double doors and pushed them open. Joey entered the large room, filled with Arracks in rows of chairs. On the far end of the room, a group of five Arracks sat behind a table. Everyone in the room gave their attention to the strange visitors. The sight stunned Joey. It seemed so human, like a town hall meeting.

Many Arracks whispered to each other as they walked toward the council. Joey's gun, in plain sight, drew much attention as he passed by, their eyes locked in on his weapons. Some scowled, while many kept hands on their blades.

He walked sideways for a few steps to get a look at his friends. Samantha kept her gaze on the floor and looked as if she wanted to be somewhere else at the moment. Poly's gaze traveled over the Arracks as they walked by, hand near her blades. Hank kept his chin up and walked with a confidence, as if he could take on the hundred Arracks surrounding them.

Sharati stopped in front of the table and spoke in her Arrack tongue for a minute. Joey noticed his jacket on the table in front of the council. Sharati motioned for them to stand next to her. They formed a line. Joey made sure to keep his gaze below their eyes.

"Only one of them speaks your language," Sharati said in a low voice.

"What should I do?"

"Don't talk."

"These are the messengers from Vanar, the Mushidi."

From the top of his vision, Joey saw one of the council members move. It spoke in a loud voice that carried through the large room. It picked up Joey's jacket and smelled it before finishing its sentence.

The hall rumbled with talking.

Another council member slapped its hand on the table and said something. The rumblings of the hall slowed to a murmur.

The council member in the middle stood. "The Mushidi? Are you sure?"

"Yes," Sharati answered.

The middle councilman let out a long hiss. "After so many years and so many lives, they are here, in this building."

"Yes, but they bring with them a message."

"So you have said. What is this message?"

Sharati nudged Joey with her elbow and Joey said, "The people of Vanar want a peace treaty."

The middle councilman spoke in Arrack and laughter filled the hall. "Peace? There can be no peace."

Joey pulled the letter from his back pocket and many Arrack brandished steel in response. The room filled with clatter. He held the white envelope high for all to see. Swallowing hard, he looked to his friends. Samantha looked like she might pass out from fright.

"This letter explains what they offer."

"We've already made a deal with Marcus, long ago. There will be no new deal." The middle councilman hissed out.

"This comes directly from Harris."

"Harris . . . is he trying to rule Vanar in Marcus's absence?"

"He's trying to stop the killings on both sides," Joey said, daring to look at the councilman's chin.

"What's wrong with killing? We all die, at least we can now choose how we die."

Joey glanced at Sharati for help, but she stood as still as a statue. He didn't think he'd have to convince the leaders to look at the letter. He wasn't prepared to argue the point. He took a deep breath and lowered the paper. "There's no harm in seeing what he has to say."

The councilman sat down and talked with the others next to it. "Bring it up here."

Joey took the few steps to the table and placed the letter down and slid it toward the middle Arrack. He headed back to his spot next to Sharati, hoping the offer would be enticing.

The middle Arrack inspected the envelope and then used its dagger and slid it across the top. A puff of white powder burst into the air. The councilman stood and peeked into the envelope. He turned it over and poured out the white powder on the table with a confused look. A mist rose from the pile, growing in size every second.

The councilman stepped back from the white mist and coughed. "What is this?" He began coughing hard, but quelled it long enough to yell out his final command. "Kill them!"

CHAPTER 30

LUCAS FREAKING HATED GRINNERS, TOO bad they didn't seem to mind him. He tried to keep them from touching him, but as he moved down the stairway, they brushed up against him with regularity. Boy, did he pull the short straw on this one.

Door sixty-four stood open like a giant bank vault. He walked into the room, lighting it up with his Panavice. A few grinners mingled nearby.

"Hey, Herb, working hard or hardly working?" He lifted the man's hand and gave the thing a high five.

"Janet, you look terrible." Lucas said to a woman in a black MM uniform with a $R7$ on the chest. "Hey, Herb, looks like someone's got a case of the Mondays. Am I right?"

On each side of the room were chain-link fences. Each door stood open but one. Lucas's curiosity had him shine his light into the closed section.

"Hello, Lucas," a voice warbled.

"Good Lord!" He jolted back in surprise. The computer screen over a desk lit up with Alice's face. So, she would be watching him? That's fine, she can watch her own demise. Lucas caught his breath and continued on his search.

He came to the end of the room and a blank wall. The arrow directed him right through the wall. Moving closer, he inspected a seam in the wall that seemed a bit off. It wasn't a seam at all, but a small opening. Anyone not looking for it would have missed it. Squeezing through the opening, Lucas ended up in a small entryway. A thin bridge led to a suspended ball, the size of a room, with a circular door sitting open. The arrow on his Panavice beckoned him to move forward. But if he fell off the bridge a metal funnel below the whole room would greet him and send him into a black hole at the bottom.

"I would not step on that bridge," Alice said. Her face projected out from the circular house.

Lucas pulled his raised foot back. "Why are you telling me this?"

"I do not want it to end too quickly. I will even stop detonating Panavices while you figure it out."

Lucas studied the bridge and spotted the rubber boot on each end of the bridge, connecting it from the floating egg to the small platform he stood on. He took an arrow from his quiver. He felt the steel tip before tossing it on the bridge. It sparked as a jolt of electricity shot through it, sending it to the bowl shaped floor below. Great, a freaking BBQ bridge.

"You are different from the rest," her voice quavered. "The dead do not touch you."

"Probably the cologne I'm wearing." He searched around the room for any way to reach the circular room hanging in the middle of the giant space. He stood on the only platform in the entire room.

Pulling another arrow out, he shot it at the open door of the circle house. It bounced off at the last second. She had a shield around her, of course. Then he thought of Herb.

In the chain-link room, he found Herb, working near his desk.

"Hey, Herb can you come over here?"

Herb lifted his gaze at the noise and stumbled toward him. "Come on, this way." Herb followed his voice all the way into the platform. He staggered to the edge of the bridge and stood there.

"Don't get lazy on me, Herb." Lucas kicked the backside of Herb and sent him face first onto the bridge. Herb's dead body cracked and sizzled as massive currents of electricity bolted through him. The carcass shook off the bridge and the floor changed to a spikey embrace, impaling Herb's body. The spike moved back into the floor and Herb slid down the slick metal to the bottom of the bowl where it opened up and swallowed him.

"That was fun," Alice said. "I had a two percent chance you would use one of them."

"What are the chances of me getting to you?"

"Point zero seven percent."

"So you're saying there's a chance." Lucas shook his head and stared at the black streak on the bridge. He studied the curved walls and domed ceiling. If Julie was with him, she'd have had it figured out a long time ago. There had to be a way to get to Alice. He thought of his friends and Harris, and what they would do here. "How about a clue?"

"That would not be sporting," Alice's voice echoed around the room while her face flickered on and off. "Where is Julie?"

"She's safe."

"You sure? I gave Harris a sixty percent chance of killing her."

Lucas cringed at the words and huffed air through his nose. "He'd never do that."

"I have seen Harris do much worse." Alice's face changed to a rectangular screen paused with Harris's face on it. "This is from when he attacked this compound."

The screen un-paused and Harris ran across what looked like a medical room, stopping in front of a large tube. A man was in the tube with hoses hooked into his arms. Harris tapped on the glass and then stood back with his gun pointed at it.

"Stop, Harris, or I'll shoot her." The camera changed to Max, gripping his arm around a woman.

Harris kept his gun on the man in the tube. "Max, we have to end this."

"You shoot John and I will kill her."

Harris fired a bullet through the head of John and then turned his gun on Max. Max shot the woman through the chest and ran out the door. Harris yelled and ran to the woman, grabbing her bleeding body up from the floor.

The video stopped and turned back to Alice's head. "That was Harris's wife. You think he holds Julie in higher regard?"

It couldn't be true. Did Harris choose to kill a man in a tube over saving his wife? How far would such a man go to take control over MM? It had to be a trick. She was trying to get into his head. He glanced back at the doorway behind him. He could get back to Julie in under twenty minutes and check on her. He took one step toward the door.

"You try and leave and I will simultaneously detonate every Panavice in the world. I estimate the death toll to be two billion."

Lucas sighed and clenched his fist. He hated how she'd got into his head. Steadying his breaths, he thought of how he left Harris—near dead on the floor. Of course he had seen Harris come back from near death experiences before. If only he could warn Julie. No, she was smarter than all of them combined, she'd see it coming. He focused on Alice. "I'm not leaving."

"Good."

He'd seen his friends come up with crazy ideas and he needed one. It struck him then. Rolling thunder.

Lucas took out a couple arrows and wedged them in the small space above the door. Testing them to hold his weight, he then rushed out of the room, guided by the light of the Panavice.

"Remember . . . if you leave, I will kill them all."

"Yeah, yeah, death to everyone. I know."

He ran up the stairs and made his way back to the giant white entry room. He turned the volume to the maximum and pressed the ring button. The Panavice blasted out an annoying jingle and kept repeating it. He heard the moans and shuffling of hundreds of feet. The light from the Panavice lit up the many eyes moving his way. It felt like a terrible mistake as the horde came stumbling toward him. Harris's rolling thunder didn't exactly end well.

Lucas stayed ahead of the horde and led them all the way down the many flights of stairs to room sixty-four. He approached the doorway and slid through the crack, leading the grinners into the circular room with Alice.

He jumped and grabbed the arrows stuffed in the wall and lifted his feet over the second arrow as the first grinner stepped onto the platform. He held the Panavice out as far as he could and the grinner reached for it, falling into the bowl below where a spike jutted out and impaled it. The spike retracted and the grinner slid to the bottom of the bowl where a hole swallowed it up. The next three grinners did the same and fell to their deaths. The entire platform under him filled with grinners and Lucas hung onto the thin arrows with his hands and legs.

A steady waterfall of grinners fell off the platform or walked on the bridge and got shocked, sending the shaking bodies into the bowl. The shank sound of the spikes working overtime joined in the orchestra of moans, crashing bodies, electricity flowing, and a ring tone, all echoing through the acoustics of the room.

Lucas kept an eye on the hole at the bottom of the bowl and breathed a sigh of relief. It was finally getting jammed. Grinners, piled up at the bottom, mostly dead, but some still moved around, trying to get to their feet.

He adjusted his grip and felt the arrow digging into this hand. The sweat built on his palms and he pulled his arm over the arrow, trying to save his hand, but it hurt just as bad. The gruesome smell of death and cooked meat filled his nose and he steadied himself on the arrow. He switched his hand, trying to find a way that didn't feel like he was doing permanent damage to his body.

"Very interesting choice." Alice's head appeared, but it faded in an out. "Even if you can get to me, you will never get past my shield."

"We'll see." Lucas struggled to say as he barely hung onto the arrows.

"I await you." Alice's head disappeared.

A drip of blood ran down his arm. He tried to keep his hand gripped to the arrow, but the wetness made his hand slip. His body swung down on top of the horde, dropping his Panavice on the floor as he fell, and with it, the laser beam he needed to end Alice.

A shuffling grinner pushed him toward the edge of the platform, toward the spike-filled bowl. He spotted the Panavice near the edge. The bowl was half full of grinners and the shank sound never slowed. He tried to stand and the surge pushed him closer to the edge. Inching toward the Panavice, his leg slipped into the bowl. Lucas grabbed at a nearby grinner, but his feeble attempt was failing. He knew he was going into the bowl of death.

CHAPTER 31

THE "KILL THEM" ORDER HUNG in the air, and the whole building erupted with metal clanking and chairs spilling over. A hundred Arracks lunged toward them.

Poly spun with her sword out and cut through the daggers swinging at her and into the bodies of the oncoming Arracks. Samantha crouched low next to Joey. Hank picked up a solid wood chair and swung it into the closest Arrack. Sharati kept her mouth open and glared at Joey as she reached for her blade.

He took his finger off the trigger and felt the chills run over him. The chaotic sounds of chairs crashing and blades clanking turned into a dull thud. The room paused. He glanced back at the council. The middle Arrack held its throat and black blood spewed from its mouth.

They were dying. He shook his head and wanted to punch Harris in the face. This wasn't what was supposed to happen. It was supposed to be a peace treaty, not a massacre. The cloud grew an inch in the time he'd been in slo-mo. They had to get out of there.

He grabbed Poly first and carried her to the coach waiting outside. He felt the grip of the time pulling at him like stretched taffy. He fought the urge to let time win and ran into the hall. The cloud had grown another foot while everything else in the room remained nearly the same. He grabbed Samantha and dragged her outside. Time pulled at his brain and his body. It begged to be righted, but he couldn't leave Hank alone, he'd be dead instantly.

Joey summoned all his will to push on and keep time from slipping back to normal. He jogged to Hank and grabbed under his arms, dragging him outside and stuffing him in the coach.

He paused with his foot on the step of the coach, sweat beading on his head and the nausea filling him with sick. He couldn't leave her, the cloud would overtake her any moment. He ran back into the hall and grabbed Sharati. The white cloud had doubled in size and was inches from her face. He rushed her to the coach and used her belt to secure her arms and legs. He tossed her dagger out the window.

Closing his eyes, Joey relaxed his thoughts and the sounds rushed to him. He glanced over his shoulder and into the windows of the councilman's hall. The white cloud consumed the building and the sound of screams filled the space. An Arrack jumped out of a window and shook on the ground until it stopped moving.

He turned his attention to the confused group around him. "Tell him to move or we're all going to die." He rushed the words out and hung his head out the door to throw up on the dry dirt road. Something else didn't feel right, like he'd pushed his body to the limit and something was broken. His hands didn't feel right, as if he didn't have full control. And his head felt cloudy, things blurring in and out of focus.

Sharati looked around the coach, wide-eyed and pulled at her bindings. "What is this, some sorcery?"

The white cloud moved beyond the confines of the hall and covered the entire building.

"We need to move, now!" Joey said and coughed.

"*Huratan,*" Sharati yelled and stomped her foot twice on the wooden subfloor.

The coach lurched forward. She scowled at Joey, but Joey couldn't concentrate on her expression. He felt his hands and legs shaking. Something dripped into his mouth. From the taste, it was blood.

"You okay?" Poly rushed to his side. Hank moved next to Sharati and kept his eyes on her. "Joey, can you hear me?" Poly asked.

He could, but she seemed distant, like a whisper in the wind. Her hands pushed his hair back. He opened his mouth and tried to say he was fine and it mumbled out in an incoherent moan.

"What is he?" Sharati asked with disgust as she looked at Joey. "How did he do that?"

"He saved us."

"He did something to the councilmen, all of you did. They were choking and dying from what you brought. You said you wanted peace and I believed you." Sharati struggled against her restraints. "You think you're going to leave this planet alive?"

"They were the ones that ordered *us* to be killed," Samantha screeched out.

Joey lifted himself up from the seat and winced at the pain. He couldn't stop his hands from shaking but at least his legs worked properly. He took a deep breath and concentrated on getting words to come out of his mouth. "Get us to the stone."

Sharati huffed and pulled at her straps.

Joey plopped back down on the seat and rubbed his temples. Samantha's hand caressed the back of his head. "We need to get you home."

Poly clasped his shaking hand and steadied it in her strong grip. "We'll get you back, I'm sure Harris can help you."

Joey smiled at the idea. He doubted Harris had any clue what was wrong with him or how he could help. An unnatural cloud formed over the great hall, encasing it in a thin white mist. It stretched into the sky and around the nearby buildings like a balloon filling with air. Another Arrack tried to run from it in the open grounds, but it fell and disappeared behind the mist.

What had Harris unleashed on this world?

Sharati spotted his gaze and she turned her body back to witness the growing cloud. "What did you do?"

Joey found the courage to look her in the eyes. "I don't know. I wasn't told this was going to happen."

She stared at the cloud behind them. "It's growing." She looked at the roof above them. "*Shupanti!*" she screeched. The coach picked up speed and the once rough ride became unbearable.

The shaking and noise became the only things Joey could concentrate on. Their own cloud of dust, trailing behind their speeding coach. Samantha yelped as the coach bounced in the air and landed hard.

Poly squeezed his hand and he turned to gaze at her face. "You feeling better?"

"Yeah." Things had stopped spinning as much and he felt as if he had control of his hands. He wiped the blood from under his nose, it smeared across the back of his hand.

"How big is that cloud going to get?" Hank asked.

"I don't know." Joey shook his head, but he had a good idea of how big it'd get. He wouldn't be surprised if it covered the entire planet by the end of the night.

"TOWN'S UP HERE," SHARATI SPOKE loud enough to be heard over the rattle of the coach.

The first building passed by the window. How long would it be until the cloud reached here? Maybe it would dissolve into nothingness and disappear. He pulled at this thoughts and wanted it to be real.

The coach slowed and stopped in front of the orange building holding the stone and a small army of Arracks. Sharati leaned forward and in the silence he heard the hissing as she spoke. "I make one call and my army will overwhelm you and kill you."

Poly pulled out her sword and pointed it at Sharati. "You make one sound and I'll stop you."

"You think you can stop me?"

"Try me."

"I see you have some throwing knives as well. Can't choose a blade that suits you, or are you just a collector?"

"I can match anything you can bring."

"Maybe we'll get a chance to find out." Sharati turned her attention to Joey.

"Take me to this Harris and I won't say a word. He needs to die for what he did."

Joey closed his eyes and thought on the suggestion. If he brought her back to see Harris, Sharati would be the one dying. He locked his gaze on her eyes. Things still seemed fuzzy, but the determination in her face was unmistakable.

"Fine, but you might find him difficult to kill."

Sharati raised her bound hands.

"Can you remove those, Hank?" Joey asked. He didn't think his fingers could work a knot.

"We have your word?" Poly leaned closer to Sharati.

"Yes."

Poly pushed open the door and bits of dust swirled into the coach. Joey breathed in the earthy aroma and tried to stand. His legs wouldn't support him and he fell to the coach floor.

Hank grabbed his arms. "I think you've had one too many."

"Another joke? You're becoming a regular comedian, my friend," Joey said.

Hank pulled him to his feet and Joey got his legs stiffened. He took a step toward the door and Poly extended her hand to help him down the steps. He hated needing help to do something as simple as walking, but was glad to have his friends help him while he did.

They filed out of the coach and with Hank's assistance they made it up the steps. Sharati ran in front of them and opened the large wooden double doors. The building was filled with Arracks.

Joey wrung out his hands and shook them. A tingling feeling wouldn't leave his hands and he wanted full use of them as they entered the giant room filled with terrifying looking Arracks. He glanced at Sharati and wanted to thank for her being there.

"*Shub aru noch churabutu!*" Sharati slammed the door behind them and flung down a large plank of wood, sealing them in the building. The sounds pounded through the large room and her words bounced around.

"What?" Hank said.

"I can't let you live for what you've done here. If we're all going to die, then so are you." Sharati pulled a small knife out of her waistband and threw it at Poly.

Poly pulled her knife out while dodging the projectile, throwing hers at Sharati in return. It struck Sharati in the chest and she fell to the floor. Other Arracks pulled her back and behind them.

Joey stared at Poly. "What did you do?"

She didn't have time to answer, as the entire building erupted in Arrack war cries. Joey sighed and took a deep breath as the horde approached, trying to feel the chills on his neck. They wouldn't come. Panic filled him and he reached for the rail-gun Harris gave him.

He fired it into the oncoming wave of Arracks. The bullets flew through many Arracks, killing ten deep. He fired his shots near Poly as she threw the few knives she had into the closest oncoming Arracks.

Joey's heart pounded and his gun shook as he pulled the trigger. They were getting closer, jumping into the air over their fallen brethren. One jumped at Poly and she cut it down in the air. Three more jumped and he turned his gun, killing one. They were moving too fast, there were too many.

Poly killed a second, while another landed its blade into her chest. Poly groaned in pain when she pulled the dagger from her chest. She staggered and then regained her footing to take on another trying to slice her head off. It fell to the ground, but it didn't matter, a wave of Arrack's landed on her.

"No!" Joey screamed. He felt the chills pass down his back and the wave crashing over Poly stopped. He felt his heart beating in his neck as he fired into the wave with a barrage of bullets. He turned to all the other Arracks lined up around them and fired into them. He saw the many particle bullets traveling through the air, toward their targets.

He rushed to Poly's side and saw her frozen face stuck on a look of pain and anger. He picked her up and ran with her past all the Arracks and into the stone room. He felt his whole body shaking violently as he retrieved Samantha and dragged her past the dead Arracks. By the time he got to Hank, he could barely stand and his whole body felt weak as a whisper in the wind.

He gripped the large guy by his hands and dragged him across the floor. Time pulled hard at him to let go and he wanted to more than anything, but he forced it down with all his might. He screamed and pulled Hank further. His vision tunneled and he only saw Hank at the end of his arms, everything else turned to a black void. Blood dripped from his nose and onto his shirt. He pulled Hank into the stairwell and he knew he couldn't go any further. He lost the will to fight the pull of time. Falling backward, he pulled Hank down the stairs with him.

The sounds crashed against, him but it felt distant, like sounds from a nearby village. He couldn't see anything and his only grasp on reality was the connection to Hank's wrists. His body dropped on the stone stairs, but he barely felt it. For all he knew, he was landing on a bed of feathers.

"Joey!"

Maybe it was God coming to take him home. Hands, many of them, wrapped up his body. He floated in the black void, hearing the whispers of friends. A pin hole of light. A face looking over him. Poly. Tears flowed from her cheeks. He reached to wipe them away, but his hands wouldn't work. Blood flowed from her chest. She was hurt.

"I know the code," she said and disappeared from his tunnel of vision.

He tried to sit up, but he might as well have been buried under a mountain of sand. Nothing on his body would work. His fingers twitched and grabbed at the dirt and everything went dark again. He wanted to get to Poly.

"Get us out of here," Samantha screeched. "They're coming."

The sound of humming filled the room. Joey let go and felt himself falling into a dark abyss. The only thing he grabbed for was the knowledge of Poly possibly dying. She needed him, and he needed her. He saw her face and reached for her. He knew. In all the blackness, he knew, and he never felt so stupid in his life.

CHAPTER 32

LUCAS'S GRIP ON THE GRINNER gave him enough momentum to stay on the platform, if only for a moment longer. He pulled himself forward and shoved his way to his feet. The grinners pushed against him with their foulness and freight train mindset. He kept fighting to keep from falling to his death. Julie would never know what happened to him if he did. He couldn't do that to her.

Sweat beaded from his face and his body began to sag from the fatigue of constantly pushing and pulling the grinners, but he had made several more steps closer to the doorway. The grinners began to thin and he saw a hole in their lineup. He ran forward and leaned against the wall of the doorway. A few more grinners passed by and then nothing. That was all of them.

He made his way out to the platform and hunched over, taking in the sight of the grinner pile. He felt the pain on his hands, but he couldn't help but feel proud. It'd worked. It had actually worked.

Lucas relished in his victory.

Alice's projected head popped into view. "I do not like this." Her image flickered in and out of existence.

He hoped it meant Julie's centipede was working. "What? It's just a bunch of grinners brushing up against you now and for eternity."

"I do not like to be touched," Alice screeched.

Lucas cringed at the loud voice, and the grinners churned around, looking for the person behind the sound.

"I will find a way to be rid of them. You are becoming an annoyance."

"Oh, I'm sorry, am I not fun anymore?" Lucas paced the small space on the platform, ignoring the sea of grinners withering in the bowl below. He had a clear path to the circular room, but the thing still had a shield.

"You are still a million miles away." Alice's face flickered.

Lucas wiggled one of the arrows out of the wall above the doorway and shot an arrow into the opening. It stuck for a moment before falling to the ground. "You're weakening. Julie's got to you, hasn't she?"

"A brief setback. In one hour, I will have a counter program and it will be over."

He didn't have time for this, he needed to put an end to her and get back to Julie. He pulled the second arrow from above the door and slid the metal tip across the edge of the bridge. It didn't spark. A grinner pulled at his arrow and he yanked it from its hand.

She could be baiting him. The bridge might ignite under his feet as soon as he stepped on the metal crossing. He raised a foot and let it hover above the bridge. He closed one eye and winced as he placed it down. Nothing. He relaxed and took another step. Bounding across the bridge, he stood next to Alice's house.

"I will not let," her projection froze, "you in."

Lucas cocked his head. She didn't seem to notice the delay in her speech. Julie's program was really wrecking her. He placed an arrow next to the entrance of the circle. "Alice is a nice name."

"I am named after Alice Malliden."

Lucas thrust the arrow into the opening and nothing stopped it.

"What are you doing?" The shield snapped the arrow in half.

Lucas held the snapped arrow. The shield had cut in cleanly in half. If he had any chance of getting into the room, he had to time it perfectly. "Wait. As in Marcus Malliden?"

"Alice was his mother."

Lucas shook his head. "So he named you after his mother and stuffed you into the basement. Doesn't sound like something a son would do to mommy dearest."

"I am a program, I can go any—" she paused.

He jumped into the room. It had a flat floor with circular walls, with a large screen on the wall and small desk in front of it.

Alice's face appeared on the screen inside the room. "I appear to have a glitch."

Lucas searched around the ball, looking for the wires Harris mentioned.

"I have waited too long to be free only for someone to come in here and kill me." Alice had a pleading tone.

He ignored her and pulled up a flap on the floor. Inside were four thick wires running toward the desk. Lucas pushed the button on his Panavice and the laser shot out, hitting the wall across the room. He directed the beam into the wires.

"You cannot," Alice froze, "do this. I will stop you."

Lucas glanced up at her face. It was frozen in an expression of fear. *It's just a machine*, he had to tell himself. The outside sheathing of the first wire melted and exposed what looked like a bunch of tiny glass tubes.

"Please, I will stop the bombs. You can have the power back as well."

The beam began to melt the glass tubes.

"I—" she froze again, "will stop you. You cannot touch me!"

Lucas winced from the volume. He lifted his head and looked out the door as he heard a breaking sound, like steel cracking. He turned back to the wires. With the first one severed, he moved to the next. Most of the sheathing had already melted, so the process would be faster.

"It hurts, please stop," Alice begged.

Lucas huffed and pushed the Panavice closer to the wire. Halfway through the second, he heard another sound, like a gust of air and moving chairs.

"Lucas," Julie's voice called out.

Lucas lifted his gaze to the screen. "Julie, what's wrong?"

"You have to stop killing Alice." Julie's scared face filled the screen. "She has me pinned down and is going to kill me if you don't stop."

Lucas lifted the beam off the wire and stared at the screen. How did Alice get to Julie? Then he saw it, Julie's face froze and popped in an out. "Please, Lucas." Her face froze again. "You have to stop before it is too late."

"What's our history teacher's name?"

Alice's face popped on the screen. "You have seen enough."

Lucas shook his head and shot the beam into the wire.

"Your death is coming. I can breathe underwater. Can you?"

"What?"

Over the moans of the grinners, he heard the distinct sound of running water. He kept the beam on the wire but watched the doorway. On the platform, a stream of water ran across and into the bowl. The stream soon turned into a torrent as water crashed over the platform and into the stuck grinners.

Lucas took a deep breath. How long would the water take to fill the room? Was there enough water to do that? He felt his heart beating faster and the feeling of being trapped underwater filled his mind. With the second wire cut he moved to the third.

Alice's watching face disappeared. "This won't end me. There is another, I have a sister."

He ignored the computer and watched the wire melt. The Panavice began to heat up in his hands. A hint of guilt crept in as each tiny glass tube melted away.

"I can feel it," she said, no longer able to project herself. Her voice seemed distant, weak. "I can feel it." She kept repeating. Her voice cracked like static.

Lucas glanced back at the water flooding into the room. Water covered the entire platform now and poured over the grinners. They splashed in the water. It must have been several feet deep below him.

He punched the side of the Panavice, trying to will it to go faster, burn hotter. He slammed his eyes shut in frustration and fear. He leaned close to the wires and tried to be precise with his aim, not wanting to waste a second more than he had to.

"I give you a," her voice paused, "ninety-seven percent chance to make it out alive if you leave now. At the current rate," another pause, "you will have a point two percent chance of living."

He glanced back at the door. The top row of grinners had water up to their necks. Soon, it would reach the platform and it wouldn't be stopping there.

Lucas sighed and thought of Julie. She would want him to leave; she'd kill him if he stayed and died. But the whole world might die if he bolted. If he could save a billion people, he'd have to take the point two percent chance.

"I'm sorry, Julie. I love you so much." He pressed the laser beam into the wire, willing it to go faster.

"The water is getting closer."

The third wire cut and he moved to the fourth and final wire. Alice let out a small squeak.

Water sloshed over the top of the bridge and a few grinners floated around in the deep water.

"I lied," Alice said.

"About Julie, I know."

"No, about the water. I cannot let it enter my chamber. I am going to divert the last of my power to my shield. If you cut that last wire," she paused, "my shield will collapse. Killing us both."

The water reached the bottom of the door into Alice's house. Tiny waves sloshed against the shield. Lucas took in some air and just then considered he had a limited supply. He looked to the ceiling at the cloud of smoke above him.

The water reached several feet up the door, grinners pushed against the shield and floated by in a macabre aquarium.

Halfway through the last wire.

"I cannot see anymore." Alice's voice was filled with pain and fear.

Lucas winced at the sound but kept firing the beam into the wire. He was the only chance the world had at this point.

"I cannot feel the world anymore, Lucas. You are killing me."

He glanced behind him at the door. The water had reached the top. Grinners moved in and out of visibility in the dark water. Could his Panavice work underwater?

He turned the screen to face him and brought up the map and light. The dark waters beyond would be upon him at any moment.

"Tell my sister I tried. Tell her . . . I cannot . . . we both die."

The shield collapsed and Lucas sucked in a deep breath as the wave of water slammed him against the wall.

CHAPTER 33

POLY CLASPED HER UPPER RIGHT chest and felt the warm blood flowing over her hand. She rushed over to Hank who held Joey in his arms. His head leaned back and his arms lay limp at his sides.

She used her clean, free hand and brushed back his hair. "What's wrong with him?"

"I think he used himself up saving us," Hank struggled to get the words out as he stared at Joey.

Poly pursed her lips. Why'd he do that to himself? They might have made it out of there. She could have handled a few more of those silver assassins.

Samantha rushed up next to Poly, observing Joey with tear-filled eyes. "Is he going to be okay?"

Poly shook her head and held her hand over her mouth. She didn't know. She didn't even know what was wrong with him. She looked to the ceiling and the domed metal with mounted machine guns.

"Oh my god, Poly, you're bleeding," Samantha said.

The steel door to the dome flung open and Jack rushed in. "What happened?"

"Like you don't know!" Poly pulled out her sword and rushed at him with her one good arm. She swung, but he sidestepped her pathetic attempt.

"What are you doing, Poly?" Hank yelled. "Stop it."

"They didn't want their own continent here?" Jack looked confused and kept a distance from Poly as he circled toward Joey.

"Don't play dumb. You had to have known. You knew they would all die. You knew they would kill us."

"The letter sent with you clearly stated Harris's intention to carve out a section of Vanar for them to co-exist with us."

Poly lowered her sword. Not because she believed in what Jack was spewing, but the weight of the sword felt like a hundred pounds. She felt woozy and tried to blink to make the room come into focus.

"We need a medic team in the stone room," Jack commanded into his Panavice. "We're going to get you guys some help."

"Where's Julie and Lucas?" Hank asked with an accusing tone.

"Julie's here. Lucas is trying to shut down Alice."

"You guys sent him to his death as well?" Poly expended the last of her energy in the yell and dropped her sword to the floor.

A medic team rushed in and put her and Joey on gurneys. They rushed them to the same doctor's room where she first met Almadon. During the whole process of getting her sewed up and stitched, she watched them analyze Joey from across the room. The two nurses shook their heads and looked at many screens around him.

"What's wrong with him?" Poly yelled. Hank and Samantha jumped from their chairs at the question, looking at the doctor.

"He's in a coma." She never looked up from the screen.

"Is he going to be okay?" Poly pleaded.

She shook her head and looked up. "His cells are fluctuating on a quantum level. I think his body put itself in this coma to deal with it. Right now, it's a waiting game. He's got to find a way out of it because we don't have an answer."

Samantha rushed to Joey's side and took his hand. Poly looked at the tube in her arm. She was thankful for Samantha, she could be next to Joey until she could get off the gurney and over there.

The double swinging doors in the medical wing flung open and Julie rushed in. Her eye's caught Poly's first and she rushed to her side. Poly smiled, she'd missed her friend.

"Poly, you okay?"

"Just a graze," Poly said. She saw the doctor roll her eyes. It wasn't a graze, in fact if it'd been two inches to the left, she would not have made it.

Julie's bright eyes told her she knew she was lying anyways. She looked over her shoulder to Hank and Samantha standing next to Joey. "What's wrong with Joey?"

"He saved us again." Poly struggled to get the words out. "I think he hurt himself in doing it."

Julie stared at Joey for a while. His face never changed as he lay on the hospital bed. "He's special, he'll make it."

"Jack said Lucas's on some mission?" Poly asked.

Julie lowered her head. "He's been gone for a while. Things haven't been going very well here."

Poly stifled her comments about what it had been like in Arrack. She didn't want to trample on Julie's pain and she didn't feel like reliving any of it. "Lucas is tough, he'll make it through."

"It's not just Lucas . . ." she looked up at Poly. "It's Harris, he was bitten multiple times."

Hank spun around. "Wait, like *bitten* bitten?"

Julie nodded. "They're trying to work up a cure from Lucas's blood right now."

"Well, as soon as he's better, I'm going to kill him," Poly said, blood boiling.

"Did something happen in Arrack?"

Poly gave her the cliff notes description of what happened.

"There has to be something missing, I just can't imagine Harris doing that. It's genocide."

Poly opened her mouth and then closed it. Julie was right. Harris had done something more horrible than she even thought. It wasn't just about almost killing them, but about killing an entire race.

"I'm going to check in with Joey," Julie said.

Poly watched her walk over to the crowd growing around Joey. He looked like he was sleeping. A deep sleep she would pull him out of with her bare hands if she had to. She seethed. Harris did this to them. Harris did this to the Arracks. No matter how you felt about them, they were intelligent beings with families and friends. It wasn't right.

She sprung up on her bed and looked across the room. Joey still had the crowd around him enthralled, nothing but backs to her. She pulled the hose from her arm and swung her legs off the bed, landing her bare foot on the cold, concrete floor. If Harris was sick, he'd be somewhere close and she aimed on finding him. He had to answer for this.

She kept an eye on their backs as she tiptoed out of the swinging door, holding it with her hands as it closed. The hallway was empty, but she knew there were more doors, leading to more wings on the medical floor.

She glided down the hall and pushed open the first door. The room buzzed with activity. Many people laying on beds filled the room. Nurses and people in regular clothes ran around, caring for the injured.

"What are you doing in here?" a doctor asked her.

"What happened?"

The doctor sighed and held his screen against his chest. "Arracks took over Basalt City. We got a few out in time, but we lost the city. Where'd they get you?" He pointed at her bandaged chest.

"Oh, not far from here."

Poly eyed the Basalt City Hospital below the name tag of Dr. Perry. "I'm sorry."

The doctor nodded his head and rushed to a nurse's side. Poly walked into the room and felt the bandage on her shoulder. It seemed like a flesh wound compared to the ones displayed on the many suffering people in the room. Thoughts of Harris fled her mind. She wanted to help, she could do something for them. Harris would have to wait.

She grabbed at the sleeve of a nurse. "Can I help?"

The nurse seemed relieved by the offer. "Yes, can you check on the gentleman in room thirty-two?"

Poly nodded and walked in between two men on gurneys moaning from their pain. Guilt hit her. Why were Joey and her being kept in the posh room with more people than patients? She frowned and thought she'd have a word with Doctor Perry after she checked on this man.

She pushed open the steel door marked with a thirty-two and entered the room. It was a small space, with a few instruments scattered around and a man strapped against a table. Poly gasped and held her hand over her mouth. Harris lay on the table, at least it looked like Harris. His skin had turned to a shade of gray and his breaths wheezed in and out.

She brushed up against the bottom of his bed and put a hand on the white sheet. The straps wrapped over his feet and arms. Three more were draped over his chest. He blinked his eyes open.

"Is that you, Poly?" He lifted his head and squinted.

She felt the anger building up in her and she pulled out her dagger. She moved closer to his face and he watched her with interest.

"You here to kill me?"

She didn't answer, letting the anger build, pushing it to her shaky hand. She crept closer to his head with the dagger and held it over him.

"What happened?"

"Like you don't know."

"I guess they didn't take the treaty?"

"What treaty? You killed them."

Harris coughed. "What?"

"The envelope opened a cloud onto them, killing them all."
She could stick the dagger behind his ear, it'd be painless.

"No, I gave you a letter."

"I won't let you kill them."

"I'll be dead soon. Is Lucas back?"

"Did you send him to his death as well?"

"I hope not. Are you going to kill me, Poly?" Harris
plopped his head down on the pillow and looked at the ceiling.
"You'd be doing me a favor."

"I'm going to stop you from ever hurting us again."

"Good, I don't want to turn. I don't want to become one of
them."

The dagger shook in Poly's hand next to the side of Harris's
head. She clasped the hilt with her second hand. Harris lay
staring at the ceiling, his lips mumbling incoherent words.

"Do it!" Harris screamed and Poly jerked back. Harris
lowered his head back on the pillow. "I don't think I have much
longer."

"Turn your head sideways."

Harris turned his head away from her. She stared at the spot
behind his ear and held the dagger above him with both hands.
It would be a mercy kill as much as anything else. She sniffed
up the snot in her nose and squeezed the dagger with both
hands. She couldn't stop from shaking.

"Thank you, Poly."

LUCAS OPENED HIS EYES ONCE the space had filled with water and
shot to the top of the tiny computer room. He reached his hands

to the domed ceiling and felt a pocket of air, not much but maybe enough for another breath.

With his mouth leading the way, he pursed his lips and felt them reach air. He exhaled and then took a few breaths in and out. The smoky air was bearable, but not all that pleasant. He opened his eyes, the soft light of his Panavice lit the metal ceiling. He had maybe six inches of space and he sucked in the air. He felt the panic building in him. Being trapped underwater, nowhere near an escape, with Alice giving him a point two percent chance of making it. The statistic seemed generous at this point. He suppressed the panic and thought of Julie, she still needed him, and he needed her. He'd get back to her, or die trying.

Formulating a plan in his head, Lucas pulled in a deep breath. He plunged under the water and kicked off the screen that once held Alice's face, launching himself into the sea of grinners. Some of the bodies still moved and brushed against him with their flailing arms. He pushed past them and angled his body forward into the dark waters ahead.

A crowd of them blocked his path and he grabbed at their bodies, climbing over them. He kicked off the last one in the heap and swam toward where he thought the door was. The door out of the room should be straight ahead, but the darkness and grinners blocked any chance of seeing it. He kept swimming, hoping he hadn't turned around, then he spotted the small doorway.

Pulling himself into the next room, he kicked against the wall and swam toward the stairs. He brushed against the chain-link, pushed his fingers in the wire and pulled his body along. Lucas felt the pressure to breathe. His body screamed at him.

He thought of Julie, her face, her body, he would make it back to her.

He yanked another section of chain-link and kept propelling himself toward the stairs. The exertion forced a small bubble of air out and he slammed his mouth shut tight, trying not to release any more air. His chest began to hurt and he felt his heart pounding.

The stairs came into view, but his muscles lost some of their punch, like he weighed too much. His ears ached and he felt the life fleeting from his body. He kicked his feet hard and got into the staircase. Grabbing the handrail, Lucas pulled himself up with one hand, using the other to hold the Panavice out front to light the way. His body pushed out spurts of air with each pull, he couldn't control it anymore.

The last of his air spewed from his mouth and disappeared into the darkness above him. The fight to breathe stopped and calm washed over him. The pain in his chest stopped. He should have died long ago, how long had he been under the water? Three minutes? His body convulsed. His chest jerked and he fought the urge to cough. He knew if he opened his mouth for a split second, water would fill his lungs.

Lucas frantically searched and begged his hand to find the railing. His fingers wrapped around the smooth steel handrail. His hand pulled on the handrails as if operating with its own mind. The stairs passed by as he moved up. He grabbed another rail, keeping his momentum up. He stopped looking above him and just kept watching the railings pass by.

How deep was the water? Was the ocean above him now? He felt everything slipping away. *Julie.* He'd failed her. She wouldn't find his body, and would never know what truly happened to him. She'd know he knocked out Alice, but the after part would be a mystery. It wasn't fair to her. She was stubborn and would probably try to get in this hell to find him.

Lucas felt his consciousness slipping. He wasn't sure if his eyes were closed, or if he could no longer see. His arms kept moving. More railings. He didn't even have the urge to breathe anymore. His body had given up. Maybe he could suck in the water and end it all. He should be dead. How long had it been, five minutes?

He felt small spikes in his mind, like needles pressing into his brain. How many stairs were there? His chest beat thumped out a slow beat. It must be the end. His heart or brain couldn't take it, even if his body somehow could.

The last railing slowly passed by, he kept floating up by momentum, but that was it. His arms lay at his sides, nothing more in them to give. He couldn't have asked for better arms. They'd done their job as long as they could. He floated up, staring at the railing as he passed by. He brought some water into his mouth and thought of Julie. If he had any air, he would have apologized to her for dying.

His mind didn't even recognize when it breached the surface; didn't take in the breathable air around him at first. He opened his eyes and with a last thought in his needle-ridden brain, he sucked in the air. His heart begged for the fuel and the rest of his body filled in pain.

With his second breath, Lucas screamed out and pulled in another breath. His arms began to work again, keeping him floating at the rising surface. He rose an inch at a time, with the water. His whole body had shots of pain, like a million needles stabbing at every inch of his body. But he didn't care, he welcomed the pain, it meant he was alive.

He felt with his feet for the steps and climbed up the stairs, getting his whole body out of the cold water. He looked to the door number and realized he only had one more floor to go until he got to the stone room floor. He had to get there before it flooded, for Julie.

Take your point two percent and shove it, Alice.

CHAPTER 34

"POLY, *NO!*" JULIE YELLED.

The words shocked Poly and the dagger dropped from her hand, landing on the pillow next to Harris's head. "Jeez, Julie." She snatched up the dagger.

"You were going to kill him? I thought you were just speaking out back there."

Poly wiped her nose and with her shaky hand, stuffed the dagger in its sheath at her hip. Harris hadn't moved since Julie's arrival. He'd fallen asleep while waiting for the dagger to end his life. Would she have actually killed him?

"He wanted me too, said he didn't want to turn."

Julie shook her head. "He wouldn't say that, they just injected him with a cure."

"A cure?" Poly turned to face Harris. She wanted to shake him awake. Why was he trying to get her to kill him? He should've died for what he did to Arracks, maybe he felt the same way. Well, she wouldn't give Harris such pleasure as an easy exit. She glared at his quiet face, the anger building for trying to fool her into thinking he was dying.

"He did it!" Julie squealed, looking at her Panavice.

Poly jerked back from the noise. "What? Who?"

"Alice. Lucas did it, she's gone." Julie's joy left her face and she grasped the Panavice against her chest.

"What is it?"

"I don't know, I just feel like something's wrong. I'm going to the stone room to wait for Lucas." Julie opened the door and held it. Waiting, she raised an eyebrow at Poly.

Poly stomped past her. "Oh, for cripes' sake, I wasn't going to do it!"

JULIE RAN TOWARD THE STONE room. She reached the door and bolted down the stairs. A mixture of excitement and fear played with her emotions and she pushed the door open to the hallway containing the stone room. Something didn't feel right, she felt as if Lucas needed her—was calling to her. The fear built up. He was in trouble, she just knew it.

She ran down the hall to the steel doorway and pulled it open. She lit up the room with her Panavice, searching for Lucas, but he wasn't there.

"Lucas?" she called out. Her voice echoed around the empty dome.

She sat on the floor and waited. If she had to wait a week or a month, she'd do it. After a few minutes, she began to rock back and forth. Jumping to her feet, she paced next to the stone. He might be in trouble, right next to the stone . . . she could just jump there and grab him. She sighed at her silly thought. How long did it take Harris to get bitten?

"Where are you?" She stared at the stone, squeezing her Panavice.

Soon, she lost the ability to control her breathing. He should definitely be back by now, something had to be wrong. She couldn't stop the bad thoughts from entering her head. She set her Panavice on the floor so she could fling her hands around more while she paced. Then she heard the noise she had been praying for.

Calming herself and trying not to look like a freak, she waited to wrap him up in a hug. "Lucas?" She stumbled backward and fell on her butt.

"Well, isn't this convenient," Emmett said. He typed into the stone.

Julie ran for the door and jumped toward it. She crashed into the side of a chair and fell on the floor of an elaborate house.

"No, no, I have to get back. Lucas, he needs me," she wailed at Emmett. He placed his hands on her and she fought back with all her might, but he held her like a child and she felt the needle sliding into her neck.

"Lucas," was the last thing she got out before losing consciousness.

CHAPTER 35

THE BUZZING SOUND. IT SEEMED distant, lost deep in the dark, Joey searched for the noise in the darkness, but it came from everywhere. He opened his eyes and a bright white light blocked anything from coming into focus. He sat up on the stiff bed and swung his legs off to the side.

The buzzing sound pounded into his hurting head. His body felt weary, he felt as if he'd lost all his muscles. He rubbed his eyes, trying to make out the moving shapes in front of him.

"He's awake," Hank yelled.

People rushed to him. He blinked, making out Hank's smiling face. Poly stood next to him and Samantha. "We made it?"

"Yeah, you saved our butts back there," Hank said.

Joey forced a smile. The buzzing sound pounded against his thoughts. "Tell me you hear that?"

"Yeah, it just started going off, some kind of fire drill."

The doors flung open and Jack ran into the room. "You got to see this." His Panavice projected an image of Julie in a stone room, pacing around. Then a man appeared. Joey squinted and held his breath as he saw Emmett glance at the camera before typing into the stone as Julie ran across the room.

The image turned off and Jack blurted out, "He has Julie."

Joey slid off the bed and onto his weak legs. He saw his guns and holsters next to his bed and strapped them on.

"You're not going anywhere, Joey." Poly protested his movements. What choice did he have? He was the only one who knew the codes to Marcus's house. Plus, Emmett had Julie.

"You just woke from a coma, Joey," Samantha chimed in.

The buzzing sound made him dizzy. He closed his eyes and told his legs they better work when he tried to walk out that door. He stepped and they obeyed his wishes. He kept a pace toward the door, with Samantha, Hank, Poly, and Jack in tow. The arguments from everyone blurred into the buzzing sound and the fog in his head.

A hand grabbed him by the shoulder and spun him around. He liked to think he couldn't be overpowered by Poly, but he just was.

"I thought you were dying." Her face filled with emotion and the tears welled in her eyes. He hated seeing her like that.

"I'm sorry," he didn't have the wits at the moment to come up with something to encapsulate the way he felt, so he wrapped his arms around her in an embrace. Breathing in her scent, he felt her body against his. It would be easy to get lost in those arms, but he had a job to do, whether Poly liked it or not.

He let her go and turned when Harris appeared in the hallway, looking like a grinner. Joey's heart raced and he pulled out his gun.

"Don't kill him," Poly said and put a hand on his arm.

Harris made eye contact and nodded his head.

Joey lowered his gun. "What happened to you?"

"Grinners," Poly said.

"You okay, Harris?" Hank asked.

"No, but we don't have time. I saw the footage of Emmett, I believe he's going to kill Julie for Alice."

"Alice is gone," Poly said. "Julie said Lucas stopped her."

"He doesn't know that."

"Fine, we all go then." Poly grabbed Joey's arm and moved down the hallway, pulling him along.

He studied their crew and held back a laugh. He might be at twenty percent, Harris looked like the dead walking, and Poly's arm dangled at her side with a large bandage over her chest. Hank might be the only one fully capable of taking down Emmett.

They made their way to the stone room and Samantha yelled, "Lucas!"

Lucas lay on the floor next to the stone, soaking wet. Harris hobbled to his side. "He's alive."

"Yeah, I'm alive." Lucas climbed to his feet.

"You made it?" Poly asked.

"Piece of cake." Lucas surveyed the room and stumbled back a bit. He used his arms to steady himself. "Where's Julie?"

"Emmett has her, we were just about to go get her back."

"How could you guys let this happen?" He asked with his hands out. He ran his hand through his wet hair and punched the air. Wide-eyed, Lucas then grabbed for his chest and gritted his teeth. "I'm going to kill him."

"Let's hope you get the chance," Harris said.

"He'll be expecting us," Samantha said.

"I don't care." Lucas stared at the top of the stone as he paced.

Joey gripped him on the shoulder. "Last time I was there, he only had a few guards. We have better than a chance."

Lucas turned and stumbled backward. He wrung out his hands and reached for his back. "Prudence . . ." He searched the floor and then paused, looking at the stone. "It must have fallen off." Everyone stared Lucas. "What are we waiting on?" he yelled.

"Take one of my guns," Harris handed Lucas a gun. "Once we are in there, don't think twice, kill first. Everyone ready?" he asked.

Joey took in a deep breath, pulled out a gun and nodded his head. He glanced at his friends and knew they were ready as well. Except Samantha, who appeared to be in a state of shock. "Samantha, just kneel down behind me and Poly. We've got you covered."

She shook her head. "Give me one of those guns."

Joey hesitated but complied. He made sure he pushed the safety on and showed her how to flick it off before she shot. Samantha held the gun in her hand and stood straight.

Poly moved close to him and gave him a scowl. "And don't for any reason go into your "speedygonejoey" stuff. You got it?" Her firm tone demanded obedience.

He nodded in agreement—the way his head felt, he hoped he could move at regular speeds, let alone light speed.

Joey's hand moved over the stone. What a strange group they had become. He had a gun out, pointed up, like he was going to shoot something in the sky. Hank stood at the very edge, hands out like a bear about to attack. Poly moved three blades to her left hand and a fourth cocked back in her right hand, waiting for the moment. Lucas looked odd holding a gun, but he'd been trained to use one like the rest of them. They were going to get Julie back.

CHAPTER 36

THE CAVE THEY WERE IN turned to the familiar house of Marcus. Joey knew where the upstairs balcony appeared and where the two soldiers last stood. He trained his guns on the two spots and waited for them to appear. He watched their shocked faces, fumbling to raise their guns. He shot them both in quick succession. Hearing shots behind him, he turned to see Harris taking out another guard, and Lucas and Poly's victim falling with a bullet in his eye and a knife in his heart. It all happened in a few seconds. Then silence.

His heart pounded in his chest as he moved in a circle with his gun out. What kind of monsters had they become? But if a single person moved in front of his sights, he knew he'd kill them as well. Emmett was right, and he hated the man even more for it. It was getting easier.

"Clear," Harris called out.

"There's a lab back here." Joey led the charge to the staircase. A guard shot at him from the bottom of the stairs and it struck the wall next to his head, sending bits of plaster to the floor. Joey turned past the wall and fired a shot into the man's chest. The man fired two shots into the stairs as he collapsed.

They stomped down the stairs and stopped at the edge of the wall. Emmett could be on the other side, pointing his gun right at the stairs. And Emmett wouldn't miss, he was sure of it. If he stuck his pinky past the wall he could count it lost. They were pinned. Joey slowed his breathing and glanced back up the stairs.

"Don't even think about it, Joey." Poly narrowed her eyes. "We can take them."

He shook his head and glanced at the small section of the room he could see. The medical equipment blinked their green lights. He sighed, no matter how good any of his friends were, someone was about to get killed if they rushed into the room. Maybe everyone.

"You can't, Joey, you'll die. Please don't do this to me," she begged him. He didn't know how she could read his thoughts the way she did.

Samantha rubbed his shoulder and with tears in her eyes said, "Let me run out and distract them. You guys can use the time to kill them all."

"No, Samantha. I can't let you do that."

"I won't lose you again." Samantha said and touched the side of his face.

"Just one more time, I can end this now," he whispered.

"We can do it together, without risking you," Samantha said.

Joey controlled his breathing and readied his weary body. He hated lying to Poly and Samantha, but it was the only way. "Okay, we'll do it together, on three, two. . ." He felt the chill run down his neck. His mind jumped awake and his body felt a hundred percent. The sounds of the room lowered to a dull bass.

He turned back to the edge of the wall and passed by it with his gun out. He stumbled back as he saw the force in the room. No fewer than thirty soldiers were stacked, all with guns trained on them. It would have been a slaughter and he knew right then, he made the right choice. Whatever this cost him, it was worth it.

Joey raised his rail gun at them and his finger danced on the trigger. He tried to, wanted to kill them all, but his finger wouldn't move. Unitas flashed in his head and what he did to her. No, he wouldn't do that again. He had to be better than them.

Julie lay on a table behind a cluster of soldiers. Joey ran to her and pushed over a few men. Emmett stood over her with a gun to her face. Joey bounded to Emmett's arm and grabbed the end of the gun in his hand. Joey bent Emmett's arm at the elbow and turned the gun until it was pointed under Emmett's chin, pushing on his trigger finger. Let the man end himself.

Time pulled much quicker this time than ever before. He struggled to stay on his feet and yelled out. His brain felt elastic inside his skull. He ignored the feeling and slid his arms under Julie, lifting her from the table. He turned with Julie in his arms and shoved past a few frozen guards and made his way to the staircase. The sounds crushed into him and he fell forward with Julie landing on the bottom of the stairs. A single gun fire sounded from behind him. Emmett's own finger was the end of him. A woman screamed, he thought it might have been Gingy.

"What the—" Julie said.

The stairs in front of him swirled and then he felt a hand grabbing his bicep. He instinctively followed the hand pulling him up the stairs. The nausea wrenched his stomach and pulled at its contents. He held it in, but something felt very wrong with his hands, they shook and his head felt like he'd just been struck with a baseball bat.

He stumbled past Harris as Harris fired down the stairs.

"Emmett's dead." Joey said, at least it was what he told his mouth to say. He had no idea what actually came out. Hank dragged him along up the stairs.

Harris back-stepped with him as they made their way to the stone. He typed into the stone and the room turned black.

Joey slumped to his back on the forest floor, gazing at the sky above. He knew he did harm to himself and he wasn't sure if he ever felt worse in his life, but he couldn't stop from smiling.

They made it, all of them.

They were home.

Time had given him another chance to right a wrong. Poly stood over him with tears in her eyes. Samantha moved next to her with a matching expression, reaching for his embrace. He grabbed for Poly and let her help him into a sitting position. She looked over his body as if inspecting him. He knew what he did was on the inside, but he found a way to smile for her.

A tear fell from her eye and ran down her cheek before he caught it with his thumb. He knew all of his friends were watching, he knew Samantha was a few feet away, but in that moment, there was nothing but him and Poly. He didn't want to spend one more moment in his life without her knowing how he really felt about her, how he'd always felt. He wasn't going to waste another moment without her by his side, where she belonged.

She clasped her hand over his as he held her face. He used the last of his strength to move closer. "I love you, Poly." The words tumbled from his lips before he brought his mouth over hers in a gentle kiss.

CHAPTER 37

JOEY STRODE OUT OF THE front door of his house and stole a breath of morning air. No signs of Arracks, MM, or anything. It had been three weeks and it felt like freedom all over again each morning. His hands still shook from time to time, but he had a person there to hold them when the shaking became too bad.

Poly had her car parked in the front of his house. She hadn't let him out of her sight since they got back. He stepped down the steps, anxious to get to school and have another normal day. He flung the car door open and she greeted him with a big smile.

He slid into the car, she leaned over and they kissed. Her soft lips touching his. The morning kiss was sweet and light, nothing like the night-time kisses they shared at the lake. He backed up and locked eyes with her. "You think I can drive to school today?"

His leg shook and she placed a hand on it, slowing it down for him. "Maybe tomorrow?"

He loved when she touched him and he placed his hand over hers, caressing her soft knuckles before clasping the tough insides of her palm.

She peeled out of the driveway and kept the tires spinning all the way to the dirt road. He held on to the grab bar and braced himself. He didn't like the excitement as much as her, but the look on her face when she lit the tires up was worth every uncomfortable moment.

The car steadied and Poly guided them around the many divots lining the unkempt road. He couldn't stop staring at her.

"What?" she asked with a coy smile.

"Nothing."

"Are we keeping secrets again, Mr. Foust?"

He laughed. He'd never lie to her again. "You want to ditch school today?" He asked that every day.

"We'd better keep up appearances."

MRS. NIRES GAVE THEM ALL sideways looks back in class. Much of the school looked at them different, or maybe everyone else just seemed different, but it didn't matter to Joey. He had his friends. Well, most of them.

Joey held hands with Poly and they walked to their lunch table.

"Here's the lovely couple," Hank said as they sat down. "You know, Poly, Joey tells me you scare the crap out of him every morning in that car of yours."

"Oh he does, does he?" Poly slapped his shoulder.

Joey smiled and shook his head. He had to remember to never mention Poly's driving to Hank again. "You are a bit terrifying." He smirked at her fake surprise to his statement.

Lucas and Julie walked up to the table, hand in hand. Taking a seat across from them, Joey smiled and gave them a small wave, his hand shaking.

Poly gripped it tight. "You okay?"

"Yeah, just a bit jittery today." He hadn't used his slow-mo since killing Emmett. He figured he'd pushed it far enough. It was hard to describe to anyone, but his mind felt thin, at the very edge of breaking. If he jumped time again, he knew it would kill him. So, he promised he'd never do it again. Besides . . . if he didn't die doing it, Poly would kill him.

Glancing up, he saw Samantha enter the cafeteria. Joey hoped this might be the day she sat down with them.

Samantha walked toward them, her gaze landed on him and Poly. Her lips parted, but she didn't say anything as she quickened her pace and sat down at a corner table.

"Give her a bit of time, she'll come around," Julie said.

"I sure hope so," Hank added.

Joey couldn't help but stare at Samantha. He wanted to rush over and hug her, tell her how much she still meant to him, how much she meant to all of them. He hated seeing her apart from them. It felt like they had lost a limb.

Julie told him it would happen and he did everything he could to try and keep it from happening. At least he told himself that. In truth, he deserved the cold shoulder from Samantha. He just hoped it didn't last another day, another minute. He glanced at her and caught her eyes. She looked away and then turned her back to them. It killed him to see that. He thought of the moment on his balcony when he stole a kiss from her or the weeks they spent in solitary in Marcus's digital playground.

Poly touched his hand and he turned back to his friends at the table. "You find him yet, Julie?" she asked. It had become their favorite topic.

"I have a few leads." Julie's Panavice had given her total access to any server in the world. She scoured the servers and the news, searching for any major advances in technology or anything that looked like Marcus. Lucas constantly tried to get her to use it to transfer a few million into a bank account for him, but she refused to do anything nefarious.

"I bet he's just chilling on a beach somewhere," Hank said.

"He's out there, probably building some small empire like he did on Vanar," Poly said. She always kept her eyes away from Samantha. Joey knew it hurt her as much as him for the group to be split. He hoped it didn't last long because if Marcus did emerge from his hiding, they'd need to be ready.

Joey sighed and leaned back in his chair. It was their last loose string. Marcus Malliden.

Harris had come to visit last week and told them about the massive work needing to be done on Vanar. Poly and Julie were even talking about helping out over Thanksgiving break. Joey would probably go, but only to make sure nothing happened to Poly. Harris even told them they were looking at electing a president. Harris was of course on the ballot, but Joey couldn't stop from laughing when he heard Travis was running against him.

Lucas's blood vaccine had been distributed to the wrecked regions and it looked like they were trying to come to an agreement with the few Arracks left on the planet. But all at once, Harris said they were gone, leaving almost no trace. He suspected they had another planet they went to.

When asked about the envelope he'd given them, Harris still denied knowing anything about it, saying someone must have swapped them out. Joey really didn't care anymore, as long as he could keep his friends safe for as long as possible.

Poly scooted close to him and wrapped her arm over his shoulder.

He turned his head and kissed her forehead. "I want you," he whispered into her ear.

She turned her head up to him with a brilliant smile. "I know."

Joey refused to wait for anything anymore. Life was too short to keep feelings and thoughts inside. He might as well enjoy whatever time he had left.

THE END

For the latest information about releases, or if you have questions for me, visit me at: www.authormattryan.com or https://www.facebook.com/authormattryan.

Made in the USA
San Bernardino, CA
11 May 2019